The House on Falling Star Hill

MICHAEL MOLLOY

SCHOLASTIC INC.

New York Toronto London Auckland Sydney
Mexico City New Delhi Hong Kong Buenos Aires

First published in the United Kingdom in 2004 by
The Chicken House, 2 Palmer Street, Frome, Somerset BA11 1DS.
Email: _chickenhouse@doublecluck.com_

ISBN 0-439-57741-1

12 11 10 9 8 7 6 5 4 3 2   4 5 6 7 8 9/0

Printed in the U.S.A.   40

First Scholastic paperback printing, October 2004

Book design by Sarita Kusuma

Contents

Eli's Gift

There was something odd about Enton. Tim Swift had felt it the moment he arrived with his dog, Josh, to spend the summer with his grandparents, Peter and Emily Bishop.

The sleepy west country village was best known for its large selection of antique shops and the advanced age of its inhabitants. Peter and Emily had moved there the year before to open a flower nursery. Their new home had once been the village school but there were no longer any children living in Enton. In recent years all the young families had moved away to find work in other towns.

Enton seemed remote, but not far beyond the fringe of hills to the north of it was a highway, and Tim's grandfather did a brisk trade with people who thought nothing of driving long distances to wander about the pretty village for a few hours. Apart from a couple of streets of flint and brick cottages, there was a Norman church, twelve antique shops, two expensive restaurants, an old-fashioned tea shop called Mistress Witherspoons, a general store, and The White Hart public house.

With the summer stretching out ahead of him, it didn't bother Tim much that he was the only boy in Enton. He was used to being alone and was content enough with Josh for company. As an only child, he tended to be a bit shy with boys and girls of his own age.

Nor did he care much for team games, although he was a strong swimmer and a good runner. The other boys at his school had mistaken his shyness for lack of courage and nicknamed him Timid, which he hated, mostly because deep down he wasn't quite sure if he was brave or not.

Tim was of average height, a bit on the thin side, and wore his thick brown hair falling forward in a jagged fringe. His gray-blue eyes were wide and set in a long, square-jawed serious face. When he remembered, he tried to smile because people were always telling him to cheer up. But he was generally happy, so his usually sad expression had little to do with his mood, it was just the way his face was made.

Josh, Tim's small black-and-white dog, was quick and clever. Tim had taught him to walk on his hind legs, dribble a ball, and lie on his back to play dead. When Tim crouched down and called, "Leapfrog!" Josh would jump over him, then circle around to repeat the action. Josh was great company, but Tim did sometimes wonder what it would be like to have a boy or girl as a friend.

In his first hour exploring the village, Tim realized what it was that was odd about Enton — something was missing.

"That's strange, Josh," he muttered to the little dog, who cocked his head to one side as if he, too, were glancing around inquisitively.

Later, Tim sat waiting for his supper in the old classroom his grandparents now used as a kitchen. It retained a lot of the old school atmosphere, and his grandfather had even kept the ancient blackboard so he could write reminders to himself about his business.

Tim nearly put up his hand before saying, "Grandad, I've realized what's odd about Enton, there are no flowers in the village gardens."

Peter Bishop, a portly man who enjoyed his food, nodded and stroked his mustache while eyeing with anticipation the sizzling steaks Emily was grilling as a treat. "I know," he replied and tapped his nose. "That's what gave me the idea to open a flower nursery when we first came here on a day trip."

Tim's grandmother placed a bowl of peas on the table, pushed a wisp of silver-streaked hair back behind her ear, and said, "Well, it's a good thing there's plenty of visitors. We'd be in even more trouble than we are if we had to rely on the villagers for business."

"But why don't they plant flowers?" Tim asked.

Peter shrugged and put his arm around his wife's waist when she brought out the buttery mashed potatoes. "The old villagers always tell new arrivals that it's bad luck to grow flowers in Enton," he said. "So they all just go along with the local custom."

"How weird," said Tim. "How did the custom start?"

"Blowed if I know," Peter answered, stabbing at his enormous steak. "But your grandmother's right; if we'd had to rely on the village for trade, we'd have starved."

The couple beamed at each other, as if they'd solved some extraordinary puzzle, rather than having left the mystery unresolved.

Tim shrugged at Josh who was sitting by his side hoping for tidbits. The lack of curiosity in some people is baffling, Tim thought. His grandparents had lived in Enton for a year and they still hadn't found out *why* it was supposed to be bad luck to grow flowers! He sighed, doubting that they ever would.

After supper, in the warm twilight of that first day, Tim walked along the quiet cobbled streets with Josh, who kept darting nosily into gardens to snuffle among the bushes until Tim called him to heel. Eventually, they reached the bridge over the village stream. Tim paused to watch the trout lying still in the shadows but they soon darted away, disturbed by Josh plunging in to splash about in the shallows.

It was a peaceful evening. Next to The White Hart was

a parking lot shaded by oak trees and no sign of any customers. The main street was deserted, until an old woman
in a long dress suddenly appeared, walking toward Tim.
Although it was a warm evening she was clutching a shawl
over her shoulders.

Tim could hear her muttering as if she were conducting
an argument with herself. The voice rose and fell, scolding
and pleading in turn.

Ignoring Tim, she drew level and crossed the bridge.
Tim saw her face was windburned and streaked with tears;
her eyes were a startling pale gray and looked wild with
grief, but she was not as old as Tim had first thought. He
was about to ask her if he could help in any way but the
woman hurried past as if he didn't exist, and Josh was tug-
ging at his trouser leg as if to hold him back.

After breakfast the following morning, Tim agreed to give
his grandfather a hand to plant seedlings at one of the long
trestle tables that ran the length of the main greenhouse.

He was alone and concentrating on the work when a
voice with a deep country accent said, "Ah, so I see I've
got competition for my job."

Tim looked up at a smiling nut-brown face. The man
wasn't much taller than Tim and quite old, judging by his
cropped white hair and deep wrinkles. But his forearms
below the rolled-up sleeves of his shirt were corded with
muscles. The man hooked the thumbs of his broad hands

into the wide leather belt around his corduroy trousers and rocked backward and forward, making his heavy boots squeak in protest.

"I'm just helping my grandfather," said Tim, unsure whether or not the man was joking, despite his cheerful smile.

"So, you'll be Tim, and this is Josh," said the man, holding out his hand. "Or is it the other way around?"

"The dog is Josh," said Tim, shaking the hand, which was as hard and rough as a stone wall.

"I'm Elijah Baldwin," said the old man. "But you can call me Eli."

"Do you work here, Mr. Baldw — Eli?" asked Tim.

Eli snorted with laughter. "I don't call tending a few seedlings work, lad. But I give your grandaddy a hand from time to time."

"Would you like a cup of tea?" Tim asked him.

Eli gave the suggestion serious consideration.

"Now, that's a great idea. You're just the kind of smart lad I like to see about the place," he replied. "Make it strong now, in a pint mug, with three big spoonfuls of sugar."

For the rest of the morning, Eli and Tim stood side by side, potting seedlings, and Eli told him stories about Enton and the surrounding countryside. Tales of mad farmers and ferocious gamekeepers, cunning poachers and eccentric landlords, likely lads and comely lasses. He told him how the country folk Eli knew as a boy used to cele-brate Christmas, Easter, midsummer, and the harvest, and how farmwork altered month by month throughout the seasons, from one year's lambing to the next.

Eli's stories were so interesting, Tim quite forgot to ask him why there were no flowers in the gardens of Enton or who the weeping woman was that he'd seen the previous evening.

When the church clock struck one o'clock, Eli wiped his brow with a red-spotted handkerchief and told Tim he was going home for his dinner but he would see him that afternoon.

"I wasn't planning to work this afternoon, Eli," said Tim.

"Nor was I," he replied with a wink. "We'll have a bit of fun, instead."

When Eli returned, he had brought Tim a wonderful gift. "That's for making me the mug of tea," he said, handing it to him.

It was the most beautiful slingshot Tim had ever seen. Made from oak, the grip was bound with a fine thin strip of leather that also secured the lengths of heavy rubber to the prongs and to the supple leather pouch.

"It's terrific," said Tim, wondering briefly if he was too old to play with slingshots.

As if he'd read his mind, Eli said, "It's mine, but I don't do much poaching these days."

"Poaching?" said Tim, interested.

Eli nodded. "You don't want to go firing off guns at night, do you? Especially if you're on someone else's land.

Pheasants perch up in the trees. We used to take them down with slingshots."

"It's really great," said Tim, giving an experimental pull. Then his face clouded over. "But I don't think I'll be able to keep it."

"Why not?" asked Eli, puzzled.

Tim thought about Peter and Emily. One minute they would tell him he was still a boy, and the next that he was too old for childish things.

"My grandparents will say it's too dangerous and I'll get into trouble, I expect," Tim said gloomily. "What they really mean is, I'll get *them* into trouble."

Eli chuckled. "You're in the countryside now, lad. Once you're over the stream and into the woods there's no windows to break. As long as you don't go shooting at people's chickens, there'll be no problem." He scratched his chin. "I want you to promise me something, though."

"Yes, Eli."

"Never kill anything with it just for fun. That's wicked. It's all right to hunt something you're going to eat or to destroy a pest that ruins a farmer's living, that's natural. But it's a poor excuse of a man who kills just for the pleasure of proving he's a good shot."

"I promise," said Tim.

Eli nodded. "Well, all you need now is ammunition. There's plenty of pebbles on the bottom of the stream. Come on."

CHAPTER 2

The Man from the Hill

At the stream, Tim filled his pockets with the round-est pebbles he could find before he and Eli entered the woods. When they came to a clearing a fair distance from the village, Eli produced an empty tin can from his jacket pocket and set it on a tree stump.

He watched as Tim walked away from the clearing and far back into the woods.

"Are you sure you can see it from there?" Eli called doubtfully.

Tim let fly with his first shot and the tin can flew off, spinning in the air.

"It seems you can," said Eli, slightly taken aback by Tim's marksmanship. "Well, lad, you're a good enough shot — but are you fast?" he asked, and threw the can into the air.

It soared high, flashing in the beams of light spearing down through the branches. When it reached its highest point, Tim hit it dead center.

Eli was delighted by Tim's prowess. He pointed out smaller targets, a tiny dead twig high in a sycamore tree, and three toadstools in the shadow of a fallen log. Whatever Tim could see, he could hit.

"Where did you learn to shoot like that?" asked Eli as they strolled back to the village.

"I've never shot a slingshot before today, Eli," he replied. "I wasn't even allowed to *throw* stones at home."

"There must be bowman's blood in you," Eli grunted.

"Bowman's blood?" repeated Tim. "What's that?"

"Once, a long time ago," said Eli, "this country had some of the world's finest archers, men who fought with bows and arrows. Maybe you're descended from one of them."

When they crossed back over the bridge the woman in the shawl was standing at the parapet, gazing down into the water. Just as she had ignored Tim the evening before, she now took no notice of them, but Eli said, "Good day, Meg," as they passed.

"Who is that lady, Eli?" Tim asked when they were out of earshot.

The old man shook his head. "Just a poor soul who lost her son," he replied. "She means no harm."

Eli did not return with Tim to his grandparents' nursery, but said he had his own work to do. They parted on the main street. As Tim approached the old schoolhouse, he saw a big bay horse tied up in the street.

Tim patted the horse's neck and it nodded, making its bit jingle softly. Animals liked Tim. The horse snuffled and nudged his shoulder. Tim wished it was the same with human beings. An uncomfortable memory came back to him and he sighed. At the end of school term there had been a dance with the girls from a local school and Tim had really liked one of them. She had dark hair and blue eyes. She'd glanced at him a few times, but he had been too shy to ask her to dance.

Too bad she hadn't been a horse, he thought ruefully as he gave it a final pat before entering the main greenhouse. He remembered just in time to tuck the slingshot into the back of his belt under his shirt. Despite Eli's assurance that attitudes were different in the countryside, he still thought his grandparents might confiscate his new prize.

There was no sign of Tim's grandfather inside, but a tall, bearded man was waiting impatiently.

"Is there anyone serving here, boy?" he asked abruptly, as if he were accustomed to being obeyed.

He was wide-shouldered, gaunt, and wore a dark blue jacket, fitted at the waist and made of a heavy, corded material. The coat had large pockets with button-down flaps at the hips and chest. His gray silk shirt was open at the neck, and his tight black-cord trousers were tucked into leather riding boots. A wide-brimmed black trilby hat was pulled low over his brow. The outfit looked oddly out of keeping in the village but obviously hard-wearing — a bit like a soldier's uniform.

The man's face was striking, its sunburned skin taut over high cheekbones. He had a firm jaw and hooked nose, and his beard was pointed and flecked with gray. Although he was quite young, there was nothing youthful about him.

Tim had a feeling the stranger had somehow been hardened by untold troubles. He appeared to be frowning, until Tim realized the deep crease between his eyebrows was actually an old scar. His hooded eyes were gray and melancholy but he smiled fleetingly when he noticed Josh, who as usual was close at Tim's heels.

"I said, is there anyone serving?" he repeated softly.

"I'll get my grandfather, sir," Tim replied, but at that moment Peter came over from the house, wiping his earth-stained hands on his green apron.

"My name is Hunter," the horseman said. "I've just moved to the village, and I want to buy your flowers."

"My name is Peter Bishop and this is my grandson, Tim," said Peter. "Are you interested in any particular variety?"

"I want all the flowers you have," said Hunter, glancing around. "In fact, far more than you have in stock."

"Really, how much more?" said Peter, surprised.

"Enough to give a good show over an acre," said Hunter. "The variety is immaterial as long as they're already in bloom."

"An acre," said Tim's grandfather, thinking. "It'll take a day or so to fill that order. I'll have to phone the wholesalers."

Hunter nodded. "Start at once. You can deliver what stock you have right away. And I'll need a worker to plant them. Can you recommend anyone?"

Peter scratched his forehead. "There's a man called Eli who helps me." He paused, then indicated Tim. "And my grandson, here, is with us for the summer. He might give you a hand."

"Do you fancy the job, boy?" Hunter asked. "I'll pay you fifty pounds a day."

"Fifty pounds!" Tim gasped. The most money he'd ever had was ten pounds — a present from an aunt the previous Christmas.

"I take it you want the work," Hunter said dryly. "When can you start?"

"We can begin delivering in the morning," said Peter. "Which house is yours, Mr. Hunter?"

"Just call me Hunter," the man replied casually, and going to the doorway he pointed to the far end of the village. "The stone buildings on the first hill you come to. You can start first thing in the morning. I'll be away. Just plant them scattered about the meadow in front of the house. Don't bother with making flower beds."

The hill he'd indicated was just on the outskirts of the village, past a rough expanse of common land that ended at a drystone wall. Beyond the wall, a wide meadow sloped up to the house and barn. Behind the house the ground rose more steeply as it approached the brow of the hill, which was crested by four horse-chestnut trees.

Hunter mounted the big bay horse and touching the brim of his hat to Peter, walked the horse down the main street. After he'd departed, Peter began checking the stock while Tim daydreamed about what he'd spend his money on.

When he was called in for supper, Tim found his grand-father standing in front of the blackboard, scratching his head and muttering to himself as he checked his notes.

"That's very odd."

"What's that, dear?" Emily asked as she cut cucumber into the salad.

"Some plants — about twenty, I'd guess — are missing from the greenhouse."

"Are you sure?"

"I checked twice. Yesterday we sold fourteen pots of begonias, five geraniums, and a rubber tree. There's defi-nitely some plants missing. And this isn't the first time — that's why I've started keeping these notes. I'm going to lock the greenhouse this evening."

"Well, I doubt if anyone from the village has taken them. It'll be louts visiting The White Hart, I expect," said Emily. "Will you cut some bread, dear?"

That night, Tim lay in bed, still excited by his good for-tune. Eventually he slept, but later in the night he was woken by the sound of Josh growling. He lay quiet, listening for a time, until he heard a soft scuffling sound coming from the street below. Josh whimpered and leaped up onto a chest to thrust his head out of the open window.

"I hear it, too, Josh," Tim whispered and, loading his slingshot, he joined the little dog. An almost-full moon glowed in a cloudless sky, clearly lighting up the greenhouse and the street. There was no one in sight.

"Can you see anything?" Tim whispered to Josh, who was tautly alert beside him.

Tim gave another sweeping glance and was about to withdraw when something flickered on the edge of his vision. Something as swift and darting as the trout in the stream. Josh gave a low throaty growl and, instinctively, Tim fired the slingshot at the quivering disturbance. Immediately, he heard a curious squeak but could see nothing that would make such a noise.

"I think I hit something, Josh," said Tim, and even more curious now, the pair ran downstairs and opened the door on to the street. It was deserted, and all was silent in the moonlight, but Josh stood on the step, still growling.

Tim was about to go back inside, when he noticed something glittering in the gutter. Josh noticed it, too, and darted forward to pick it up.

"Give it here, boy," ordered Tim, and Josh obediently dropped it into his hand.

It looked like a piece of glass crystal, about the size of a peach pit but shaped and polished like a piece from a chandelier.

Must be from one of the antique shops, Tim thought, taking it up to his room. He placed it with the smooth pebbles on his bedside table, went back to bed, and was soon asleep. But Josh remained at the open window, staring out into the moonlit street.

CHAPTER 3

The Legend of Joseph Mossop

Early the following morning, Tim began loading a large handcart with potted plants. It was going to take several journeys to wheel them to Hunter's house. His grandfather was already telephoning the wholesaler for more flowers when Eli arrived.

Tim told him of Hunter's huge order and that he would need help to plant all the flowers but Eli said he wasn't interested in the job.

"He's paying me lots of money, Eli, and I'm just a boy," Tim explained. "I should think he'd give you even more."

"I don't want his money," said Eli firmly.

"Why not?" asked Tim, puzzled by the old man's sudden gruff attitude.

"Because I ain't going anywhere near that house on Falling Star Hill," said Eli. "It's bad luck."

Peter Bishop came back from telephoning and heard Eli's refusal.

"You don't have to plant them, Eli, if you don't want to stay at the house," he said. "Just give Tim a hand to get them up the hill."

But Eli was adamant. "No hard feelings, Peter," he said finally. "But I don't *need* the work."

"Please yourself, Eli," said Peter, shrugging. "But will you stay here and keep an eye on things while I give the lad a hand?"

Eli agreed to this arrangement. It took Tim and his grandfather nearly all morning to transport the flowers. There was no sign of Hunter. They placed the loads of potted plants on an overgrown lawn in front of the house.

Later, during their lunch break, Tim brought Eli a mug of tea in the greenhouse. The old man was eating a slab of hard cheese and a huge Spanish onion, which he sliced with a pocketknife.

Tim accepted a piece of the cheese and asked Eli why he wouldn't go near Hunter's house.

"Because the land is haunted," Eli replied shortly.

"Haunted?" Tim echoed, intrigued.

Eli nodded.

"By what?" Tim wanted to know.

"It's a long story."

"We've got all lunchtime," urged Tim.

Eli closed his knife and took a long swig of tea before he began.

"Long ago, when my great-great-grandfather was a boy, even younger than you are now, a stonemason called Joseph Mossop and his wife, Anne, lived on the hill. One night, about this time of year, a strange thing happened. The sky was full of falling stars. No one had ever seen anything like it.

"'Like fireworks for giants,' they always used to say. The villagers came out and stood in the street to watch. It lasted for nearly an hour. Then they saw one last star fall to earth on the hill."

He jabbed his knife in the direction of Hunter's house.

"They thought it might have hit Mossop's place. But when the villagers ran to look, they could find no sign of damage, nor any trace of the falling star. Mossop and his wife weren't even there. They were away visiting relatives at the time.

"No one thought any more about it. But then, strange things began to happen about the village. At first, all the wildflowers vanished from the meadow in front of Mossop's house, and it had been thick with them for as long as anyone could remember.

"In those days, folks in the village prided themselves on the flowers in their gardens. They say the displays were a picture. But then their flowers also began to vanish overnight.

"Folks thought practical jokers must be at work, so they kept watch. Some people claimed they saw strange little men taking blooms from the gardens. Already superstitious folk, the villagers rooted up their remaining flowers and from then on never planted anything but vegetables. After that, people stopped seeing the little men."

Eli paused to drink more of his tea and, after wiping his mouth with the back of his hand, he continued.

"Years passed. Joseph Mossop had quit being a stonemason. But he always seemed to have plenty of money, and the house became famous for the grand style in which the Mossops lived.

"Then, one day, Mossop and his wife just vanished. After a time, folks looked inside the house, but there was no sign of them. The odd thing was, no one had heard or seen any moving vans, and there was still a good deal of stuff in the house: fine furniture and suchlike.

"But on a mantelpiece they found something extraordinary: a strange flower that looked as if it was made of glass. They say it turned to dust when it was moved.

"The house on Falling Star Hill stayed unoccupied for many years. Another couple moved in for a time; that was in my parents' day. The story was, they planted some flowers. But they only stayed a few months and no one in the village really got to know them. Since then, the house has been deserted."

"Why hasn't it fallen down?" asked Tim.

Eli shrugged. "It's well made. Mossop built it himself,

using the best-quality stone and slate, oak beams and boards. Nothing much is going to rot those. It'll still be standing a hundred years from now, I shouldn't wonder."

"What's the house like inside?"

"I don't know, lad, I've never been up there. We old villagers always kept away."

"Everyone?"

Eli paused before he answered. "Well, not everyone. Remember Megan, the woman I spoke to on the bridge the other day?"

Tim nodded.

"That's Megan Tagg. She grew up around here, married, and had a child — young Tom. Her husband was a village lad, but he died when Tom was a baby. So the boy became more than ever the apple of Megan's eye. She laughed at the old stories, said they were silly. She used to take young Tom up onto the hill to play. She even planted a few wildflowers. One November, a few years ago, when they were up there to let off Tom's fireworks, the child disappeared. Megan always claimed he had chased a little man, and they both vanished. All she could say was that 'a devil lured Tom away and the earth swallowed him up.'"

Eli sighed. "Since then, Megan just wanders about the village looking for her little boy." He handed his empty mug to Tim. "So, you see, that's why I don't go up to the house on Falling Star Hill."

The Girl in the Meadow

The following morning while his grandparents were still asleep, Tim got up before first cockcrow and didn't bother with breakfast. Walking through the village with Josh trotting confidently ahead, he felt as though they were alone in the world. Curtains were still drawn in the cottage windows and in the center of the road a fat tabby cat stalked along in the slanting early morning sun. The cat stopped and watched the little black-and-white dog warily as they passed, but Josh had no interest in cats.

When they were halfway up the gravel path that led to Hunter's house, Tim heard a clashing sound as if steel were striking stone but he couldn't see what was causing it.

As they approached the imposing house, Tim noted that it was connected by a high wall to a barn of roughly equal size, and each building was at least as big as two of the village cottages put together. They were partly covered with ivy that had recently been cut back to reveal large sash windows. The front of the barn, the connecting wall, and the house were all faced with roughly dressed granite.

Set into the connecting wall were high double gates, wide enough for an old-fashioned horse-drawn dray to pass through. Tim knew from his deliveries the previous day that the gates led to a wide cobbled yard between the house and barn, which was mostly built of oak planks.

The curious, clashing sounds continued and, as Tim reached the half-open gates to the yard, he saw Hunter was practicing some kind of violent exercise.

Armed with a glittering sword that he held with both hands, Hunter was whirling about the yard, his movements as light and graceful as a ballet dancer's. The sword flashed as the sunlight caught its curved blade. Slabs of mossy stone, left in the yard since Joseph Mossop's time, rested against the barn wall. Occasionally, Hunter struck the blade against one of them and chips of granite flew off it in a shower of sparks. Eventually, he stopped and stood quite still, his back toward Tim. Then, with a sudden swift movement, he sheathed the sword in the scabbard at his waist.

Without turning around he said, "I didn't think you'd be this early."

Hunter spoke evenly, though Tim had expected him to be out of breath.

"I can come back later, if you like," he replied.

Hunter turned swiftly and shook his head, "No, you can make a start immediately."

Tim hesitated, curiosity overcoming his shyness.

"Did you damage your sword on the granite?" he asked.

Hunter beckoned him over and unsheathed the weapon. Tim expected it to be jagged with nicks, but the edge was unmarked and honed as sharp as a razor.

"This was made for me by Namanatuka, one of the greatest sword makers in Japan," he said. "It's the finest steel in the world."

"Did he teach you to fight with it?" Tim asked.

Hunter shook his head. "No, that was someone else."

He waved Tim back through the gate. "Come on, I'll show you where I want the flowers planted."

Hunter explained that the flowers were to be scattered around the hill with just a few near the house. Tim set about the job, cutting through the meadow's turf with a spade he'd brought with him. It was hard work. Hunter watched him plant a few flowers and nodded with satisfaction.

"I've got to be away for most of the day," he said. "I would slow down a bit. Easy and steady is the way to do this kind of job. Otherwise, you'll be exhausted in a few hours. There's a long way to go."

Hunter stayed a few minutes longer, then went to the cobbled yard and saddled his horse.

"I'll be back later," he called out as he cantered down the hill.

* * *

Tim took Hunter's advice, working steadily while Josh played in the meadow, chasing bees and butterflies. Despite his even pace, Tim was tired by the time his grandfather arrived with a packed lunch for him.

"Did Hunter want them planted like this?" his grandfather asked, surveying the work Tim had already done.

Tim bit gratefully into a cheese and pickle sandwich before answering. The work had certainly sharpened his appetite. "Yes," he replied. "He doesn't want flower beds. He wants them scattered randomly."

When Tim had finished his lunch he strolled up to the house. The day was warm and he'd noticed an old-fashioned pump in the cobbled yard. He went over to splash his face with water before resuming his work.

Josh stayed with him until they were passing back in front of the house, where Hunter had left one of the ground-floor windows open. Barking excitedly, the dog leaped straight through it.

"Josh! Get back here," Tim called, peering into the gloomy interior. But Josh had gone even farther into the house. Tim could hear him in the distance. Following the dog, he clambered in. The shaded rooms were swept clean but were quite bare. The walls were hung with old silk coverings but the patterns were so faded he could only just make out the flowers on them. Tim's footsteps sounded loud on the bare floorboards as he wandered through, calling Josh.

He found him panting at the head of the stairs. Unlike

the ground floor, the first floor hadn't been swept. In the dust on the landing, Tim saw Josh's paw marks and there were also some pointed footprints that were smaller than his own.

"What was it Eli said about little men, Josh?" Tim said with a slight shiver, then he shrugged. "It was probably some woman with small feet from the village who Hunter hired to clean the place," he said firmly. "Come on, Josh, we shouldn't be up here."

Returning to the first room he'd entered, Tim paid more attention to the surroundings. It was a kitchen with bare whitewashed walls, gray with age, and appeared to be the only room Hunter used. The conditions were hardly comfortable. There was a plain table, two wooden chairs, and a sleeping bag on a camp bed in one corner. Two battered tin trunks, covered with labels from foreign parts, stood against a wall. The walk-in pantry was stocked with canned food and an old iron cooking range stood opposite a large stone sink. On the floor was a packed haversack and coils of climbing rope. Hunter's sword and two leather-bound books lay on the table, one much older than the other.

Casually, Tim opened the older-looking book. Its pages were brown with age and on the title page, written in copperplate script, were the words *The Diary of Anne Mossop*. Tim flipped open the second book and saw it, too, was a journal. He guessed it was written by Hunter.

Aware that he was already invading Hunter's privacy by being in the house, he didn't read any of the contents. He ordered Josh outside and returned to his work.

Tim had gotten his second wind by now and plodded on throughout the afternoon. The work was boring but his mind was happily occupied with thoughts of all the things he would be able to do with the money Hunter was going to pay him.

He'd lost track of the time when he heard Josh growling softly beside him. He looked up, blinking, and could just make out a girl standing close by. It was impossible to see her in any detail because she was silhouetted against the sun. Tim laid down the trowel he was using and wiped the perspiration from his eyes. When he looked again she was gone. He stood up to scan the meadow but there was no sign of her. All was quiet but for the hum of bees in the clover.

He'd almost finished planting the last of the flowers when Hunter returned and unsaddled the horse before turning it loose in the meadow. After a time he called Tim to join him outside the house.

As Tim walked up the slope, he noticed some of the flowers he'd planted earlier in the day were missing. In one hole he examined, there was a piece of crystal glass similar to the one he'd found the night before.

Handing it to Hunter, he said, "Someone's been here. I think they may have taken some flowers and left this."

"Did you see them?" asked Hunter, passing Tim a mug of freshly brewed coffee. He hardly glanced at the piece of crystal.

Tim drank thirstily. The coffee tasted delicious. "Just a girl," he answered,

"What kind of girl?" Hunter asked sharply.

Tim explained that he hadn't got a good look at her. He also told Hunter how he'd had to follow Josh into the house, and of the small footprints he'd found on the first floor.

"They could have been left by a girl," he said. "They were more pointed than the kind of shoes any boy would wear."

Hunter was not annoyed by the news of an intruder. Instead, he seemed pleased by the information. "You've done well today," he said, taking a banknote from his pocket and handing it to Tim. "I'll see you when the rest of the flowers arrive."

Tim walked home elated, examining the money Hunter had given him. It was the first fifty-pound note he had ever held!

Hunter watched Tim's retreating figure for a few minutes, then with the glittering gemstone Tim had found, he casually scratched a long curve on the windowpane.

CHAPTER 5

The Visitor Returns

Next morning, Tim was woken by a loud banging on the front door. From his bedroom window he stared down at the top of a man's head. A truck was parked by the door, its engine throbbing.

"Yes," Tim called out.

Glancing up, the man replied, "I've got a load of flowers for Mr. Bishop."

"Can you hang on, please?" Tim said.

"Not for long," said the man. "I'm blocking the street."

Tim and his grandfather, who'd also been roused by the knocking, hurriedly dressed and went down.

"We may as well unload the truck at Hunter's house," said Peter. "It'll save wheeling load after load up the hill."

The driver was no longer in a rush, as Emily was making

him a cup of tea. Luckily, it was too early for his truck to cause any difficulties with other traffic in the narrow street.

A few minutes later, Tim and his grandfather climbed up into the driver's cabin and rode to the house on the hill with Josh on Tim's lap. There was no sign of Hunter but when they were halfway through unloading the flowers he arrived on horseback, looking tired, as if he'd been up all night.

"We'll plant these farther down the hill," he said. "I can give you a hand for a while."

The three of them worked steadily until lunchtime, when Tim's grandfather said, "I've got to get back to the nursery now. I'll bring you up some sandwiches soon, Tim."

"He can eat with me," said Hunter but there was no friendliness in the offer. "Take a break, boy," he added to Tim. "I'll call you when the food's ready."

Tim stayed outside throwing a stick for Josh while Hunter clattered about at the iron cooking range. When Josh eventually tired of retrieving the stick, he ran into the cobbled yard. Tim followed, and a short bark told him that Josh was in the barn.

Inside, the barn was much as it must have been in the days when Joseph Mossop worked in it as a stonemason. In a clear area by the doorway a half-carved angel stood as if on guard, her face, arms, and wings emerging from a block of roughly hewn marble. Looking up, Tim saw that huge oak beams supported the roof slates. Beyond the clear area by the door there was a strange barrier. The vast floor space was filled with a labyrinth of pillars standing at various heights and made from huge oblongs of rough stone, some reaching up as high as the oak crossbeams.

From somewhere beyond the closely stacked pillars came a cheerful bark. Tim knew it was Josh challenging him to come and find him. Light from a high window was flooding into what seemed to be another space farther back in the barn. But Tim couldn't find his way to it. Although the pillars of stone seemed to be placed haphazardly, it was as if someone had deliberately created a maze to stop anyone from reaching the far end of the barn. Each time Tim tried, he found his way blocked by a dead end.

"The food's ready, boy," Hunter shouted just as Josh reappeared, and they returned to the front of the house.

Hunter had brought the chairs and table from the kitchen out onto the overgrown lawn so they could eat in the sunshine. The food was simple. Canned beef stew, a bowl of baked beans, a loaf of dark bread, and a plate of pears.

They ate in silence. As Hunter finished the pear he'd peeled with a horn-handled hunting knife, he stretched and said coldly, "I'm going to get some sleep now. You can carry on with the work this afternoon, can't you?"

Tim nodded, suddenly tired of Hunter's graceless attitude. "Yes," he replied curtly.

Usually, Tim was more polite but Hunter's dismissive attitude reminded him of certain teachers he'd had who always seemed to be in a foul mood. It wasn't just Hunter's bad temper that riled Tim, it was the man's apparent indifference to his presence — he obviously cared nothing for Tim's good opinion. So Tim decided not to bother remembering his own manners.

Hunter went inside, lay down on the camp bed, and almost immediately Tim heard his breathing change. He'd fallen asleep.

Tim resumed his work as the sun continued to beat down. He worked rhythmically, cutting the turf, peeling it back, removing a spadeful of earth, pushing a plant down into it, then filling around it with the trowel. He became mesmerized by the repetitive tedium and hardly noticed the time passing, until the church clock chimed three. He glanced up and saw the girl was once more standing in front of him.

Even though she was so close he could easily have reached out and touched her, she'd made no sound as she approached. This time, Tim could see her clearly. Her long, wheat-colored hair hung down below her shoulders and parted to reveal a solemn, oval-shaped face. Tim was surprised by how beautiful she was. Her nose was slightly snubbed and she had high cheekbones, pale golden skin, and a full mouth. But her eyes were strange. They appeared to change color. First, they were a dark blue, then a lighter green, then gray, then they turned blue again.

She was slender and wore a gray-blue silk dress slit at

the sides so her legs could move easily. As Tim stared in astonishment, the material kept changing color to match her eyes. Her little pointed boots were also made of silk and shimmered in the sun. A fringed leather pouch was slung from her waist.

This time she spoke to him. Her voice was clear, with a slight accent he could not place.

"Did you make these flowers?" she asked.

It seemed such an odd question, Tim smiled. "No, my grandfather grows them," he answered.

"How does he *grow* flowers?" she asked, puzzled.

"From seeds."

"Seeds? What seeds?"

Judging by her accent and the way she spoke English, Tim guessed she was from somewhere abroad. "Seeds are what you plant in the ground when you want to grow flowers, or vegetables, or anything really. You must have seen them in your own country. They're those tiny things that form after a flower has bloomed."

"Can you show me?" she asked.

"I don't have any with me, but if you come to my grandfather's nursery, I can."

The girl frowned and her eyes changed color again. "What is a *nursery*?"

Tim stood up and saw she was about his height. From where they stood on the hill they could look down on the village. He pointed to the greenhouse.

"That's it," he said. "Where the sun is glinting on the glass roof."

"I can't come now," said the girl wistfully. "But I could come tonight. When the bell strikes one."

Tim realized she was referring to the church clock. "Won't your parents mind you being out so late?" he asked.

"No one minds," she said.

"Are you staying in the village?" he asked.

"No, nearby."

It seemed unlikely to Tim that she'd come so late.

"I'll be in bed," he said, "but my window is the one over the front door of the house next to the greenhouse. Throw a pebble up at it if you come."

"I shall," said the girl, leaning forward hesitantly to pat Josh. "I like your creature," she told Tim. Before he could ask her name, she had run toward the house and vanished through the gates in the connecting wall.

Tim decided he'd done enough for the day and walked back up to the house, too. Through the window he could see that Hunter was still asleep. He was about to leave when Josh, who was peering through the gates into the yard, gave a sharp bark.

Hunter woke instantly and sat up, rubbing his beard. "Are you finished?" he asked, seeing Tim at the window.

"For today," Tim answered. He was about to leave but added, "I saw the girl again."

Hunter leaped from the bed and came over to the window. "Where?" he asked urgently.

"In the meadow," said Tim. "She wanted to know if I'd made the flowers."

Hunter slapped his hand on the windowsill. "What else did she say?" he demanded almost angrily.

Although the girl was obviously important to Hunter, Tim was reluctant to tell him of their intended meeting. He couldn't be sure that Hunter meant the girl well.

Hunter saw he was holding back. He vaulted through the window and took Tim by the shoulders.

"Listen to me, boy," he said in an urgent voice. "This girl is the daughter of my friends. She's not right in the head, she keeps running away. I promised them I'd take care of her. Help me, please; it's important that I find her — before she does herself any harm."

Tim was uncertain now. Hunter's story sounded plausible. The girl was certainly odd. The strange way she talked and arranged to meet in the middle of the night was not normal behavior for a young girl. Perhaps she was a danger to herself, thought Tim. Hunter was a grim sort of man, but he did sound as though he had the girl's best interest at heart.

Reluctantly, Tim told him that the girl was coming to the nursery at one o'clock that night. Hunter closed his eyes, relaxed his shoulders, and inhaled deeply, as if receiving good news after a worrying time.

"Will you bring her up to the barn, Tim?" Hunter said, using his name for the first time. "It's for her own benefit."

"I'll try," Tim answered.

Hunter put his hands on Tim's shoulders. "Don't tell your grandparents about this," he said. "They won't be keen on your being out after midnight."

Tim nodded — he'd already decided to keep the girl's proposed visit a secret from his grandparents — and set off for the nursery.

The village street was more crowded now. Day-trippers to the village antique shops strolled in pairs along the sidewalks and gazed into the windows. Tim was almost home when he saw Megan Tagg, the woman in the shawl, hurrying toward him, her eyes blazing. When they were a few paces apart she raised her arms and screamed, "You're dealing with the devil, boy! You'll bring the demons back to Falling Star Hill!"

Tim was transfixed with embarrassment. The woman looked possessed. Several elderly couples stopped to stare, puzzled by the woman's extraordinary and violent accusation.

"You don't know what you're doing, boy," Megan Tagg screamed in anguish. "They took my son, stole my only child. They're devils."

Before she could shout more, old Eli turned up. He crossed the road and put his arm around her shoulders. "Come along, Meg," he soothed. "There's no need for all that. Leave the lad alone, he doesn't know what he's doing."

Eli gestured for Tim to pass by as he guided the madwoman away. Disturbed by the encounter, Tim hurried back to his grandparents' house to eat and wait for night to fall.

CHAPTER 6

A Strange Meeting

When Tim went upstairs for the night, he slipped off his shoes but didn't undress before getting into bed. He pulled the duvet up to his chin and pretended to be asleep when his grandmother looked into his room. He did doze off for a time but woke the instant the church clock began chiming midnight.

Some hours seem much longer than others and the one Tim now waited through seemed more like an entire evening. He tried to read but couldn't concentrate. Then he remembered he'd packed a model airplane kit to put together while he was in Enton over the summer. It was enough to absorb his attention until he heard a noise in the quiet street below. He switched off the desk lamp and went over to the open window.

All was silent outside. A full moon, which seemed brighter than any he'd ever seen, shone from a clear, star-filled sky. Tim could see every detail of the street below. There was a movement.

Farther down the street a figure was heading in his direction, but it was too tall to be the girl. It was Megan, the madwoman who'd shouted at him earlier. She was walking down the middle of the road crooning and muttering to herself as she passed his window. Then there was silence again.

Tim lay down on the bed and waited. A shaft of moonlight, so bright he could read the lettering on the box of his aircraft kit, shone into his room. The church clock chimed one, but the silence continued.

Suddenly, he felt something land on his stomach. Surprised, he glanced down and saw a piece of the polished crystal. He leaped up and over to the open window. The girl was standing in the street below.

Tim waved and, tucking his slingshot into his belt, he picked up his flashlight and slipped on his shoes. He crept downstairs and located the row of hooks where his grandfather kept his keys.

Leaving the front door closed but unlocked, he beckoned to the girl to follow him to the greenhouse. He didn't switch on the main lights but she was enchanted when he shone the flashlight along the rows of trestle tables. His grandfather had retained some stock for his other customers, so there was still an abundance of flowers.

"I have heard of this place," said the girl. "Friends have

been here and they told me of it. But I did not imagine it would be so wondrous."

Wondrous, thought Tim. What an interesting choice of word. Where *had* she learned her English?

"Why are they in these things?" she asked, pointing.

"Flowerpots keep the flowers fresh until you want to plant them in the soil," Tim explained.

The girl looked up sharply. "You mean the life of the flower is longer if they stay in these containers?"

"Of course," replied Tim. Then he said, "My name's Timothy. People call me Tim. What's your name?"

"It is Sarre," she said, pronouncing it like a sigh of the wind.

"Sah —" Tim attempted.

She shook her head. "No, *Sarre.*"

This time he did better, and she smiled. "That is so," she said. "Now, will you show me some flower seeds?"

Tim found several packets and handed them to her. She shook one, looking puzzled at the soft rattle.

"Put out your hand," Tim said as he tore open a packet and shook a few seeds into her palm. She studied them, then clasped her hand shut. When she opened her hand again, Tim was astonished to see the seeds had sprouted.

"How did you do that?" he asked.

"I do not know," she answered.

"You can keep those packets," Tim said.

Sarre placed them carefully in the pouch at her waist. For a time she wandered between the tables, gently touching various plants. It was as if she were visiting an art gallery filled with fabulous paintings. Then she stopped, suddenly alert, as though she'd heard a distant noise.

"I must go now," she said.

Tim remembered his promise to Hunter. "Where to?" he asked anxiously.

"Back to the house of stones," she replied.

Tim was puzzled, until he realized she meant Hunter's barn.

"Is that where you've been hiding?" he asked.

She nodded. "Now it is time to return to my home."

"May I come with you to the barn?" Tim asked.

She hesitated slightly before answering, "If you wish."

They hurried through the moonlit village to the hill, with Josh prancing merrily about their feet, excited to have this unexpected outing. When they'd passed the drystone wall, Tim had the odd sensation that there were other people close to him. Josh felt it, too. With the hair on his back bristling, he kept stopping and giving low warning growls. Tim could see every detail of the meadow, and there was a strange flickering at the very edge of his vision. Twice he thought he'd caught a glimpse of what looked like a little man.

As they crossed the meadow going up toward the house, Tim saw that more of the flowers he'd planted earlier had vanished. Sarre stooped to pick up three stacks of the plastic flowerpots, some still containing earth, that Tim had discarded earlier. She placed most of them in a silk sack she'd taken from her pouch. Many more were still on the ground. Sarre produced another silk sack, and handing it to Tim, said, "Please, help me to carry more of them."

It was odd behavior, but he did as she asked and gathered up more of the empty pots.

No lights shone in Hunter's house. They passed the front door and before Sarre entered the barn she turned, reached for the sack Tim carried, and said, "I was very glad to meet you, Tim, but you must go now."

He followed her into the barn but before he could say anything, a battery of powerful lights blazed down on them. Each one shone with a different color of the rainbow. Startled, Tim gasped when he saw what they revealed.

Close by were five little men, none of whom even came up to his shoulder height. They were dressed in tight leather trousers, brightly colored silk shirts, and long laced coats that came to just above their knees. They wore soft leather hats shaped like large berets and high boots with pointed toes. Each one carried a pack on his back filled with flowers.

The little men's features were extraordinary. They had long, narrow, pale faces, framed by straight, fair hair that hung to their shoulders. Their almond-shaped eyes slanted over high cheekbones. Their noses were long and pointed, and their chins were sharp. And they looked just as startled and frightened as Tim did in the bright light.

They began to scatter, but just then a finely webbed net fell from the ceiling, trapping them along with Tim, Josh, and Sarre. As they all struggled wildly to free themselves, Hunter stepped out from behind the angel carving, wearing his sword and carrying his large haversack and the coils of rope.

"Please don't be afraid," he said, holding up his hand. "I mean you no harm."

The little man standing closest to Sarre replied crossly, "I am Almat, Chief of the Treggers. What do you want with us?"

Hunter replied in a gentle voice, "I want you to take me with you to Tallis."

Despite the net draped over his body, Almat managed to look extremely dignified. He stood straight, folded his arms, and said, "Impossible. It is forbidden to *invite* humans to Tallis. They can only come by chance. That is the law."

"If I cannot go, then neither can you," Hunter retorted with a warning edge to his voice.

"Remember the moon, Almat," urged one of the little men, and as they all looked anxiously toward the window high in the barn wall, he added, "We must hurry."

Just then, Tim smelled the powerful fumes of gasoline. As he glanced about looking for the source, a sudden roaring sound and a wave of heat engulfed them. Tim scooped up Josh and stuffed him into his shirt. As if recognizing the danger, the dog lay quite still next to Tim's thumping heart.

Hunter kicked open the door and immediately retreated from a searing wall of flame. The barn was on fire! Beyond the doorway Tim could see the madwoman, Megan. She held a blazing torch aloft and was shrieking triumphantly.

"I'll kill you all. Just as you killed my Tom. Burn, all of you, *burn!*"

With a few rapid sweeps of his sword, Hunter cut through the net. The little men scrambled free, and urged on by Almat and Sarre, they disappeared into the maze of stones in the barn.

"Come back! You'll get trapped in there!" Hunter shouted.

But Sarre shook her head as the flames blazed even higher.

"Follow me," she shouted above the roar, and she, too, slipped into the stone maze. Hunter pushed Tim in after her, snatched up his haversack and rope, and followed them. Guided by Sarre, they twisted and turned through the narrow passageways. The heat and choking smoke grew so intense, Tim doubted they would survive. But all of a sudden they were standing in another clear space. The one Tim had been unable to find when he'd first explored the barn.

In the center was a strange shimmering pool, more like quicksilver than water. Reflected in its surface was the full moon, shining down through the high window. Without the slightest hesitation Almat leaped into the pool and vanished.

There was no splash. It was as if he'd simply melted into the surface. Tim stood staring down at the pool, looking too shocked to move.

"Come, Tim," said Sarre calmly as she took his hand, and they leaped together into the reflection of the moon.

Hunter followed, still clasping his haversack and ropes.

CHAPTER 7

The Rim of Tallis

Tim had closed his eyes, expecting to plunge into
something similar to water, but the sensation he
experienced was very different. It was as though
he and Sarre had been swallowed by a gigantic creature
and were now hurtling through a great, churning stomach
lined with velvet. They tumbled over and over, propelled
by some unseen force along a soft dark passageway until
they were suddenly ejected.

Tim, still clasping his silk sack of flowerpots, opened
his eyes to find himself lying next to Sarre on soft ground
in a strange alien landscape unlike anything he'd ever seen
before. They were surrounded by the Treggers.

Sarre tugged Tim aside, and Hunter emerged from the

ground in his place, leaving no sign of the passageway through which they had just traveled.

Tim now felt a new sensation that made him think there was something wrong with his sight. Every few seconds his vision was momentarily obscured by a pastel-colored flash of light. Each flash, in turn, was a different color of the spectrum.

Above their heads a dark lead-gray sky appeared to be part of a hazy opaque bubble that stretched over them to infinity. High in the strange sky, Tim could see two weakly glowing orbs, one paler than the other. It came as a shock to realize they were a sun and a moon, but he could see no stars, and it was icy cold. The landscape was generally flat but with an uneven surface. There was no direct light, just a pale diffused glow that seemed to come from the ground itself. The air was filled with the smell of ashes.

Around them stretched a nightmarish vista, heaped with oddly familiar shapes. Some were as large as houses, others smaller than Tim. But everything, including the ground beneath their feet, was covered in a gray-green lichen that softened and rounded all outlines. Scattered everywhere among the lichen were countless numbers of glittering stones the color of rubies, emeralds, and diamonds.

Tim picked up a ruby and an emerald, each the size of a pigeon's egg, and held them out to Hunter who was adjusting the coil of rope and the haversack on his back.

"Are these real?" Tim asked.

Hunter nodded and loosened the sword in his scabbard. "Real, right enough," he replied, sounding disinterested.

Just then, Tim felt Josh poke his head out from inside his shirt and lick his chin.

"Stay in there," Tim ordered, still unsure of the disturbing landscape.

Maybe it's a dream, he told himself, but he knew it wasn't. He was about to ask more questions, but Almat spoke.

"We must keep moving," he said. "It is dangerous here."

"Before you do, Treggers," said Sarre, emptying the sacks of flowerpots onto the ground, "put your flowers into one of these."

"Is it important?" asked Almat, looking about him anxiously.

"*Very* important," replied Sarre, so they all hurried to do as she instructed.

After potting the flowers, they set off in single file with Almat leading. Without pausing on their march, the Treggers produced more silk sacks and stooped to fill them with the precious stones that lay everywhere. Sarre handed Tim another sack and told him to do the same.

"What's over there?" Tim asked Sarre, pointing to a thick gray mist on the horizon.

"Nothing," she replied. "We can't go there."

"Why not?"

"There is no air, just the gray fog."

To his astonishment and despite the flickering light, Tim

began to recognize familiar shapes in the disconcerting jumble all about them. It was as if they were passing through an endless rubbish dump of things from his own world.

Sown in the dreary wasteland were fragments of buildings, cars, household goods, toys, trees, boats — an infinite variety of ill-matched objects, all randomly scattered yet unified by their covering of gray-green lichen.

The Chief of the Treggers led his men, with Sarre, Tim, and Hunter following, in a direction that was away from the ominous gray mist. Josh was still stuffed inside Tim's shirt and for the time being seemed glad to be there.

"Where are we, Hunter?" Tim asked, glancing over his shoulder.

"The Rim of Tallis," he replied.

"How am I going to get home?" Tim wanted to know, growing more anxious.

"You can't — not until the next full moon," answered Sarre. "Watch your step, this ground is treacherous."

As they hurried on, they became aware of a distant rumbling sound. The column of walkers stopped, everyone looking about them. The rumbling grew into a roar and the ground trembled. Tim could see fear on the faces of Sarre and the little Tregger men.

Suddenly, a mighty ball of fire erupted from the ground, less than fifty paces from where they stood. As it tore out of the earth and hurtled into the air, a great shower of precious jewels, like a gigantic firework exploding, burst forth to carpet the ground. The flaming ball soared far into the sky and curved to die away on the distant horizon. The Treggers rushed forward to where the comet had emerged, and to Tim's astonishment, an old-fashioned bicycle materialized.

"Hurry, hurry," cried Almat. "There may be more coming."

One of the Treggers retrieved the bicycle and pushing it along, rejoined the column. Despite their small stature the Treggers set a hard pace. They hurried on, winding through the bizarre landscape for more than an hour. Occasionally, Tim saw darting movements close by but it was hard to make out shapes because of the flickering light.

"There's something alive out there," Tim said to Sarre. "What is it?"

She shrugged without pausing in her stride. "Good things, bad things, Tim. We do not have time to look."

"Where are we going?" he asked.

"There," she replied, pointing.

Ahead of them, Tim now saw that the lichen-covered landscape came to an abrupt end and the ground fell away in a steep precipice. It faded to the horizon in both directions. Beyond the cliff's edge, an ocean of blackness stretched before them.

The Tregger wheeling the bicycle walked close to the abyss and threw it into the void.

Without pausing, the Treggers swarmed over the edge. Sarre hesitated and asked, "How well do you climb, Tim?"

"Don't worry, I'll take care of him," said Hunter, who was securing his rope to the axle of an ancient, lichen-covered truck that lay on its side nearby.

"How did we get here?" Tim asked Hunter.

"Through a hole blasted by a falling star, boy," he replied. "I thought that much would be obvious by now."

Tim waved to encompass the weird landscape of random objects that lay behind them. "And all that just fell in after other falling stars?"

"That's right. Just like that bicycle."

"This is a dreadful place," said Tim, shivering with cold.

"It gets better," said Hunter, "but there's a way to go." He clipped a harness he'd taken from his haversack around Tim's waist.

"Hold the rope," he said, "and pay it out through the ring on the harness to lower yourself. I'll be following, so be quick."

Hunter threw the coiled rope over the precipice. Tim checked on Josh who was still snuggled inside his shirt, then launched himself over the edge and began to descend the cliff.

It was so smooth, Tim was astonished to see that Sarre and the Treggers were climbing down without ropes. It did not seem possible. He lowered himself quickly, slowing down when he saw Sarre immediately below him.

She was descending with astonishing agility, as were the

Treggers. They found hand- and toeholds where Tim saw only smooth rock. There was no hesitation in their descent; it was as rhythmical as dancing.

Tim could not judge how far they had come, it seemed to be taking hours, but eventually he became aware that it was growing lighter, and the cold wasn't nearly so intense. Every so often, Hunter took spikes from his haversack and banged them into the rock face. Then he released the rope above and resecured it for the next section of their descent.

As more time passed, Tim noticed the dreary gray rock face was slowly becoming the color of lavender. The smell of ashes had long gone and the air here was fresh and unscented. Looking up, he saw the sky was now blue-black, and the flickers of light had ceased. He saw other colors far below. A mist of red and gold, but he couldn't make out if it was the ground or something else. A warm breeze began to blow. The sky gradually lightened to a brilliant yellow, shading to turquoise and sapphire blue at the horizon.

Below, the gold-and-red mass was slowly revealed to be the tree canopy of an enormous forest. Farther away from the face of the precipice, the red-and-gold treetops merged into greener foliage. They were descending into a mighty forest that spread to the outer limits of Tim's vision.

CHAPTER 8

In the Great Forest

It wasn't until they reached the forest canopy that Tim appreciated just how breathtakingly huge the trees were. Each red or gold leaf was the length of his forearm and at their widest were equal to the span of both his hands. They felt dry and warm to the touch.

The Treggers had stopped to take a rest. They were lying back along the massive branches, their faces turned to the wind, which was stronger now. The branches sprouting from the main trunk of the tree were at least ten paces wide. Hanging from smaller twigs were silk sacks left by the Treggers on their outward journey. They were filled with food — some dark green fruit the size of melons that looked unripe but tasted delicious — a bit like a cherries, Tim thought.

There were also pies. Biting into one cautiously, Tim was delighted to find it tasted like steak and kidney. What was happening was so utterly strange it was comforting to find something familiar, even if it was only a pie. He fed some to Josh, who wolfed it down.

Hunter unhooked Tim's harness and tugged on the rope in a well-practiced way until it came free and began to fall all around them. After he'd secured it around a branch, Hunter fed it down the trunk of the tree. Then he lay along one of the massive branches to rest, his hat pulled over his eyes.

Tim was tired, too. He'd carried Josh for the entire journey and the extra weight was telling. Sarre moved closer to the branch on which he was sitting.

"Give me a shoulder sack," she instructed one of the Treggers. The little man unslung his backpack, and being careful not to damage the flowers it contained, he rummaged around and produced a silk bag with loops of cord attached as shoulder straps.

"Will you cut some leaves with your sword?" Sarre asked Hunter.

Tim realized she intended to fill the sack, but he was puzzled about the need to use Hunter's sword. He reached out to pluck a leaf and was surprised. It was completely dry, with a texture like linen, and no matter how hard he tugged, it was impossible to break the stem.

The Treggers laughed at his efforts.

"These are not living trees," Sarre explained. "No one

knows how old they are. The trunks and branches have turned to stone, but the leaves are soft — and they fly."

Hunter demonstrated, slashing through the leaf stems along a branch. The moment a leaf was cut free it floated upward. Astonished, Tim reached up and caught three of them. Immediately his hand felt lighter. Sarre stuffed the leaves into the sack and let it bob in her hands like a gas-filled balloon. She held it out so Tim could wriggle his arms through the shoulder loops. As soon as it was secure on his back he felt buoyed up by its lightness.

"Take care the wind doesn't blow you away," said Almat, laughing. "And when you pull yourself down through the trees, watch out for broken twigs. They're as sharp as knives."

Giant trees with leaves that fly and branches sharp as knives, Tim thought. What other surprises lay in store in this incredible world?

After a brief rest, the Treggers resumed their descent of the tree. Judging from the width of its trunk and the mighty branches, Tim had expected the trees to be tall but he was not prepared for just how vast they really were. The trunk of the one they were climbing down was even wider than his grandparents' schoolhouse, but at least its petrified bark made for easy handholds. Almat was right about the broken twigs, though. Despite taking care, Tim tore his shirt in a few places and ripped his jeans at the knee. But having the silk sack full of leaves made the descent feel almost like a game and the sense of weightlessness was exhilarating.

They climbed down for hours, taking two more rest breaks.

"Just how tall are these trees?" Tim asked Sarre as they stopped for one of their breaks.

"We measure them in time," she answered casually. "This one is a day and a half's climb."

Eventually, Almat called, "Night is coming, make yourselves secure."

There was virtually no twilight. A few minutes of grayness, then dark. But Sarre and the Treggers had quickly produced oblongs of silk from their knapsacks and tied them to the stone branches to fashion hammocks. The silk was finer and smoother than any material Tim had ever seen and it appeared to be very strong. Hunter cut two lengths of rope and showed Tim the best way to tie himself to the fork of a massive branch just below Sarre's hammock.

"Are there other humans like you in Tallis, Sarre?" Tim asked her in the darkness. "Or are the rest of the people like the Treggers?"

"Most are like me, I am told," she replied with a yawn. "But I have always lived with Bethen among the Treggers."

"What is a bethen?"

"Bethen is a person, that's her name. She is one of the Chanters. They have special powers. I am to be a Chanter one day."

"Do you have special powers?" he asked, but Sarre was already asleep.

Tim's head was filled with questions but he was also exhausted and, despite the hardness of the stone branches and the warm wind, he, too, was soon fast asleep.

When the Treggers roused themselves, Hunter was already up and trimming his beard. He used his bone-handled knife and splashed water on his face from a canteen in his haversack. Tim had woken up with the idea that he should give Josh more freedom and make him his own leaf-filled balloon. While the others breakfasted on more of the dark green fruit, Tim borrowed another silk sack and with Hunter's blade managed to hack off more leaves.

The little dog waited patiently as Tim tied the sack to his back. As a precaution against him floating off in the strong wind, Tim tied a length of string around his own waist and the other end to Josh's collar. As they resumed their descent, Josh quickly learned to use his paws to avoid being bumped against the branches. The Treggers, who at first had been nervous of the little dog, were now greatly amused by his valiant efforts.

"They like your creature," Sarre told Tim as they climbed. "Usually, when they visit your world, such animals chase them."

"Don't you have dogs here?" asked Tim.

"Not in Tallis," she replied.

* * *

Finally, the long climb ended. They had reached the vast, gnarled tree roots, tall as houses and arching up in grotesque shapes from a carpet of gigantic ferns that emitted a sharp, musky scent.

The Treggers hunted about for a time and eventually found the bicycle they'd thrown from the top of the precipice. Incredibly, it had not become caught in the branches of the tree, but it had been knocked about a lot during its fall. The wheels were buckled out of shape.

"You won't be able to ride that," said Tim.

The Treggers produced tools from their haversacks and in a few minutes had taken apart the bike and distributed the pieces among them. They were all heavily loaded now with knapsacks of flowers, bags of jewels, and bicycle parts.

Sarre suddenly held up a warning hand, and the Treggers stood quite still. She closed her eyes and appeared to be listening intently. All Tim could hear was the sigh of the strong wind blowing through the forest.

Almat whispered, "Are they near?"

Sarre nodded. "A few, but more are on their way."

"We must hurry," said Almat.

They quickly reformed in single file with Almat taking the lead. Twisting their way beneath the vast roots of the stone trees, they hurried on, the wind blowing against their backs.

CHAPTER 9

A River Journey

The forest changed as the gigantic stone trees merged with a living forest that bore some resemblance to the woods Tim knew at home, albeit on a vast scale. The trees were massive but recognizable: sycamore, hornbeam, elm, and oak towered above him and the forest floor was carpeted in a thick soft layer of leaf mold.

They hurried on, the strong wind still blowing, marching hour after hour without rest. Eventually, they came to the edge of a wide, lazily flowing river fringed with reed beds and overhung by the branches of mighty trees.

"Rim River," Almat announced.

Tim, too exhausted to speak, slumped down on the bank and saw large rainbow-striped fish darting through the crystal-clear water.

Even Hunter seemed to be tired but the Treggers and Sarre were apparently unaffected by the rigors of their long march, and Josh looked fresh, too. He was still wearing his floating bag of red-and-gold leaves and Tim had easily towed him along like a balloon.

Resting with his back to a tree, Tim watched Almat stroll down the riverbank and onto the surface of the water. "What the —" Tim cried, and leaped up to see better. Only then did he realize that, carefully concealed in the reeds, there was a sunken pontoon just below the surface.

One of the Treggers took off his knapsack, jewel bag, and the handlebar of the bicycle that was slung about his waist, then swiftly climbed up an oak tree overhanging the river. From the fork of the tree, Tim was amazed to see him lowering an ancient tuba to Almat. The brass instrument was green from lack of polishing but the stops still worked.

Almat blew a long, melodious note on the instrument before the Tregger in the tree hoisted it back up to its hiding place.

Looking back anxiously, Almat asked Sarre, "Are they still following?"

She closed her eyes for a moment of concentration, then nodded.

"What do you think is following us?" Tim asked Hunter.

"Nothing good," he replied shortly, just as Tim spotted a long, single-masted boat with eight oars on each side being rowed rapidly downstream toward them. As in a

Viking ship, the rowers were protected by large, round, leather shields that were fixed along the sides of the craft.

Its crew of Tregger people skillfully brought the boat alongside the submerged jetty so that Almat and his party could climb onto its deck. Swiftly, the rowers pulled away and returned to the middle of the stream. At its widest the river was about forty paces from bank to bank but where they were it narrowed to half that width.

Almat's Treggers took off their loads and two of them hoisted the sail. Caught by the strong wind, it snapped open and the boat's speed increased immediately. The rowers shipped their oars, all the while keeping careful watch on the trees along the riverbank. Sarre beckoned to Tim and Josh to keep down with her behind the protective shields. Realizing they expected to be attacked, Tim loaded his slingshot with a ruby from his jewel sack.

"What are we hiding from?" Tim asked.

"The wild children," she replied simply. "They live in the forest and try to kill us."

"Children!" said Tim, slightly relieved. "Are they *that* dangerous?"

As he spoke, a shower of tiny arrows thudded into the deck close to Hunter.

The Tregger at the rudder gave a warning shout. Up ahead, shadowy half-naked figures, their bodies smeared with pigment, were concealed in the branches of the over-hanging trees. One of them aimed his bow directly at Hunter as the boat passed close to the tree in which the savage child was crouching. He was about to release his arrow, when Tim's ruby hit him square in the forehead. He fell with a scream into the river and they watched him swim to the bank.

"The boy saved your life, tall man," Almat called out, and laughed.

Tim was doubtful. "I don't think that little arrow would have killed Hunter," he said.

Almat plucked one of the arrows from the deck and threw it like a spear into the stream ahead. In the wake of the boat, Tim saw dead fish float to the surface as they sailed on.

"There is enough poison on the tip of just one of their arrows to kill us all," said Almat.

Hunter nodded his thanks to Tim but said nothing.

Sarre drew another of the arrows from the deck and wrapped it carefully in a silk sack.

Gradually, the river widened and by steering a course in the middle of the stream, the boat kept out of arrow range. Satisfied that they'd reached safer waters, the Treggers set about making themselves more comfortable. After showing the crew the potted flowers they had taken from Falling Star Hill, one of them produced a round object, blackened with soot, and some bundles of firewood.

Placing the blackened car hubcap on a square of metal at the rear of the boat, the Tregger lit a charcoal fire in it. While they waited for the flames to die down to hot embers, three Treggers trailed fishing lines in the boat's wake. Within a few minutes they had made several catches.

It seemed to take ages to cook them but eventually they were all eating the grilled fish, which had a delicious smoky flavor. The Treggers fed tidbits of fish to Josh and laughed with delight when he snapped down each mouthful. The daylight faded fast but they sailed on, the strong wind filling their single sail. Then the moon rose, bathing the river in silver light. At last, without the threat of danger from the riverbank or any hard marching to do, there was time to talk.

Sarre was in the prow of the boat with Almat when Tim asked Hunter about Tallis. "You've been here before, haven't you?" he began.

"A long time ago," Hunter replied.

"Where exactly are we?"

Hunter shrugged. "Tallis exists close to our world but you can only reach it through the passages made by falling stars. The only people who can see these starways from Tallis to Earth are the Chanters and Warlocks. That's why the Treggers brought Sarre with them. They don't have the ability."

"So Sarre is a Chanter," said Tim.

"One day she will be. She's still learning, but she can already see the starways."

"Can anyone here learn to be a Chanter or a Warlock?"

Hunter shook his head. "No, only very rare children are born with the gift. The parents know when the child is

about five years old. That's when their eyes are developed
enough to change color."

"Can boys become Chanters?" asked Tim.

"The power is different in boys and girls. It seems to go
to the bad in boys. They become Warlocks. Some of them
are *very* unpleasant. But with girls it turns to goodness.
They often become great healers."

"What exactly can Chanters do — apart from heal?"
Tim asked. "Sarre says she lives with one."

Hunter shrugged. "They can send and receive messages
by the power of thought, and they can sense danger. The
powerful ones can read minds and sometimes change the
way people behave without them knowing the reason why."

"Sarre can do all that?" said Tim, impressed.

Hunter chuckled. "I doubt it. As I said, she's still learning. Not all of her powers will be fully developed yet."

"Tell me more about the Warlocks," said Tim.

Before Hunter could reply, Sarre interrupted them.
"There are no Warlocks anymore. The Duke killed them."

"All of them?" said Hunter, surprised. "I thought they
numbered among his supporters?"

"Only the Duke's personal Warlock, Stryker, survived."

"Things *have* changed," said Hunter.

"What kind of place is Tallis?" asked Tim, still deeply
puzzled by his whereabouts.

"You'll see," said Hunter. "Sometimes it's like our world
and sometimes completely different. Not everything that

passes through the starways comes out the same as it was on Earth. Things can alter on the way through."

"Why do they speak English?"

Hunter shook his head. "I don't know. But I've traveled about the world a good deal. All civilizations have legends about places similar to Tallis. They always speak the same language as the country in which the legend exists."

"Are there roads? Do they have railways or airplanes?" asked Tim.

Hunter laughed wearily. "They don't have many machines here. If you want a rough idea of what it's like, imagine you've traveled back in time to the Middle Ages."

"Why don't they have machines?" asked Tim. "If they can get into our world, why haven't they copied things?"

"There's no gasoline or coal. So no cars nor even steam power. Besides, things just don't always work in the same way here — you'll see." Hunter gave a long yawn and stretched his arms, saying, "I'm going to rest now. I'd advise you to do the same."

Hunter was asleep within moments, but Tim needed his questions answered and Sarre was still awake.

"Why do you help the Treggers to take flowers, Sarre?" he asked.

"We do not have living flowers in Tallis," she answered, looking toward the tall trees on the moonlit bank. "They only grow where you come from."

"And only the Treggers take them?"

"Yes, the Treggers have always lived near the Southern Rim. The strange light has affected them. It is very hard for you to see a Tregger in your world. Some humans do, but not many. So Treggers go there to hunt flowers. Flowers are one of the greatest prizes in Tallis. They are treasured. But the Treggers must be quick to trade them for goods, because the flowers die so soon."

"What about the jewels we collected?"

"They are also useful for trade. They have value because hardly anyone but the Treggers dare go to the Rim and collect them."

"You dare, Sarre."

She raised her head. "One day I shall be a Chanter. I must learn to fear nothing. Besides, I have the power to see the starways into your world."

"Will I ever be able to get home, Sarre?" he asked.

"Do not worry, Tim. I will take you when we go back to the Rim."

"When will that be?"

Sarre shrugged. "The next full moon or the one after that, maybe."

Tim sighed. "My family will be frantic."

"Do not be concerned," said Sarre. "I can arrange it so that no time will have passed when you return."

Tim was intrigued. "How can you do that?"

"By consulting a Time Map."

Seeing his blank expression in the bright moonlight, Sarre laughed. "Tallis and Earth have different times," she explained. "In ancient days the Chanters made Time Maps. We can return to any monthly anniversary starting from when the starway was made. But we can only visit the past. Do not concern yourself, Tim. Your family will not worry about you. They won't even know you are gone."

Feeling a little more at ease, Tim finally lay down in the bottom of the boat. His mind still teemed with unanswered questions, but he was too tired to talk anymore. And with Josh curled up beside him, he soon fell asleep.

CHAPTER 10

In the Tregger Village

Sarre shook Tim awake. He blinked up into a brilliant blue sky where snatches of wispy clouds were being blown in the same direction as the boat. Despite the wind, the early morning sun was strong enough to make the planks of the boat feel warm to the touch.

The river was even wider now and faster flowing. The forest lay farther back from it, with swathes of flat sandy land shelving away from the embankment. The river's edge was thick with a wide growth of tall reeds. After a time, Tim spotted a high wooden stockade built close to the tree line.

The helmsman steered the boat toward the bank, where dozens of boats were moored at long wooden jetties that reached out into the water.

There were several larger craft, the same size as their own smaller sailing boats, skiffs, rafts, and clusters of red-and-gold painted canoes. The Treggers lowered the sail and rowed the final distance to the shore, where a crowd had gathered to greet them. Women and children crowded the jetties. The women wore silk dresses, similar to Sarre's, and the children were clad in plain linen smocks.

They all gazed at Hunter in fascination as he stepped from the boat — he was twice as tall as most of them. Tim was given only a passing glance but a gasp of surprise went up when they saw Josh. Children clung to their mothers' skirts, some hiding their faces, until the Treggers, who'd grown used to him on the long journey from the Rim, patted the little dog to show there was no danger and encouraged the children to do the same. Josh scampered from one to another, wagging his tail and enjoying all the attention.

From the jetty, Tim could see more of the high stockade. Watchtowers flanked either side of the two great gates facing the river.

A wide pontoon, built of planking and resting on the sandy soil, stretched from the landing stage to the stockade. Sarre explained that at certain times of year the ground was as treacherous as quicksand. They crossed the pontoon and entered the stockade. There was nothing of the Treggers' village to be seen at ground level, just a vast expanse of packed, sweet-smelling earth.

The Treggers had hollowed their houses out of the giant trees of the forest, with only the irregularly shaped doors and windows visible in the mighty trunks. Walkways fashioned from vines, ropes, and planks ran between them. The door of every house was painted red and gold.

"They're the same colors as the leaves of the great stone trees," said Tim.

Sarre nodded. "The Treggers make paint by boiling the leaves. When the color is extracted, so is the lightness. They use the leaves for clothing, and paint the red-and-gold dye on their doors and boats to bring them good luck."

"Does no one live on the ground?"

Sarre gestured for Hunter and Tim to follow her up a wooden staircase.

"The river floods in the spring," she explained.

They reached the walkways and she led them farther into the stockade.

"How high does the river get?" Hunter asked.

"Never higher than the platforms," said Sarre. "And when that happens we can step straight from our doorways into the boats."

Finally, Sarre stopped in front of a tall, strong-looking woman, dressed in a long, white silk robe and sandals, who stood with folded arms on the walkway ahead of them. Thick silver-gray hair framed the woman's broad features. Tim could tell she was very old but there were few wrinkles marring her smooth pink skin. Her expression was serious, almost grim, as they approached. Her eyes were just like Sarre's and changed color as she stood watching them.

"I am Bethen," she said in a deep voice with the same accent as Sarre's. "And you are Hunter, Tim, and the dog, Josh. Sarre has already told me about you."

"How could sh — ?" Tim began. Then he remembered that Chanters were able to send messages over great distances. He'd had his doubts when Hunter had told him about this ability. But here was the proof!

To Tim's surprise, Josh immediately trotted forward and leaped into the woman's arms. Smiling down at him, she scratched behind his ear.

"It is a long time since I last saw a dog," she said and, cradling Josh in one arm, indicated they should enter the open doorway beside her.

It was surprisingly large and light inside the tree. In the main room there were four large easy chairs, upholstered in red leather. The floor was covered in thick rugs woven with floral designs. A kitchen, tiled with clay, led off the main room, and a carved spiral staircase led upstairs into the branches where there were more rooms.

Bethen set Josh on one of the chairs next to a wall that consisted of row upon row of shelves, all packed with scrolls of parchment and three large leather-bound books. An elaborately carved table and six chairs stood under the window. Another table was covered with jars of herbs. Beautiful relief carvings of plants and farm animals covered the walls. Images of wheat sheaves, vines, pigs, cows, chickens, and ducks were entwined in intricate detail. Tim wondered if the woman had carved them herself.

"This house was given to me by the Treggers long ago," Bethen answered, as if Tim had asked the question aloud. "It is typical of their homes. They have little to do in the hard winter, so they make furniture and carve walls."

Tim felt hungry, and his shirt and jeans were grubby and torn. Bethen looked at him, saying, "The food is nearly ready. If you would care for a bath after your journey I will wash and mend your clothes for you."

Hunter had taken off his pack but was still standing when the old woman reached out to touch his face.

"This has been a long journey for one with such a heavy heart," she said, as if she knew all his secrets.

Hunter smiled bitterly. "And still a long way to go," he answered.

"You have visited Tallis before," Bethen said. It was a statement not a question.

"Some time ago," Hunter replied. "But I came here then by a different starway."

She touched the hilt of his sword but quickly withdrew her hand as if she'd received a shock.

"A special weapon," she said. "I'm glad it is in your hands."

She smiled again and said, "There's food and clothing to attend to. Sarre, will you show Tim to the bathroom, please?"

Before they climbed the spiral staircase, Sarre handed Bethen the arrow she had taken from the deck of the Treggers' boat. Bethen placed it on the table among the various bottles. "A new poison?" she said, sighing.

"I think so," replied Sarre.

Then Sarre led Tim upstairs and into a smaller room where a deep, bath-shaped depression was hollowed out in the floor. The wood was smooth and polished, like the inside of a salad bowl. Sarre pulled on a length of plaited rope and warm water cascaded from above to fill it.

"Where does the water come from? And how is it heated?" Tim asked, fascinated.

"Rainwater is trapped and channeled along the higher branches. It's heated by the sun and warm wind," she explained.

Tim handed his clothes out to Sarre before stepping into the bath. He scrubbed himself with handfuls of sweet-smelling herbs from a dish that Sarre had shown him. The herbs made a rich lather and caused his body to tingle pleasantly. His weariness began to melt away, along with all the aches and pains he'd acquired on the journey.

Sarre returned with a white linen robe for Tim to wear until his own clothes were dry.

"Now you look like one of us," she said, smiling at him as he came out of the bathroom.

Embarrassed, Tim looked intently at his feet.

In the large room, Hunter had taken a tin of polish from his haversack and was working it into his riding boots. When he had finished, Bethen took a small glass bottle from a shelf and handed it to him.

"Wipe this over them," she said. "It will protect the leather better than any other potion."

Bethen returned to slicing a long green vegetable with a razor-sharp knife while Hunter did as she'd instructed. When he'd finished he looked down at his boots as if trying to see some difference.

Suddenly, Bethen slashed her blade across one of the boots. Startled, Hunter drew back, but as he looked down at his boots he smiled. There was no sign of a cut in the leather.

"Effective, isn't it?" said Bethen, as she resumed her cooking.

After Hunter had bathed they all sat at the table to eat the meal Bethen had prepared.

"Gurneys will be here tomorrow," Bethen said. "I received a message yesterday."

"Oh, good," said Sarre. "Gurneys are always interesting."

"What are Gurneys?" asked Tim.

Hunter answered, "Traders, they travel all over Tallis."

"Do they use wagons?" asked Tim.

Hunter shook his head as Bethen ladled more stew into his bowl. "No, they don't have wagons, they live in tents. Tomorrow, I'll ask if I can travel with them."

"Will Tim not go with you?" asked Sarre.

Hunter shook his head. "Tim is here by accident. I came by choice. I have business I must attend to in Tallis."

After the meal, Hunter took Anne Mossop's diary from his backpack and sat in one of the easy chairs reading, while Bethen examined the arrow Sarre had brought from the boat. After a time, she got up and began preparing a mixture of herbs at her workbench. Josh jumped onto the bench and with his head cocked to one side he sat watching her intently as if jealous of her attention being elsewhere.

He began to show off, standing on his hind legs and pawing at the arm Bethen was using to mix the herbs. Finally, she laughed and ordered him to sit quietly. They obviously liked each other, so when Sarre asked Tim if he would care to look around the village he accepted, happy to leave Josh with his new friend.

First, Tim and Sarre went up to walk all around the upper perimeter of the stockade. It was made of logs, each one as thick as a man's body and, at regular intervals along the broad platform that was set below the parapet wall, there was a series of watchtowers. Looking out from one of them into bright sunshine, Tim could see there was a wide grassy clearing between the fort and the edge of the dense forest. Every few meters along the wall was a recess stocked with weapons, including shields, clubs, and bows with quivers of arrows.

Tim stopped to examine them and noticed that the arrowheads were blunt. He picked up one of the clubs and was surprised that it was so light, and that the thicker end was covered in tiny needlelike spikes. He was about to test their sharpness when Sarre grabbed his hand.

"Don't touch it," she warned. "The spikes are tipped with a potion Bethen made. The instant they pierce the skin, the person receiving the blow falls into a deep sleep.

We don't want to harm the wild children, we just want to capture them."

Nodding, Tim replaced the club and they walked on. Sarre seemed more lighthearted since they'd reached the village. During the journey her responsibilities had made her seem almost like an adult. Now she was humming a tune and calling out greetings to various Tregger families. Often giggling at their answers, she seemed much more like a girl of his own age.

The walls of the stockade protected more than a hundred of the Tregger houses that were cut into the tree trunks. At the center of the compound there were three massive lime trees. From their branches hung hundreds of round, whitish, papery pods the size of beehives. Tim was about to ask what they were, when there was a sudden torrential downpour.

Blown in slanting torrents by the driving wind, the rain had come on so swiftly Tim hadn't even noticed the clouds gathering. Within moments, the light turned dimly gray and the rain was hammering all about them. Pounding down on the roof of the stockade, the water ran off it in sheets. The cloudburst lasted only a few minutes but it left large pools on the bare ground inside the perimeter. When the sun streamed down again, it lit up myriads of incredibly fine lines, sparkling with rainwater and stretching from the round, white, papery pods to the windows of the homes hollowed out of the trees.

"What are those lines?" Tim asked Sarre.

"The thread that the Tregger women weave into silk."

"Are there silkworms in those white things?" Tim asked.

Sarre laughed. "Not worms — but *spiders*. The Treggers use their yarn to make cloth. Would you like to see them?"

Tim shook his head; he'd never been too fond of spiders. Changing the subject he asked, "Why do you have such powerful defenses yet have no one standing guard?"

Sarre laughed again. "There *are* people standing guard. When the wild children are ready to attack, Bethen and I will warn the Treggers."

"You said *when*. Are you sure they're coming?"

Sarre nodded. "Bethen and I can feel them gathering together in the forest. With any luck, they'll probably attack while the Gurneys are still here. That will help us; the Gurneys fight well."

"Why do the children attack you?" asked Tim.

"It is the work of the Great Duke and his Warlock, Stryker," she replied. "They send the wild children here to try to destroy us."

"Where does the Duke live?"

"In the Palace of the High King of Tallis, in the north," said a voice behind them. Hunter had come to join them.

"They say the High King is unwell and the Great Duke rules for him," said Sarre.

Two Treggers, who were carrying more weaponry to the wall defenses, passed on the parapet and as they did so Hunter, almost absentmindedly, raised a hand and made a cutting motion in the air in front of his forehead. Both Treggers made the same gesture in response.

"You have known Treggers before?" said Sarre, surprised.

Hunter nodded. "In the north, there were still some Tregger servants. They were the sons and daughters of slaves," he replied. "These are the first free Treggers I've ever encountered."

"Slaves?" said Tim.

"Yes," said Sarre. "The Great Duke's ancestors used to capture Treggers and sell them as servants to the other aristocrats."

"Not all the nobles kept slaves," said Hunter. "Some even helped to free the Treggers."

"You know the history of the Tallis slaves?" asked Sarre.

"A little — not much," replied Hunter.

"What happened?" asked Tim.

"The Treggers ran away, a mass escape, most of them came back here to hide in the Forest of the Southern Rim," answered Sarre.

"Just the ones here in the village?" Tim asked.

Sarre laughed. "No, there are many Treggers scattered throughout the forest. This is just one of the bands. The Great Duke's father sent his army to pursue the ones who had escaped. But the army was defeated in the forest."

"By the ghost army," said Hunter, "according to legend."

"What was the ghost army?" asked Tim, totally enthralled.

Sarre shook her head. "Nobody knows for sure. Sur-

vivors of the old Duke's army said they were attacked in
the forest by ghosts."

"I thought you would know everything, since you can
communicate with thought messages," said Tim.

Sarre stopped for a moment and looked toward the
river. "We used to learn a great deal of news from the outside. But Stryker the Warlock now has great power. He
can read our messages and know where they come from,
so he can hunt down Chanters. Even Illya, the High King's
Chanter, no longer sends thought messages. Bethen has
not received word from her for a long time. We know the
Duke and Stryker have hunted the other Chanters almost
to extinction. That is why Bethen came here, to be near
the Southern Rim of Tallis. Even the Great Duke fears the
forest and its legendary ghost army."

"After all this time?" asked Tim.

"Yes," said Sarre. "There is some force here that may
yet defeat him. Not long ago, the present Duke chose to
ignore the legend and sent his men to invade the forest.
But, once again, something strange happened. Almost as
soon as they entered the forest they broke ranks and fled."

"Did the survivors say what had attacked them?"

"There were no survivors," said Sarre.

"Oh . . . ," said Tim. "But I still don't understand. Why
does the Duke want to harm you, anyway?"

"The Duke wants to control the Southern Rim. He
already controls the Northern Rim, and to the east and
west there are only oceans."

"What makes the Rim to the north so different?" asked Tim.

"The Northern Rim is bound by mountains. And there are no free Treggers there," said Sarre. "The Duke realized he would have to devise some new tactics to gain control of the Southern Rim. So, instead of sending armies, Stryker the Warlock takes children from the peasants and, somehow, drives them mad. He takes their minds from them so they become savages. Then he releases them into the forest to hunt us and the Treggers."

"Why doesn't the ghost army drive off the wild children?" asked Tim, puzzled.

Sarre shrugged her shoulders. "We don't know."

They had reached the main gateway, where they descended the stairs and walked out onto one of the jetties. The Treggers were down there preparing for the expected attack. They were hauling the boats out of the water and rolling them across logs into the compound so the wild children wouldn't be able to set fire to them.

"I must return to help Bethen with the sleeping potions," said Sarre.

"Has she always lived here?" asked Tim. "I got the impression that Chanters were always part of some noble household."

"They usually are," agreed Sarre. "But Bethen always wanted to be independent — and she's very fond of Treggers."

They set off back to the house. This time, the three of

them walked across the compound, and Tim gingerly took hold of one of the strands of spider thread as they ducked beneath the lime trees.

"It feels very strong," said Tim.

Sarre nodded. "Try to break it," she said.

Tim pulled the thread as hard as he could, until it cut deeply into his hands. "That's extraordinary," he said, letting go. "I would need all my strength to break it."

Sarre laughed. "More than that," she replied.

"Where do the spiders come from?"

"The stone trees we climbed down," explained Sarre. "The spiders were everywhere. You just weren't looking for them."

"Probably just as well," said Tim with a slight shudder. "But, Sarre, if it's so strong, how do you harvest it?"

Sarre took a small ring from her pouch and handed it to Tim. There was a gap in the band and the inside of the ring was set with rows of tiny diamonds, like teeth. Sarre took it from his hand, threaded the fine silk thread into the center, gave a hard jerk, and the thread parted.

"We do not have knives sharp enough to cut it," said Sarre.

"Let me try," said Hunter, drawing his sword. The blade easily parted the fine thread.

Tim laughed. "Hunter's blade seems to cut through anything."

As they walked on, Tim noticed something odd near the three spider trees. Set on a pole and protected by a canopy of woven leaves was an old-fashioned gentleman's top hat! The Treggers working on the boats gave it a slight bow each time they passed it.

"What's this?" asked Hunter, taking the hat from the pole.

"Put it back, please," said Sarre sharply. "It's the village's most precious possession."

Tim saw the Treggers nearby flinch anxiously when Hunter touched the hat.

Before replacing it, Hunter flipped it over, and Tim saw a name written on the headband in a copperplate hand. It was *Joseph Mossop*.

"Good grief! So Mossop was here," said Tim.

"You have heard of Mossop?" asked Sarre.

"Yes," replied Tim. "He used to live in our world — in the house Hunter lives in."

"He is the Treggers' greatest hero," said Sarre.

"So it seems," replied Hunter, replacing the hat on the pole.

CHAPTER 11

The Coming
of the Gurneys

The following morning, down in the compound, Tim and Sarre watched the Treggers erecting long rows of tables and heaping them with trade goods: smoked river fish, exquisite animal carvings, dried forest fruit, elegant furniture, bolts of linen made from the washed red and gold leaves. One table contained various metal items gathered at the Rim, including the bicycle parts. There were huge bowls of gemstones, rolls of spider-yarn silk, and most precious of all — the pots containing the flowers that, under Tim's instruction, the Treggers had kept well watered.

The villagers were intrigued by the flowerpots.

"Why do they have these?" a woman asked Tim, tapping the pot of one of the plants that had been taken from his grandfather's greenhouse.

"They protect the roots of the plant, stop them from drying out," Tim answered. "As long as you keep watering them they'll stay alive and keep growing."

"For how long?" chorused several Treggers.

"Well, weeks, months, and some will even flower again next year," answered Tim, not quite sure how long a potted plant could survive.

"Surely not," said one elderly Tregger, shaking his head in disbelief.

"The boy's right," said Hunter, who had followed them down to the trading place. "The flowers will last all summer in those pots."

The Treggers appeared delighted by this information. They all put their hands on their hips and gave a little jig as they nodded and grinned at one another.

"That's a Tregger joy dance," Sarre explained to Tim. "You don't see that very often."

A sudden noise in the distance distracted them, a repetitive thudding interspersed with a brassy, braying sound. It was repeated three times, then the sound of strange marching music reached them.

The villagers hurried from the compound to the grassy area between the stockade and the river. Hunter, Sarre, and Tim followed and were just in time to see the head of a great procession emerging from the fringe of woods far-ther downstream.

At first, Tim thought the approaching figures were mounted on elephants, but then he realized they were rid-ing gigantic pigs!

The great creatures were reddish brown in color and wore bridles, like shire horses. Some of the riders played extraordinary instruments: vast brass trumpets, long flutes, a variety of drums, tambourines, stringed gourds like huge mandolins, and a few wailing contraptions similar to bag-pipes. After the initial shock, the cacophony was reason-ably pleasant, if extremely loud.

Also loaded onto the pigs were massive, bulging sad-dlebags, vast leather boxes, rolled carpets, long poles, cooking pots, griddles, and coils of rope.

As they came closer, Tim noticed there were no women among the Gurneys. The men were stocky and powerfully built, with pale skin, broad chests, and curly red hair that hung in long ringlets to their shoulders. All wore dazzlingly decorative clothes: vividly colored shirts beneath leather waistcoats that were heavily studded with patterns of rubies, emeralds, and diamonds. Each leg of their tight trousers was a different color and their leather boots reached high above the knee. Their wide-brimmed hats were black, and they wore vast bunches of colored heather in the bands.

Draped about their bodies were all sorts of weapons:

short swords, clubs, bows and arrows. Each wore a small round shield strapped to his upper arm and encrusted with a pattern of precious stones.

They looked both formidable and welcoming, simultaneously giving off a sense of good fellowship and danger.

The procession came to a halt with the Gurneys blowing a long, trumpet fanfare. As it died away, Almat hurried forward.

The broadest Gurney, mounted on the leading pig, slid to the ground and lifting the little Tregger Chief off his feet, embraced him warmly.

"Almat," he bellowed. "By my left leg, it is good to see you again."

"And you, too, Charto," replied Almat when his feet were once more on the ground. "Are you ready to trade? Or would you like to eat first?"

"Trade, of course!" shouted the Gurney. "We can eat the whole night long."

The Treggers carried more of the long trestle tables out onto the flat, grassy area outside the stockade so the Gurneys could display their wares.

In an amazingly short time, the Gurneys had unloaded their great pigs and were laying out the goods they'd brought with them to trade. Mounds of raw hides, weapons, tools, nails, ropes in a variety of thicknesses, barrels, pottery, and tinware.

The pigs were tethered near the landing stage where Tregger children, in exchange for rides organized by four of the younger Gurneys, fed them from the baskets of fruit they'd gathered from the forest.

Bargaining was hard. Hunter and Tim watched as arguments raged between the little Treggers and the powerfully built Gurneys. Fists were shaken in faces, accusatory fingers pointed, angry shouts exchanged. Sometimes a Tregger or a Gurney would storm away, only to return a few minutes later to resume the haggling. When a bargain was finally struck, the Tregger would hold both hands above his head and do a little jig, while the Gurney would violently slap himself on the left thigh. Then they would shake hands and exchange the goods.

The flowers were the last to be traded. The Gurneys were deeply impressed when the Treggers told them they would last for months in their little pots. Hunter and Tim were brought forward to testify that it was the truth. Then Charto spotted Josh dashing about excitedly at Tim's feet.

"And what is this?" Charto asked, twirling his long red mustache and pointing at Josh. The little dog stopped cavorting and fearlessly gazed up at the Gurney Chief.

"My dog, Josh," replied Tim.

"Dog!" repeated Charto. "What does it do — this dog?"

Tim crouched down and demonstrated Josh's leapfrog trick. All the Gurneys roared with laughter.

Then Charto crouched down and Josh obligingly jumped over his back, too.

"I'll give you my best pig for the dog," Charto offered.

"No, thank you," replied Tim hastily.

"You're right, it is not enough for such a creature. I'll give you two pigs and your choice of weapons."

"Tim, you must tap your heart when you refuse," Hunter warned, "or he'll think you're just bargaining."

Charto looked shrewdly at Hunter. "You have bargained with Gurney before?"

Hunter nodded. "I have, and I have something to offer."

He took a round object, like a fat pocket watch from his pocket and handed it to Charto. The Gurney held it in his hand, puzzled until Hunter reached out and sprung it open. It was a compass.

"North is magnetic in Tallis, too," Hunter said as an aside to Tim.

"What does this do?" asked Charto, watching the needle quiver.

"This needle will always point to the north. You will never be lost in winter, at night, or in fog. This will always tell you which way to go."

Charto was not convinced. He saw Sarre in the crowd and beckoned to her.

"Which way is north, young miss Chanter?"

Without a moment's hesitation, Sarre pointed. Charto looked at the needle and nodded to his companions.

"Does he speak the truth? Will it always work, even at night and in fog?"

"He speaks the truth," replied Sarre.

"What do you want for this?" asked Charto.

Hunter placed his open hand on his heart to signify that he would accept only what he was about to ask for, and said, "I want you to allow me to travel with you when you leave."

Charto nodded, slapped his left thigh, and held out his hand.

The Treggers and Gurneys bargained on until nightfall. Then the Treggers lit lanterns that they placed all around the walls of the stockade and hung from the walkways and in front of the house doors. Their glowing light shone over the village.

Charcoal pits had been dug in the center of the compound, next to the three lime trees. Now succulent smells were rising from the rabbits, game, fish, and fruit being grilled over the embers. The trailing spider yarns had all been severed for the occasion.

The tables, used for trading goods earlier, were soon loaded with food, and everyone sat before heaped platters. The feasting had just commenced when Bethen and Sarre both stood up.

The chattering died away and in the silence, Bethen said. "The wild ones are approaching the tree line."

Almat knew what to do. "We Treggers will be on the walls," he told the Gurneys. "We will allow them to think they have overwhelmed us and will apparently fall back into the center. Then you Gurneys attack."

Charto nodded, then signaled for his men to spread out around the compound and stand close to the wall of stockade.

"I'll stay with you," said Hunter, gripping the handle of his sword.

"Don't fight with that weapon," said Charto. "Use one of Bethen's clubs. They're only children; we want to capture them, not kill them."

"Will they be trying to kill us?" asked Hunter grimly.

"For sure," said Charto with a chuckle.

Clutching Tim's hand, Sarre hurried him across the compound with Josh at their heels.

"Stay with me in the lime trees," said Sarre. "The wild children are frightened to go near the spiders' nests."

Tim wasn't too keen on the spiders himself, but this was no time to be squeamish. He had his slingshot and a pouchful of jewels at his waist. Scooping up Josh and thrusting him inside his shirt, he climbed up into one of the lime trees with Sarre.

From their vantage point, Sarre and Tim could see over the stockade. The Treggers on the parapet were lighting fire arrows.

"Here they come," said Sarre.

Tim could see nothing. Beyond the light of the lanterns on the stockade was a wall of darkness. Bethen was on the parapet with the Treggers. Tim saw her give the order to shoot. Fire arrows curved through the sky and fell into piles of underbrush that the Treggers had raked up earlier.

Fires blazed on the tree line and illuminated two waves of wild children charging the walls of the stockade.

The attackers looked terrifying in the flickering fire-light. Their bodies were daubed with jagged patterns of colored mud and their tangled hair stuck with feathers, bones, and scraps of fur. They were armed with spears, bows and arrows, clubs, and short swords.

The first wave of screaming children carried ropes with grappling hooks attached. As they came forward their cries sounded like those of wounded animals. When they were close to the walls of the stockade, the second wave hurled spears and fired a heavy volley of arrows at the defending Treggers, causing them to duck away from the poisonous missiles. Then the first wave of savage children threw their grappling hooks up to catch onto the ramparts and began to swarm up the stockade wall.

The Treggers sent off a volley of their blunted arrows, then retreated from the rampart walls to the middle of the compound. Screaming in triumph, the savage children leaped from the parapet in pursuit.

The Treggers and Gurneys retreated across the open compound to form a circle, their backs to the massive lime trees where Sarre and Tim were concealed. The Gurneys and Treggers had taken up Bethen's clubs and were fight-ing with great determination — but they were heavily out-numbered. Tim could see Hunter, shoulder to shoulder with Charto. Hunter's club rose and fell methodically, never missing a blow.

The defenders of the village fought only with clubs and blunted arrows, while the savage children slashed with swords, thrust with spears, and fired poison arrows into the circle. From up in the lime tree, Tim hurled gemstone after gemstone at the attackers, each missile striking home. Even so, the battle looked lost.

Then a strange thing happened. The savage children closest to the fighting began to drop their weapons and fall to the ground, struggling against an unseen power that was forcing their arms and legs to their bodies.

The silk spiders! They had dropped from the trees and were winding their thread around the attackers, binding them helpless. Most of the savage children fell in heaps, screaming and weeping. The others, terrified by the strange turn of events, ran to scramble back over the walls and vanish into the forest.

Most of the Treggers and Gurneys were wounded, some still had arrows stuck in their bodies, others bore deep cuts from swords and spears.

"Are all their weapons poisoned?" asked Tim anxiously, remembering the dead fish in the river when Almat had thrown the arrow into the stream.

"Don't worry, Bethen has made an antidote," replied Sarre. "I gave her one of their arrows, remember?"

Tregger women hurried down from their homes with bandages, and Bethen appeared carrying a large iron pot filled with steaming liquid. After sewing up the deeper cuts with spider yarn, the women dipped the bandages into the solution and began to bind up everyone's wounds.

The screams of the helpless wild children continued long into the night, while the wounds of the Treggers and Gurneys were still being dressed. Eventually, when all the Treggers and Gurneys had been attended to, a weary Bethen came to where the savages lay, guarded by Hunter and Tim.

Standing before them motionless to gather her strength, she then reached up, arms outstretched, and closed her eyes.

"What's she doing?" Tim asked Sarre.

"Treating their damaged minds," Sarre answered.

A shimmering aura of white light began to form around Bethen's body. It pulsed about her briefly before spreading out across the writhing bodies of the children. Finally, the last of their screams died away and they all fell into a deep trancelike sleep.

"I have taken the worst of the madness from them," she said wearily. "But it is just a beginning; it will take more time for their minds to heal completely."

Bethen's usual pink complexion was suddenly as white as her Chanter's robes. Even the skin of her powerful hands looked translucent. She stood very upright for a moment, then collapsed.

Sarre reached her side as a group of Treggers were already lifting her onto their shoulders to carry her up to her house. Tim followed. The Treggers laid Bethen on her bed and left Tim and Sarre with her. Sarre took her hand.

Bethen slowly opened her eyes and looked into Sarre's face, smiling. "Time for me to go home," she said softly.

Josh, released from Tim's shirt, stood whimpering by the bed Bethen lay on. The Chanter touched his head and the little dog grew quiet.

"What's happened, Bethen?" Sarre asked gently.

"My work here is done," she answered. "Now, hold my hand tightly."

She closed her eyes and said, "Put my body on the river. Almat knows how it must be done. Then you must go with Hunter."

"He's leaving with the Gurneys tomorrow," said Tim.

"You two must make the same journey."

"But Sarre was going to take me home," protested Tim.

Bethen smiled again. "Your time in Tallis has only just begun, Tim. Hunter will take you with him. He does not know it yet, but he has great need of you both."

"I can feel your spirit in my hand," Sarre whispered sadly, and just as Almat, Charto, and Hunter entered the room, Bethen gave a long, final sigh.

"She's gone," Sarre said bleakly. Then she looked up at Almat. "Bethen said we must place her on the river."

Almat nodded. "I know what to do. She told me long ago."

"Who will read the minds of the savage children now?" Charto asked.

"I shall," replied Sarre. "Bethen passed the power to me."

"All her powers?" asked Hunter.

"All I need for now," answered Sarre quietly.

They carried Bethen through the village, with the Treggers and the Gurneys following as far as the riverbank. Almat instructed them to place her in a canoe. By the light of lanterns they watched as he pushed the craft away from the bank. It caught in the fast flow of the stream and soon vanished into the night.

Tim noticed that Sarre didn't seem to grieve, apart from smiling thoughtfully as they walked back together from the river.

"Chanters cry inside," she said simply.

The following morning most of the Gurneys were down on the riverbank loading the giant pigs with the goods they had traded. In the compound the captive children stood like sleepwalkers. There was no fight in them nor any interest in their surroundings. There had been no protests earlier, when some of the Tregger women had taken them to the river so they could wash before putting on the new linen clothes they were given.

"Their minds are still asleep," Sarre explained to Tim. "They will obey orders but they can't think for themselves yet."

Charto sat at a table on which there was a great map drawn on silk. Sarre stood beside him with Tim and

Hunter looking on. As each child was brought in turn to stand before Charto, Sarre reached out and laid her hand on the child's forehead. Then she gave Charto the name of a village, which he marked on the map.

"More than one hundred children," said Charto when the last of the captives had been identified. "They'll bring us a tidy profit."

"You're selling them?" asked Tim, horrified.

Charto laughed. "No, not selling them, but their villages will gladly reward us for their safe return."

"That's a fine map of Tallis," said Hunter, looking over the Gurney Chief's shoulder.

"You like it?" said Charto, pleased. "It is a Mossop map."

"*Mossop!*" repeated Tim, exchanging a glance with Hunter.

"Yes, a Mossop map," said Charto. "Mossop was a friend of the Gurneys. He gave my ancestors maps of the forest so we could find Tregger villages and avoid the ghost army."

"You've seen the ghost army?" Tim gasped.

Charto shook his head and bellowed with laughter. "Never. That is the point of the forest maps: to avoid the ghosts." He gently pinched Sarre's cheek. "Thank you for reading the children's minds, Chanter girl," he said. "I shall bring you a special present when next we come to this village."

"But I'm coming with you, Charto. So are Tim and Josh," Sarre replied.

The Gurney Chief folded his map and slipped it inside his waistcoat. "You could be useful," he mused. "Can you foresee danger? Send messages on the wind?"

"I can. Bethen taught me."

"Then you'll earn your keep."

"The boy should stay here," said Hunter. "He can go home when the Treggers next journey to the Southern Rim."

"Tim must come with us," Sarre spoke firmly. "I will see he gets home when the time is right."

Hunter shrugged. "It's up to Charto. He's in charge."

Sarre said, "Will you show me your map again, please?"

Charto produced it and Sarre pointed to the towns and villages marked. Tracing a route on it with her finger she said, "You should go this way so you can trade the children and eventually sell the flowers to Lord Tredore."

"You already know I intend to sell them to Lord Tredore?" said Charto, surprised.

Sarre smiled. "You need me to tell you when storms are coming, which parts of the country are at war or are flooded, so you can get the flowers to Lord Tredore while they are still fresh."

"Yes, that would indeed be useful," said Charto.

"I can show you the route you must take, and Tim will keep the flowers alive."

"You can do that, boy?" asked Charto.

"I think so," said Tim. "My grandfather says I have green fingers."

"Your fingers are white," said Charto suspiciously.

"It's a saying we use on Earth," said Tim. "It means I'm good at growing flowers."

Charto slapped his hand on the table. "That settles it, you both come — and the little dog, too. Excellent!"

He stood up and laid a hand on Almat's shoulder. "We made good trade, my friend. Until the next time we meet, farewell."

They walked to the river embankment where the great pigs were tethered and Charto inspected the caravan. When he was satisfied that all their trade goods were securely loaded, he climbed onto the lead pig and held up his hand. There was a roll of drums and the Gurneys began their marching tune. The Treggers waved and children ran alongside the caravan until they reached the tree line, where they stopped to wave as the traders departed into the forest.

Quite close to the waving children, a figure stood hidden in the undergrowth at the edge of the forest, but none of them noticed him there in the dark shadows. Had they seen the man they may only have recognized him from their nightmares, so frightening was his appearance.

He watched the Gurney caravan intently and, as the pig carrying Hunter passed by him, some creature beneath his long garment began to twitch about agitatedly. The hideous figure reached inside his robe and withdrew a long brown-and-black snake. Caressing it, he held it up to his

The landlord poured a pewter mug of ale for Hunter and a sweet, purple-colored juice for Sarre and Tim.

"So, how are things in Tallis, landlord?" asked Hunter in an unusually friendly voice.

"Mustn't complain, Sir," the landlord replied.

"I saw some uniformed men mounted on fighting boars at the gate," continued Hunter.

"Oh, yes, the Great Duke's police," the man answered warily. "A fine body of men, recently formed. We always feel safe when they're about."

"Do you see much of them?"

"Whenever an honest citizen is in need of them, Sir."

Hunter didn't carry on the conversation. He drained his ale and when the landlord moved along the counter to trim a guttering candle, murmured, "It's useless trying to learn anything from this man."

"Let me try," said Sarre, holding up a hand to cover her eyes. When the landlord returned she took away her hand and gazed directly into his eyes. The man attempted to look away but could not take his eyes from hers.

"Tell me all the gossip," she said casually, and in the dim light Tim could see her eyes changing color.

"My name's Reginald Bunton," he said. "I come from London."

"London on Earth?" asked Tim, surprised.

"That's right," said Bunton. "I'm a wanted man back there. Nothing serious, of course. Just a bit of burglary."

ear. The snake hissed and the man closed his eyes and concentrated. Then he stared malevolently after Hunter.

"Perhaps our luck has changed altogether, little one," he muttered happily.

The watcher was tall and gaunt with long, tangled black hair, streaked with gray. The flesh on his face was like a pitted stone, and a straggly, forked beard hung to his waist. He was dressed in a long robe made of snakeskins belted at the waist with leather pouches dangling around his cadaverous body. Tall boots reached his knees. His face and bare arms were burned dark by the sun and his eyes changed, just as Sarre's did, but there was no color in them. Just flickers of black and shades of dirty gray.

He leaned for a moment on the long twisted staff he had raised while the Gurneys passed, then he bent down and released the snake into the undergrowth.

"Watch him wherever he goes," he whispered as the snake curved away. Then the hooded man turned to several companions who had risen from the undergrowth, where they, too, had concealed themselves while the caravan passed. They wore the black uniform of soldiers but they were a sorry, defeated-looking group, all of whom had been wounded in a recent battle.

The figure in snakeskins beckoned to one of the men.

"I think the girl with the Gurneys was a Chanter, Sir," the soldier said anxiously. "I could see her eyes changing."

"A mere child," the bearded figure replied contemptuously. "I blocked her powers easily. Now, take a dispatch to the Great Duke."

The soldier took a square of parchment and a pen from his pouch. Crouching, he rested the parchment on his knee and looked up expectantly.

"Your Grace," the bearded man began. "I must report that the expeditionary force I led to the forest of the Southern Rim has been wiped out. Only six members of your heavy cavalry regiment have survived and the five war pigs are destroyed. However, I have succeeded in all I set out to achieve."

The soldier held out the document and the man scribbled a signature, saying, "Give this only to the Duke."

He nodded, and two of the other soldiers held out a harness in which they strapped the soldier bearing the dispatch. The man nodded again and four soldiers slashed through ropes that tethered a large balloon concealed in the trees. The hard wind caught the floating contraption and jerked the messenger high into the sky and blew him northward like a dead leaf.

The bearded man watched him until he was out of sight then turned to the remaining soldiers. "Follow the caravan — but keep your distance," he instructed.

Six of the soldiers were carrying a large wooden box made from rough branches. It was shaped like a coffin.

"Be careful with that," snarled the leader as one of the wounded men carrying the load stumbled. "It's more precious than you are."

CHAPTER 12

The Journey to Milchen

After a week's march, the Gurney caravan reached the edge of the forest. The great trees gave way to a scrubland of bush and bramble that reached all the way to the horizon. About halfway across it, they began to follow some narrow paths that eventually led into stony lanes bordered by the hedgerows that surrounded fields of ripening crops. Tim recognized wheat and barley corn, but some of the fields contained immense plants with vast, fleshy leaves and others—strange, oddly shaped vegetables, some smoothly round and others spiked like cactus.

It was beautiful countryside — rolling hills and sweet valleys were crisscrossed by meandering streams. There were orchards and thatched cottages of flint or brick, bearing vines heavy with purple fruit. Small woods lay on the sides of hills, and there were wide rolling meadows where sheep and cows grazed. But there were no horses. Instead, all the farmworkers they saw were using black pigs to pull their carts. The breed was smaller than the Gurney pack animals but wider in the shoulders.

Tim was struck by the intensity of the colors here. The earth was dark, rich brown or red, and the trees as bright as the colors in a paint box, their foliage yellow, dark red and a variety of olives, emeralds, and blues. It was as if the landscape itself was compensating for the lack of flowers.

The strong wind continued to blow, constantly changing the sky. Rain clouds would appear and vanish after a brief shower. Sometimes great banks of pewter-colored clouds would roll over them, and a sudden storm with thunder and crackling lightning would rend the sky.

They often saw people working the fields, their clothes looked homespun and simply made. The men in long smocks and wide straw hats and the women in long, calico dresses with puff sleeves and bonnets. At night, Charto would ask permission to camp on some farmer's meadow and pay a rent with trade goods. Sarre was as fascinated by their surroundings as Tim. All she had known was the forest and the Southern Rim, so it was all just as new to her.

With Sarre's help, Charto led them to the villages he had marked on his map. They were always the same — clusters of thatched, single-storied cottages, mostly made of wood, the gaps filled with whitewashed mud, and the chimneys built of bright red brick. Nearly all were the homes of craftsmen — wheelwrights, blacksmiths, thatchers, carpenters — who provided services for the local farmers.

At each stop, the Gurneys would hand over some of the captured children — and were usually rewarded with money, sometimes with food. The children were still in the same trancelike state but when their parents stepped forward, Sarre would touch each child's forehead and his or her memory would be restored.

The villagers would watch the reunion of the children with their families, then stand openmouthed, gawking at the Gurneys and pointing with alarm when they saw Tim's little dog. Sometimes the caravan saw the smoke of distant fires but the Gurneys kept well away. Twice they had come across a burned-out village.

One day, when Tim and Sarre were gathering berries, they found a ragged, half-starved young man hiding in a wood. Reluctantly, he came into the camp because he was so hungry, and the Gurneys fed him in return for information.

"Why are they burning villages?" Charto asked him.

"The Duke's police are punishing people," the young man answered as he stuffed bread and cheese into his mouth.

"Why are they after you?" asked Hunter.

"I openly praised Lord Charltren," he replied bitterly.

"I remember Lord Charltren," said Charto. "I thought the land about here was his estate."

"It was," continued the young man, "but he was declared a traitor by the Duke and all he owned was confiscated."

The young man vanished immediately after he had eaten, frightened that the Gurneys would hand him over to the Duke's police.

As they moved farther north, Hunter asked Charto why all the farm buildings they were passing now seemed to have fairly new additions to them.

"The shelters next to the farm buildings, you mean?" said Charto in a matter-of-fact voice. "Don't you know about the Killing Wind?"

Hunter shook his head. "There was no Killing Wind when I was last in Tallis."

Charto sighed. "Yes, I can remember those days. It started ten or twelve years ago. Well, you know the wind usually blows from south to north. But sometimes — no one knows why — it swings about and blows very hard for a short time from north to south. When that happens, some kind of deadly dust is borne on the wind. If you breathe it, you die. We have trained the pigs to dig pits and we protect ourselves by breathing through Tregger silk. The silk is so fine it stops the dust. We do a good trade in it."

Hunter shook his head. "Things have changed here a great deal," he said softly.

As they journeyed on through the southern lands of Tallis, Tim and Sarre shared a pack pig. Josh spent quite a lot of the time during the day dozing on Tim's lap. At first, Sarre was concerned that Josh slept for such long periods.

"Is he ill?" she asked anxiously as she leaned over Tim's shoulder to study the sleeping Josh.

Tim shook his head. "You're obviously not used to dogs," he said, sounding condescending. "They sleep a lot. Then they wake up and want you to play with them."

"I may not know about dogs," replied Sarre quickly. "But I know about manners. Who taught you yours, the grumpy one?" She nodded toward Hunter, astride his pack pig. Tim knew what she meant. Hunter rarely spoke to anyone, and when he did it was usually just a few curt words.

Tim blushed. "I'm sorry, Sarre," he said quickly, realizing that he may unconsciously have been following Hunter's example. "I didn't mean to be . . ." His voice trailed away and he looked directly ahead. Tim often wanted to chat with Sarre but then felt so tongue-tied he didn't know how to start the conversation. So instead of being friendly he behaved gruffly and became even more shy.

Seeing his blush spread to the back of his neck, Sarre smiled. "You need to laugh more, Tim Swift," she said, suddenly tickling his ribs.

Tim gave a yelp of laughter and Josh woke up and wagged his tail. Maybe, Tim thought, he could begin to relax in her company after all!

The days began to fall into a pattern. The caravan would plod on, stopping from time to time at a village to return a child to his or her parents. They would eat a light meal by the roadside in the middle of the day and at night pitch their camp of leather tents. When the pigs were fed, baths taken, and the evening meal eaten, everyone would sit around the cooking fires with the Gurneys playing their instruments and singing. The Gurneys loved to bathe and eat. They carried huge, collapsible leather baths that they liked to fill with extremely hot water.

Hunter had traded a small pair of powerful binoculars for a service from one of the Gurneys called Luxo. Renowned for his skillful leatherwork, Luxo was making Hunter a suit of hardened leather armor. He had already fashioned the boots, gauntlets, and breastplate. When they were cut and stitched together, Luxo affixed precious stones to them for added protection.

Each evening, Charto admired the work's progress. When the armor was finally finished he took a large bundle from one of his own saddlebags and handed it to Hunter. When he unwrapped the gift, Hunter found it was a helmet studded with rubies.

Tim gasped. He'd never seen anything so magnificent.

"Now you will look like one of the High King's fighting Lords," said Charto.

"Who exactly is the High King?" Tim asked. "Mostly, people only talk about the Great Duke."

"The High King is the rightful ruler of Tallis," replied Charto. "At least, he was in better days."

Then Charto called for Sarre and produced his map.

"The rest of our people should be somewhere about here," he said to her, running his index finger around a small area on the map. "Can you find them?"

Sarre closed her eyes and held her hand over the silk map, then she pointed to a name.

"Milchen," said Charto. "That's a fair-sized town. We could be there in two, maybe three days."

"Milchen!" Hunter exclaimed. "I want to go there."

"You've heard of Milchen?" asked Charto.

"Yes," said Hunter. "I intended to pay it a visit."

"Charto, your people are on good camping ground to the south of Milchen, next to a wood," said Sarre, still holding her hand over the map.

"Do you hear that, my friends?" Charto called to his men. "A few days and we'll have a meal cooked by Gurney women and all the comforts you could ask for."

A cheer went up from the men. Gurneys were usually cheerful, but now they were all positively beaming with anticipation. There was a great deal of joking and laughter around the campfires that evening and the countryside rang with wild songs. Only the last of the captive children sat silently — waiting for the reunion with their parents that would finally free their minds.

The countryside changed as they approached the town of Milchen. It was flatter and mostly meadow in which large flocks of sheep grazed. They could see the town from a fair way off. Its walls were defended with high stone battlements. Unusually for Tallis, there was hardly any wind so smoke drifted over the rooftops. Also, suspended in the sky above the town were some great bulbous-looking shapes.

Tim borrowed Luxo's binoculars and focused on one of them. All he could make out through the haze of smoke was something that looked like a vast, irregularly shaped balloon.

Charto pointed to the edge of a faraway meadow next to a wood, where they could see campfires. "There are our people," he said with satisfaction. "We shall remain outside with them."

"Aren't you coming into town, Charto?" Tim asked.

The Gurney Chief shook his head.

"We don't get on too well with townsfolk — they're different from villagers. We do trade with them but there's no love lost between us. It's better if we men stay outside the walls. The women go into town to buy and sell small things. If the townsfolk want bigger trade, they can visit us."

A welcoming turmoil erupted in the Gurney camp when the caravan arrived laden with riches. Children and women swarmed over Charto and his men, whooping with delight, and the old men cheered. There were tears of joy and passionate embraces. The Gurney women were beautiful and as wild-looking as their men. Their long, curly red hair was plaited with colored ribbons and their faces bright with makeup. Like Tregger women, they wore silk dresses, but theirs were dyed a rainbow of colors and ended above the knee, leaving their legs bare. They wore diamond-encrusted sandals, and necklaces and bracelets of emeralds and rubies. And the Gurney children were dressed in similar fashion to their parents.

Before supper, the Gurneys showed their families the goods they had traded on their travels and there was much cheering and sighs of appreciation, but the greatest gasp of admiration came when Charto asked Tim to show some of the flowers. The women were astonished they had stayed fresh so long.

After a feast of roast sheep and fruit, Tim was called upon to do some of his tricks with Josh. The Gurney women and children marveled at the little dog's cleverness and asked Tim to repeat the tricks over and over again, until even Josh grew tired of performing. The Gurney men and women sang celebratory songs long into the night, and as the campfires were getting low, Charto asked Sarre to sing.

"You're a Chanter," he said. "Everyone knows Chanters have beautiful voices."

"I don't know many songs," she replied hesitantly.

"Go on, Sarre," Tim urged.

"Do you know this one?" Charto asked, plucking a melody on the strings of his gourd instrument.

Sarre listened, her head to one side, then nodded, saying, "Yes, I think I do."

She began to sing in a voice purer than any Tim had

ever heard. A hush fell over the camp as the sweet melancholy tune rose and fell. The only words Tim could make out sounded like:

My lost love was more than life.

As she sang, Tim noticed Hunter was staring into the fire with an inconsolably bleak expression on his face.

The next day, Tim, Sarre, and Hunter prepared to go into town. They'd decided to leave Josh in the camp, where he was happy to stay with Charto and play with the Gurney children.

Sarre was unusually excited, and watched Hunter impatiently while he exchanged jewels for the coins Charto assured him were used as money in Milchen. Tim seemed almost indifferent to the intended visit.

"Aren't you looking forward to seeing a town, Tim?" she asked. "All I've ever known is the forest and the Tregger village."

"I *live* in a town at home," Tim replied. "It's not that great."

"Don't you miss your friends?"

"I don't really have any — just Josh."

"Why?"

Tim looked away and shrugged. "I never know what to say. I try, sometimes, but . . ." His voice trailed away.

"Is it because you're shy?" Sarre asked gently.

"I suppose it must be," he smiled mirthlessly. "My parents say I'll get over it — but they never say when that will be."

Sarre suddenly looked serious. "I know a Chanter cure for shyness," she said.

"You do?" said Tim hopefully.

Sarre nodded. "But you have to use your imagination."

"How?"

"Close your eyes and think of someone you've found it difficult to talk to."

"I'm thinking," he replied.

"What's he like?"

"It was a girl, not a boy."

"Is she pretty?"

"Not as pretty as you."

Sarre looked surprised. "Am I pretty, Tim?"

He opened his eyes and nodded. "Go on, what do I do next?"

But Sarre had another question. "If I'm pretty, how is it you can talk to me?"

"I don't know," he replied. "Probably because you're the only girl who has ever tickled me."

"Well, there you are," said Sarre. "Next time you have to talk to a girl, just imagine she's me."

"What about Hunter?" he asked, grinning. "He's difficult to talk to."

"You don't have any trouble talking to Josh; just imagine Hunter is a dog."

Tim chewed thoughtfully on a blade of grass. "It might work," he said slowly.

"Perhaps you can practice in the town if we meet any girls."

"The girls in Milchen will be in school, like all the children," said Charto, who had come up to them with Hunter. "You two will be the only ones on the streets."

"And an odd couple you make," said Hunter, noticing their clothes.

Sarre always looked presentable in her spider-silk dresses and Hunter's clothes looked as good as new. But Tim's were in a sorry state. His jeans and old shirt had been patched several times and were so ragged he thought he probably looked like a beggar.

Hunter had an idea. "Where's that bag of floating leaves?"

Tim retrieved it from one of the saddlebags.

"Let's see if we can find a tailor in town," said Hunter.

While she waited for them, Sarre had been standing alone, looking over the meadow, obviously concentrating. She turned as Tim and Hunter approached, and they could see that something about her was different. Her eyes were no longer changing color, as they usually did, and were now a constant blue.

"What have you done?" asked Tim.

She smiled. "You noticed."

"I would have to be blind and unconscious not to," answered Tim.

"It's just a trick," she replied. "I can do it anytime. But

when my eyes are not changing color I have no Chanter powers."

Hunter nodded. "It's best if no one in town knows you're a Chanter," he said. "If anyone questions either of you, tell them I'm your father, a trader from Earth."

"Are there traders from our world in Tallis?" asked Tim, surprised.

Hunter nodded. "There are traders everywhere. Just stay close to me and keep quiet."

They set out for Milchen along a road partly paved with ancient stones. There was no sign of the strange balloons Tim had seen in the sky earlier. Just before they reached the town wall, they passed a sinister-looking group of men mounted on ferocious-looking black boars.

Despite their immense size, Gurney pigs were gentle and placid, whereas these creatures were a very different breed. They snorted and snuffled at the ground, their deep-set eyes fixed on Tim, Sarre, and Hunter as they hurried past. Their vicious yellow tusks looked threatening, even though their riders were holding them in check. The mounted men wore tight, black leather uniforms and were heavily armed.

Hunter walked straight ahead, avoiding any eye contact with the men, and Tim saw him surreptitiously ease his sword in its scabbard.

"I wonder who they were?" said Tim, as they entered the town through tall iron gates.

"I think they may be some of the Duke's police force," said Sarre.

"Not people we want to deal with," added Hunter, stopping to take stock of their new surroundings.

Milchen seemed oddly familiar to Tim, as did some other parts of Tallis. It was similar to the illustrations of medieval towns he'd seen in his school history books. The narrow, winding streets were cobbled, and the houses widened where each story jutted out to overhang the one below it. The steeply pitched, tiled roofs almost touched across the street.

The streets were filled with people, some strolling leisurely, others hurrying about their business. Men and women were peddling goods from handcarts or walking around shouting the advantages of the wares they carried on laden trays.

The clothes of the townsfolk were far more elaborate and carefully made than the styles worn by the country people. Most of the citizens of Milchen seemed to favor styles that were worn in Tim's world during the eighteenth century. The women wore long, low-cut dresses of satin or silk with their hair piled high and powdered white, while the men looked elegant in long coats with wide sleeves, breeches, stockings, and buckled shoes.

Every so often, the trio passed a pitiful-looking, sightless man or woman dressed in rags and shuffling along, tapping with a stick. Tim was shocked to see each one wore a sign about their neck that read: I AM AN ENEMY OF THE HIGH KING.

He was about to comment on these pathetic figures but Hunter frowned and shook his head slightly, saying loudly, "Look at the splendid shops. We owe all this to the Great Duke, you know."

The business conducted in each shop was proclaimed by a sign made in the shape of whatever they were selling: a shoe sign for a cobbler, bottles for an apothecary, a quill pen writing on a scroll of paper for a stationer.

"Have you ever seen anything like this?" said Sarre breathlessly.

"I've seen pictures of places a *little* bit like it," answered Tim.

"Not quite like this," said Hunter. "What can you smell?"

Tim and Sarre each took a deep breath.

"Bread," said Tim. "And roasting meat."

"I can smell candles and fruit," said Sarre.

"This town is much cleaner than it would have been in the Middle Ages in our world," said Hunter. "The stench then would have been appalling because they threw all the sewerage out on the streets. But the plumbing in Tallis is surprisingly modern."

As if to confirm his comment, a curious thing happened. Just in front of them the cobbled paving stones suddenly erupted and a powerful, throbbing machine, almost as tall as Hunter and shaped like a sausage, clawed its way up through the ground. It came to a stop, leaving a tunnel behind it. The head of the machine was revolving at great speed while the body of it continually expanded and contracted with a great clanking noise. Tim, Hunter, and Sarre stepped back in alarm, and were still staring at it in amazement when a man in work clothes and carrying a large bag of tools arrived almost at a trot.

"Ah, there you are," he said to the machine. Then he smiled at Hunter. "Wonderful things these," he said. "But I think this one's getting old. It should have come up in the next street — or maybe I accidentally entered the wrong setting."

"What is it?" asked Sarre, fascinated.

"You must be from the country, young lady," the man replied with a grin. "This is a Mossop Mole."

"A Mossop Mole," repeated Tim. "What does it do?"

The man bent over the machine and flipped open a panel. "When I set this dial," he said, "it will bore a hole into the next street. As you can see, the front end spins around to chew through the earth with these metal teeth while its retracting claws pull it forward. As it moves along under the ground its body expands and contracts so powerfully that it impacts the disturbed earth to make it set as hard as concrete, so there's no need to lay a pipe."

"That's marvelous," said Tim, impressed. "And where does the power come from?"

"A universal Mossop clockwork motor, of course."

"What do you want with the holes it makes?" Sarre asked.

"Sanitation," answered the man, as if surprised by her

question. "All the sewers in Milchen were dug with Mossop Moles." He flipped a lever and the machine began to hum, then it burrowed back down the same hole and disappeared.

"Let's hope it comes up in the right place this time," said the workman, departing with a friendly wave.

Hunter suddenly seemed very cheerful. "I think we could do with some refreshment," he said, stepping across the alley and reaching out to push open a tavern door.

CHAPTER 13

The Mystery of the Enton Arms

The tavern door swung open before Hunter's hand touched it.

"Good day, Sir," said the thin, smiling, gap-toothed man who greeted them. His greasy hair was tied back in a pigtail and he wore a long leather apron. "Won't you come in and enjoy a glass of ale?" he urged.

Hunter nodded, and Sarre and Tim followed him into a low-ceilinged room smelling of yeast and wood smoke. It was dim inside. Hardly any light penetrated the thick green-glass windows but there were candles burning on the tables and counter. There were no other customers.

"How did you get here?" asked Tim.

"I leaned against a wall in Hackney one night, a full moon came out from behind the clouds, and I just fell in through a starway."

"What do you *really* do here?" asked Sarre.

"I'm an informer for the Duke's police," he told them.

"Why does he need informers?"

Bunton spread his hands on the counter. "Revolutionaries are everywhere. Didn't you see the sightless ones on the street?"

"Yes," answered Tim.

"They're just the ones who have spoken against the Duke." He came from behind the counter and walked across the tavern to throw open two shutters. Light streamed in from an open square outside.

A terrible sight was revealed to them. A fringe of anguished people stood watching as black-uniformed police chained prisoners to gigantic, irregularly shaped, gray linen bags. The cries of the victims were so pitiful, Sarre and Tim looked away.

"Balloons stuffed with floating leaves," said Hunter.

"That's right," said Bunton. "That's how the Duke deals with criminals. Tidy, eh?"

"How long do the balloons stay up?" asked Tim.

"Forever, I'd guess," said Bunton with a snigger. "Because we never see them again."

As he spoke, the black-clad policemen released one of

the vast balloons and it rose into the air, looking like some bloated, primeval creature. A moan of dismay went up from the watchers in the square.

"They keep them on a rope above the town for a few days to give the people a good look, then they release them and they fly north," said Bunton.

As the balloon ascended, the people chained to it moaned pitifully and thrashed about in a futile attempt to get free.

"What news is there of the High King?" asked Hunter as Bunton closed the shutters on the dreadful scene.

"The High King is unwell," said Bunton briskly. "Some say he's gone mad with grief. The Great Duke had to proclaim himself Regent, and he now rules from the High King's great palace."

"What of the other nobles?" said Sarre.

Bunton shrugged. "Most have left their own lands and nearly all of them now live in the High King's castle."

"It must be a big castle," said Tim.

"That's just a name," said Hunter. "It refers to a vast estate. The High King's castle is more like a town."

"And what of the noblemen's Chanters?" asked Sarre.

Bunton shrugged. "Most are in hiding. There's still one or two about but no one even mentions Chanters now. Someday they will be forgotten completely, even in legend."

"Do you still keep Mossop's rooms here?" Hunter asked.

"Indeed we do," said Bunton. "He was a famous character

in this town. A surprisingly modest man. He could have lived in a castle, he was so rich. But he preferred it here. Did you know he owned this tavern?"

"So I've heard," said Hunter. "May we see his rooms?"

"Certainly," said Bunton. "Follow me." He led them up a winding, narrow staircase and along a wood-paneled corridor.

"Mossop's personal suite of rooms," said Bunton, slapping his hand on the door.

"There's no need for you to wait," Hunter said. But Bunton ignored him and reached for the door handle.

"You may go back to the counter," said Sarre clearly.

This time, Bunton strolled away, whistling.

The interior of the tavern was much larger than it appeared to be from the outside. They passed through room after room, a kitchen, scullery, servants' quarters, sitting rooms. One was furnished as a draftsman's office with drawing boards and document chests. Hunter opened some of the drawers. They were crammed with elegant plans of bridges, strange machines, extraordinary buildings. One of the machines even looked a bit like an early motorcar. Each drawing had a wax seal in the bottom right-hand corner with the name *Mossop* pressed into it and the words: *COPY. Original in the Temple of the Chanters.*

Tim read aloud the caption on the plan that looked like an automobile, "*The Mossop Pigless Carriage, built as a birthday present for His Majesty, Erlan the III, High King of Tallis.*"

"I've actually seen that," said Hunter. "It was the only

one ever built. The roads of Tallis are more suitable for pigs' trotters."

"Where did you see it?" asked Tim, intrigued.

"In the north, a long time ago," Hunter replied shortly.

Eventually, they came to a large, square, oak-paneled room with three other doors off it. Through an open doorway they could see a magnificent four-poster bed hung with tapestry curtains and facing a small fireplace. The dark, uneven floorboards were wide and scattered with soft rugs. The walls were almost completely covered in framed paintings of flowers. Only the one hanging over the fireplace was different, it showed a smiling couple. The man wore side whiskers and a high collar, and the woman's hair was intricately piled up on her head. She wore a dress with leg-of-mutton sleeves, puffed at the top and tight on the forearm.

"Joseph and Anne Mossop," said Hunter. "They must have liked it in Tallis."

One of the other doors led to a large dark room that was quite empty, and another to a small dining room equipped with a dumbwaiter that would have carried food up from the kitchen.

"Why have you brought us here, Hunter?" asked Sarre.

Hunter was busy examining the decorative paneling above the fireplace. "Joseph Mossop was a remarkable man," he answered as he ran a hand over the wall's wooden surface. "He frequently visited Tallis. First to trade in flowers. Then he and his wife actually settled here and they went on to do many other things. According to his wife's diary he left some papers here."

Hunter applied pressure to the center of a wooden rose, and there was a click. A section of the paneling swung open to reveal the contents of the dim interior: an old-fashioned deep-sea diver's helmet, several boxes of matches, and a large sheet of parchment. Hunter exchanged a puzzled glance with Tim, then reached past the helmet to take the sheet of parchment, which bore the Mossop wax seal. He rolled it up and stuffed it inside his jacket. On impulse, Tim took three boxes of matches, thinking they might be useful. The Gurneys lit fires from their tinderboxes and it sometimes proved difficult in wet weather.

Hunter, Sarre, and Tim returned downstairs to the bar, where the landlord was sweeping the floor. Sarre's eyes had become bright blue again.

"There you are," said Bunton. "You didn't take long."

"Any other customers?" Hunter asked.

Bunton shook his head. "Quiet as the grave."

"Come on," Hunter said to Tim. "I've got to find you a good tailor."

They had almost reached the door when Bunton called after them, "Try Needle Lane, third street on the right."

As they left, Tim glanced up at the painted sign above the door. He hadn't noticed it when they entered. It read: THE ENTON ARMS and had a picture of a star falling on a hill.

"Mossop must have missed home when he was here," said Hunter.

"What do you think he wanted with a diver's helmet?" asked Tim, mystified.

"I haven't the faintest idea," replied Hunter briskly. "Come on."

Following Bunton's directions, Hunter led them away from the tavern and turned down an alleyway where they found a tailor's shop.

It was a narrow, wood-paneled establishment, but the back part of the shop looked much larger due to the two tall mirrors reflecting each other to infinity on the side walls. In the front part of the shop, bolts of cloth lay on shelves from floor to ceiling.

A tall, thin old man with his hair drawn back in a pigtail secured with a silk bow stood behind the counter. A tape measure hung around his neck, and he wore a flowing silk shirt, a long skirted waistcoat, breeches, stockings, and buckled shoes.

Hunter lay the bag of leaves on the counter and asked, "Can you make a suit for the lad with these?"

The tailor glanced at Tim and opened the bag. As three leaves floated out he snatched them from the air with a long hand.

"Tregger leaves," he said with a smile. "I haven't seen any of these in their natural state since I was an apprentice. These days, I'm told the Great Duke uses all supplies for the punishment balloons. We get the cloth, of course, but the dye has always been boiled out by that stage."

"But can you make the boy a suit?" Hunter asked impatiently.

"Of course," replied the tailor with a sniff. "Will the young gentleman want a light suit or not?"

"What's a light suit?" asked Tim.

"I could leave all the dye in the cloth, in which case you might float about a bit. Or I could boil it lightly. Even then, it would still put a spring in your step."

"That sounds like fun," said Tim. "Lightly boiled, please."

The tailor swiftly ran the tape measure over him, writing down measurements and humming quietly as he worked.

"It will be ready in three hours," he said finally.

"That's fast work," said Hunter. "Will it be a good fit?"

"Like a Lord's best glove," said the tailor. "And the material will stretch to allow for growth. Always essential in clothing for boys."

With time to spare, the three now wandered about the town, exploring the narrow streets, alleyways, and squares. The first square was where they'd seen the police launch the punishment balloons. They crossed it quickly and found another where livestock was being traded.

A third was filled with food stalls bearing a variety of vegetables, fruit, great cheeses, cooked meats, pies, and drinks in stone bottles. Gurney women, carrying large baskets, were moving through the crowd selling silk masks.

"Wind changers," they chanted. "Buy a wind changer."

"What are wind changers?" asked Hunter.

"These," replied Sarre, taking a square of silk from her pocket. "Don't you have them?" she asked, suddenly concerned. "They keep out the dangerous Killing Wind. We didn't need masks in the forest, but the farther north we travel, the deadlier the wind will become."

"Charto told me about the Killing Wind. It didn't exist when I was last in Tallis," said Hunter.

"You'd better get yourselves one," said Sarre.

One of the Gurney women recognized them and smiled. Hunter tried to buy a mask for himself and Tim, but the woman laughed as she handed them each one and waved away his coin.

There was still hardly any wind, apart from an occasional light gust, and the air smelled of wood smoke. It curled up from the chimneys and hung in clouds above the town. The faint moans of the prisoners dangling from the balloons continued to drift down from above.

To fill their stomachs and the time until Tim's suit was ready, Hunter bought pies and drinks from the stalls and they went up to the town battlements to eat. But Sarre and Tim didn't feel particularly hungry. The distant cries from the dangling figures above them seemed to have dampened their appetite.

After eating a few mouthfuls, they went back down to look in more of the shop windows. One was a sword maker whose wares included a variety of blades, spears, pikes, knives, and daggers all set out in rows or fanlike displays. There was obviously a brisk trade in weapons. All the townsmen wore swords.

Something puzzled Tim. "Why are there no guns here, Hunter?" he asked. "Surely, people must have brought them from our world at some time?"

Hunter nodded. "They have, on many occasions. But guns don't work in Tallis. It's not the mechanical part. That functions perfectly well. It's the ammunition that won't fire, nor will plain gunpowder explode. Many people have tried. It just burns brightly. Fine for a pretty display, but not forceful enough to fire a projectile. A man with a gun in Tallis would stand no chance against you and your slingshot."

Finally, they returned to the tailor's shop, where the finished suit lay on the counter. The tailor had added a darker brown dye when the leaves were boiled, so the original red and gold showed only faintly through a sort of tan color. Tim was shown to a curtained cubicle to put on his new suit. The trousers were close fitting, but the upper garment was looser, more like a long shirt with baggy sleeves and a wide collar. He put on his belt and felt quite smart. The material was comfortable and he did feel wonderfully light on his feet.

"Excellent," said Hunter.

"You do look smart," agreed Sarre.

Tim glanced down at his feet. "My old shoes look pretty shabby, though."

They stepped from the shop in high spirits with Sarre and Tim taking the lead. But as they entered the narrow alleyway they saw four figures striding toward them. The Great Duke's police walked with the menacing swagger of bullies looking for trouble. Tim recognized them as the ones who had chained the prisoners to the balloons.

"Out of the way, scum," one of them snarled.

Tim and Sarre stepped aside to let them to pass in the narrow alleyway. The four policemen didn't keep going but stopped at the tailor's shop and crowded around Hunter in its doorway.

The leader spat on Hunter's boots as they all stood close together, blocking his exit. Hunter ignored the insult and glanced away. He gave a slight indication with his hand that Sarre and Tim should go on. But the men bearing over him deliberately misinterpreted the gesture.

"Are you insulting the Duke's men?" the leader asked, thrusting his face close to Hunter's.

Hunter gave a slight bow, saying, "Forgive me, I am a stranger here."

"Look a Duke's man in the face when he speaks to you," another of them snapped.

"My deepest apologies, gentlemen," Hunter replied softly. "I don't want any trouble."

The leader reached out to take hold of Hunter's sword, "This looks like a gentleman's weapon. What's a piece of scum like you doing with a sword like this? Show it to me."

Before the man could touch the handle, Hunter seized his hand in an iron grip, saying, "You don't want to do that."

Immediately, the men bristled like angry dogs. It was

clear they were about to attack and Hunter had little space to maneuver in the confines of the doorway.

"Tim, Sarre, run!" Hunter commanded.

Without answering, they disobeyed. Tim swiftly drew his slingshot and fired three times. Each jewel struck a policeman on the back of his neck, the sharp missiles drawing blood. The men staggered back in confusion, clutching at their stinging wounds.

Before Tim could fire again, Sarre darted forward and kicked the fourth in the seat of his pants. He spun about, his face contorted with rage at the insult, and lunged toward her.

All four policemen drew their swords. It was a mistake. Hunter acted with such astonishing speed, it was as if the Duke's men were moving in slow motion. There was a rippling clash of weapons as Hunter, his sword gripped in both hands, whirled among them once. Then he stood quite still in a half crouch as all four of his opponents slowly toppled forward and fell to the ground.

Tim and Sarre stared in amazement.

"Are they dead?" asked Tim.

Hunter shook his head. "Only stunned. I used the back of the blade."

Suddenly, two other men were in the alleyway — the tailor and the mechanic who had controlled the Mossop Mole. Hunter held his sword at the ready but the tailor held up his hands. "Friends," he muttered.

"You must go," said the mechanic urgently.

"What about them?" asked Hunter, pointing with his sword at the fallen men just as the Mossop Mole broke the surface of the alleyway.

"Go," said the tailor. "We'll use the Mole tunnel to hide them, then soak them with ale. Their officer will think they were drunk. But you must get away from here."

"Thank you," said Hunter.

"Thank *you*," said the mechanic. "These vile creatures took my brothers for execution today."

He was already dragging the first body toward the gaping hole made by the Mole.

Hunter nodded, and taking Tim and Sarre by the arm, hurried them away into a wider street that was thronged with people. When he thought they were safe, Hunter stopped. "What you two just did was very foolhardy," he said, frowning. "They could easily have harmed you."

"But they were going to kill you, Hunter," said Tim. "We couldn't let them do that."

Hunter shook Tim gently and actually smiled, while at the same time still looking sad. "That's the second time you've probably saved my life," he said. "It's getting to be a habit. Come on."

He strolled on ahead of them and Sarre said, "You see, you talked to him just like you do to Josh."

When they returned to the Gurney camp, Luxo had a surprise waiting. Hunter had paid him to make Tim a smart pair of high boots and a hat, both fashioned from leather.

The hat had a low, pointed crown and a wide brim that could be rolled up on each side when the weather was good.

Luxo had also made him a new belt with a loop to hold his slingshot on his hip, and a large ammunition pouch. Even Josh seemed impressed. He circled around Tim, barking excitedly at his new appearance.

The Castle of
Lord Tredore

Next day, the wind blew relentlessly as the Gurney caravan left Milchen and resumed its journey north. To begin with, the country they passed through was hilly with massive outcrops of granite and only a few trees. Grazing on the hills were great flocks of sheep tended by shepherds. As they traveled from village to village, returning the wild children and striking camp at a different place every night, the landscape gradually changed to rolling hills, woodland, and small farms. Occasionally, they saw roaming bands of black-clad policemen mounted on fighting boars but they kept their distance.

Eventually, one hot windy evening the Gurneys returned the last of the captive children to their village near the sea. The water lay in a fat blue line beyond the farmland that rolled gently down to the coast.

After supper, Charto consulted his map by the flickering light of the campfire. "There's a good road going north along the coast," he said. "We'll follow that until we reach the River Tredore where there's a ferry we can take across its estuary."

He beckoned to Sarre, "I'm hoping the Great Lord Tredore will receive us. He usually buys all the flowers we manage to get this far; although sometimes that only amounts to a few wilting blooms. We used to pack them in ice and bring them by sea in racing schooners. And he always took them, even when the petals were falling."

"What do you want me to do?" asked Sarre.

"Lord Tredore used to have an old Chanter living at his castle. See if you can contact her. I think her name was Ellath, Aella — something like that."

"Her name is Ellath," said Sarre. "Bethen has told me of her."

"Do you think you can contact her mind?"

"I can try," said Sarre, and she sat down under a tree, closed her eyes, and laid her hands in her lap. Charto waved for everyone to keep their distance.

Nearly an hour passed before Sarre opened her eyes.

"We have been followed all the way from the Tregger camp," she said flatly.

"Followed?" said Charto. "Impossible! I always send out scouts to keep watch when we're traveling."

"It's something they couldn't see," answered Sarre. "I should have realized. I'm sorry. I'm not as experienced as the Chanter at Lord Tredore's castle. She has just warned me that there is a creature spying on us."

"Does she know what it is?" asked Charto.

Sarre shook her head. "Only that it is not human."

"So, the old Chanter still lives."

"Yes, under the protection of Lord Tredore. The Duke's police know of her presence and want to gain entry to the castle to arrest her, but they are prevented by Lord Tredore's soldiers."

"What about us?" asked Charto.

"We are most welcome. Although Lord Tredore doesn't believe you can have fresh flowers with you. He says it's a typical Gurney exaggeration."

Charto grinned. "Well, he's in for a big surprise, isn't he?" Then he looked anxiously at Tim. "They *are* still fresh, aren't they?"

"Fresh as a daisy," said Tim confidently.

"What is a daisy?" asked Charto suspiciously.

"Something I could sell to you for a fortune," said Tim with an innocent smile.

The following morning, after loading up the pigs, the caravan made its way to a fishing village called Gulla, where the Gurneys paused to trade for dried fish. Tim and Sarre, exhilarated by the smell of the sea, hurried through the tiny collection of stone cottages and ran shouting onto the sandy beach. Josh raced after them, yapping excitedly at their heels. They paused just long enough for Tim to pull off his boots, then dashed into the sea to splash each other with the warm salty water. Josh swam between them, barking joyfully until they returned to the beach and went to inspect the small fishing boats that were drawn up on the sand above the waterline.

Fishermen were repairing their nets and gossiping in the shelter of a breakwater. They were hard-looking men, their hands and faces dark from the wind and sun. Standing near them, Hunter was honing the blade of his sword with a pebble he had specially selected from the beach.

Sarre was fascinated by it all; she had never seen the sea before. They wandered along the shoreline throwing stones into the water for Josh, who loved to dash in after them. Eventually, Charto called them back to the caravan to resume their journey.

The road they took was made of ancient slabs of granite and wide enough for five of the pack pigs to walk abreast. Vast chestnut trees lined each side to provide shade.

"Who built these roads?" Tim asked Charto.

"The ancient ones," he answered. "The road has always been here."

"Why do you ask, Tim?" said Sarre.

He shrugged. This road is so big, yet we're the only

people using it. I guess it must have been much busier in the past."

After a time, the road curved away from the coast and they followed the southern bank of an estuary. Eventually, the road led to a large gatehouse overlooking the wide mouth of the river. It was crowned with battlements, fortified to guard a wide jetty.

Clustered about the gatehouse was a detachment of the black-clad mounted police. Tim counted ten of them. Their boars snorted aggressively at the Gurney pack pigs, which would only approach when they were goaded on. However, keeping some distance between them, Charto brought the caravan to a halt in the shade of the chestnut trees.

Sarre tugged at Tim's arm and pointed across the wide expanse of water. Coming toward them was a massive ferry propelled by mighty paddle wheels, each one higher than a two-story house.

At the gatehouse, two tough-looking old soldiers in gray leather armor stood resolutely barring the gate while the leader of the police shouted at them.

"I told you yesterday, we are acting under the orders of the Great Duke Galeth. My instructions are to present a tax demand to Lord Tredore."

One of the old soldiers, obviously unimpressed by the policeman's ranting, replied, "And I'm telling you, Lord Tredore's answer is: 'The only person who can come onto

Tredore land uninvited is the High King himself.' And you're not the High King, laddie, despite your fancy clothes. So, clear off."

The policeman grew even darker in the face. He was clearly used to people reacting fearfully to his anger. "Do you want me to arrest you and seize the ferry?" he raged.

"You can try," the old soldier answered calmly. "But I wouldn't advise it." He gave a piercing whistle and the battlements immediately bristled with archers, bows drawn.

"Now, you be on your way, laddie," said the old soldier.

Seeing they were outnumbered, the policeman reined his boar about and, waving petulantly to his men to follow, he galloped toward the caravan, scattering the Gurneys and causing the pack pigs to squeal in alarm.

The old soldier waved the caravan toward him.

"Lord Tredore is expecting you, Gurneys," he said. "When you've crossed the estuary, you can camp in the great meadow to the right of the main gate. There's plenty of wood and good water."

"Thank you, I remember it well," said Charto.

With Josh at their heels, Tim and Sarre hurried through the gatehouse with Hunter to watch the great ferry dock at the jetty. Puzzled by what power caused the mighty paddle wheels to turn, they waited as the deckhands made the ropes fast, then eagerly crossed the lowered gangplank. The deck was as wide as a tennis court and at least twice as long. In the center was a small wheelhouse with just enough headroom for a man to stand up in it. At either side of the stern there were stairs leading below.

While Hunter stayed on deck to gaze across the wide estuary, Tim and Sarre went down the stairs to find out what powered the paddle wheels. They were confronted by a massive array of cogs and wheels, all whirling and turning — it appeared to be a giant clockwork engine! Intrigued, they returned to the deck and went to the wheelhouse. A small man wearing a jaunty cap was effortlessly turning two handles. He smiled at them.

"Excuse me, Sir," said Tim. "Can you tell us what powers the paddle wheels?"

The little man nodded. "This machine I'm winding up," he answered.

"It *does* work by clockwork," gasped Tim. "That's incredible."

"A magic machine," said Sarre softly.

Tim shook his head. "Not magic, just mechanics. But the most incredible example I've ever seen. Whoever built it must be a genius."

"You have seen clockwork before?" said Sarre.

"Only working small things. Nothing on such an enormous scale," said Tim.

At last, all of the Gurney pack pigs had been persuaded to board the ferry and stood swaying on the deck. Sarre and Tim watched as the captain pulled a few levers and the crew cast off. The craft slowly turned out into the estuary and headed for the distant shore.

With much yelling and goading of the pigs, they disembarked at a similar jetty on the other side. They traveled on through a deep wood of oak trees until they emerged into gently undulating farmland. Farmworkers stopped to watch the spectacular caravan of pack pigs and Gurneys making its way along the lanes between fields of wheat, barley, and a variety of vegetable crops. They passed orchards, dairy farms, a large windmill, and a building that smelled like an alehouse. People on the vast estate looked happy enough and their children stared and waved at them.

The farmland eventually led into a great park, where herds of deer and other game were grazing. In one huge clearing they saw more than a thousand soldiers practicing with their arms. Massed archers sent flights of arrows hissing toward their targets, other companies fought mock battles with spears, swords, and shields. Farther along the road, they passed and exchanged cheerful greetings with two green-clad rangers, armed with bows and arrows and mounted on lean sporting pigs.

After passing through another fringe of woodland they came to a sudden deep-sided valley. At the bottom was a great meadow through which a stream meandered to fill the wide moat surrounding Tredore Castle, which rose on an outcrop of rock.

The castle ramparts were high and shaped so gracefully it looked to Tim more like a cathedral than a fortress. He counted fifteen stories of honey-colored stone.

"It must have a lot of stairs?" said Sarre.

"Imagine if your bedroom were on the top floor," said Tim, laughing. "You'd be really tired by the time you got to bed."

Charto led the caravan down into the meadow where the old soldier back at the gatehouse had instructed them to camp. While Hunter gave the Gurneys a hand unloading the pack pigs, Tim and Sarre went with Josh to explore the castle.

Once across the drawbridge, they passed through a short tunnel and emerged to find that the high edifice they had seen from outside was actually not of any great thickness. It was built around a much older, smaller castle, which was only three stories high. They crossed the space between the two buildings and entered the courtyard at the center of the older castle.

Josh started to wander off, sniffing the unfamiliar surroundings, but Tim called, "Stay!" and he obediently returned to heel.

The walls of the ramparts overlooking the old castle courtyard supported tier upon tier of viewing boxes. They had obviously been built high up so that spectators could view events taking place in the courtyard. To reach the boxes there was a system of elevators.

A group of people, who had not noticed Sarre and Tim enter, stood in the center of the cobbled yard. They were looking up at a robust, silver-haired figure who was four stories up the wall of the ramparts, slowly edging his way along a narrow parapet between two of the viewing boxes.

But for a blue silk sash, he was dressed completely in white. He wore a shirt with billowing sleeves, a long waistcoat, silk pantaloons with long stockings, and satin shoes with gold buckles. Two serving maids watched anxiously. One was carrying a long black robe trimmed with fur.

"Oh, do be careful, My Lord," called out an elderly footman with a powdered wig, holding out his hands beseechingly. A stout old soldier in bejeweled armor seemed less agitated than the others.

"Be careful, My Lord," they all chorused as a tall thin woman wearing a conical hat and a long blue velvet dress with tight sleeves came bustling out of another doorway.

"What are you doing up there, you old fool?" she scolded in a powerful voice.

"Trying to get Podger," the white-clad figure replied gruffly as he continued to edge along the parapet.

"How did he get up there?" she demanded.

"The same way I did. Up those blasted stairs. The elevators are still not working."

"Come down at once. One of the guards can get him."

"They're all out on exercises," he answered. "I'm the only man of action on the premises."

"Well, you'll be a dead man of no action if you're not careful," said the thin woman. "Come down!"

"I can't, I'm stuck," the man replied.

A fat man in a long velvet coat ran gasping for breath into the courtyard. He was carrying several lengths of silk curtain cord that he had tied together. "We can use this as a rope," he called. "If I can get it to His Lordship he can climb down."

"You'll never get up there," scolded the stout soldier. "The timbers of those old wooden staircases are rotten. They should have been replaced years ago. I don't know how His Lordship managed it."

"May I help?" said Sarre.

"You're just a girl, go away," snapped the fat man in the velvet coat.

Ignoring him, Sarre reached into her pouch and took out a length of spider yarn. She picked up the curtain cords that he had discarded on the ground and tied one end of them to the spider yarn. Without a moment's hesitation Sarre ran to the rampart wall and began to climb. Her movements were swift and smooth.

"Good gracious," the woman in the high conical hat proclaimed. "The girl climbs like a chimney sweep's apprentice!"

Sarre was soon above the stranded man. She hauled on the spider's yarn to pull up the cord rope, then quickly secured it to a strong oak beam that supported one of the viewing boxes.

"Can you get Podger?" the old man called out to Sarre as he swung himself quite nimbly down the rope.

Sarre swung over to rescue something that Tim could not yet see clearly. Within seconds, she had tucked it into her pouch and skimmed back down the rope.

* * *

Podger turned out to be a tiny pink pig. The old man had another one tucked into his waistcoat. Lord Tredore was a handsome man with a strong jaw, a broken nose and, apparently, a fondness for pet pigs. He peered at Tim and Sarre with piercing gray eyes set below bushy white eyebrows.

"This is Pidger," he said to Sarre, taking the other pig out of his waistcoat. "A nasty creature chased them onto the ledge when I was inspecting the Royal Box."

"Was it a large rat?" asked Tim, who for some reason seemed very interested in the rampart wall.

"Yes, with big yellow teeth. How did *you* know?" asked the old man. Then he noticed Josh sitting quietly at Tim's heel. "By a Gurney's left leg! What is *that* creature?"

"My dog," said Tim, still looking up at the wall above. "He won't harm your pigs, Sir."

Snatching the slingshot from his hip, Tim suddenly aimed high and let loose a swift jewel. Something came tumbling down the wall, bounced off one of the viewing boxes, and landed at their feet. It was the body of a huge black rat.

The tiny pigs ran around the upturned body squealing as if they were responsible for the victory.

"Well done," said Lord Tredore. "That's one accounted for, can you see the other?"

"Find the other, Josh," said Tim, letting the dog sniff the dead rat for a moment. Josh circled the yard, his nose twitching, then darted into a dark shadowy corner, from which came a snarling sound that was followed by a hideous squeak. Finally, Josh emerged backward, dragging the body of the other huge rat.

"Oh, well done," said the old man. "What a capital creature. You young pair have done me a great service today. Where do you come from, one of my farms?"

"We are traveling with the Gurney caravan, Sir," replied Sarre.

The old man squinted at them shrewdly. "You're not Gurney children, though, are you?" Then he looked over their shoulders as Charto and Hunter entered the castle yard.

Both men swept off their hats and bowed deeply before the old man.

"I remember you," said Lord Tredore. "It's Charto the Gurney, is it not?"

"It is, My Lord. May I present my traveling companion, Hunter."

"You're an Earther," said Tredore, looking him up and down.

"I am, Sir."

"And these young people are with you?" asked Lord Tredore.

"They are, My Lord," said Hunter.

"Well, they've done me a great service. I hope it sets a precedent for the rest of your visit."

Lord Tredore studied Hunter carefully. "In what order of chivalry were you knighted?" he asked.

Hunter hesitated.

"Come on, man," said Tredore. "You may be an Earther but I can tell by the way you wear your sword that you are also a knight."

Sarre and Tim exchanged surprised glances. Hunter hadn't mentioned that he had any kind of title.

"A Companion of the Dragon," he answered.

"A Dragon!" exclaimed Tredore, surprised. "The Imperial Order of the High King. That's a high rank for an Earther. Well, I'm a Dragon, too, so welcome, brother knight."

"What about the flowers?" interrupted Lady Tredore. "Is it true what Ellath told me? Are they really still fresh, or is that just a Gurney exaggeration?"

Charto bowed again. "You may judge for yourself, My Lady. When would you care to inspect them?"

"Bring them along to the courtyard now," said Lord Tredore. "I want to see them."

"I thought you would say that, My Lord," said Charto, and he gave a loud whistle. Immediately, there was a fanfare of Gurney trumpets from beyond the moat, and two great pack pigs led by Gurney women crossed the drawbridge and entered the courtyard.

Both pigs were decked from hoof to snout with the potted flowers: geraniums, petunias, lobelia, polyanthus, all glowed in a vivid mass of color.

Lord and Lady Tredore were transfixed by their beauty. The women led the pigs around and around the couple, who kept applauding like delighted children.

"It's true," said Lord Tredore finally. "They *are* fresh. And the most beautiful I have ever seen."

He lay a hand on Charto's shoulder. "How long will they last?"

"Ask the lad, My Lord. He knows all about flowers."

Tim answered the question. "Two to four months," he said confidently, but crossed his fingers hopefully as he spoke.

CHAPTER 15

Lord Tredore Plans a Tournament

That evening, at the Gurney camp, Tim and Hunter took special care with their appearance. They had been invited to dine, along with Sarre, at the table of Lord Tredore. Sarre always looked presentable no matter how hard the day's march had been. She had several silk dresses and washed them, as well as herself, whenever an opportunity presented itself.

Tim and Hunter kept themselves clean, but their clothes had become somewhat travel stained in recent weeks. While they took turns to scrub themselves in one of the Gurneys' collapsible leather baths, Charto's wife had their clothes washed and pressed and Tim even gave Josh a bath, as he was also invited to the dinner.

Charto sat by the fire, binding the handle of a beautiful knife he'd made. The blade was curved several times, like a wriggling snake.

"Why aren't you coming with us, Charto?" Tim asked.

Charto laughed at the idea. "Lords don't dine with Gurneys," he replied.

"Then why did he invite Sarre and me? We're no better than you."

Charto shrugged, unconcerned. "Sarre is a Chanter and you have a dog to amuse Lord Tredore. All people have their own customs," he said easily. "There are occasions to which Gurneys only invite other Gurneys."

He worked at a strand of the leather for a few seconds, then continued. "Besides, Hunter is socially equal to Lord Tredore. The old man probably doesn't have many people he can talk to who are on the same footing."

"Hunter is equal to Lord Tredore?"

"Oh, yes," said Charto. "The moment Hunter told him he was a Companion of the Dragon, Lord Tredore's attitude changed."

"I didn't notice."

"You probably don't have to look out for these things. We Gurneys are highly observant when it comes to spotting people's attitudes toward us. A lot of folk don't like Gurneys. We seem to make them nervous."

"Well, I'd rather spend my time with Gurneys than sitting about in a dreary old castle surrounded by silly men and women," said Tim. "Gurneys are much more fun."

Tim gave a few hops in his suit; it somehow always felt lighter after a gentle wash. "What exactly are Companions of the Dragon?" he asked.

"Members of a sort of noblemen's club," said Charto. "You'd better ask Hunter if you want to know more details."

But Tim didn't get a chance to raise the subject because as they walked to the castle Sarre was instructing him in manners and etiquette.

"So how is it *you* know which knife to eat fruit with?" Tim mocked. "I thought you grew up in a forest living in a tree house."

"Because I am a Chanter and I was instructed by a Chanter," said Sarre grandly. "Most Chanters come from the aristocracy of Tallis. It's you who is the odd one out on this occasion."

"All right," he sighed. "What is it I mustn't do again?"

"Don't tell anyone older than yourself they're wrong, even if what they're saying is nonsense. In fact, *never* correct anyone older than yourself. And you mustn't refuse any request from Lord Tredore."

"Suppose he wants me to sell him Josh?" said Tim, alarmed. "Lots of people have tried to buy him."

Sarre thought. "In that case it would be best to say: 'My

Lord, you are welcome to have my unworthy dog for nothing, but I must warn you, I fear he may be the bringer of ill fortune.'"

"Do you think that would work?"

"Probably, the old nobles of Tallis are dreadfully superstitious."

"So it doesn't matter if I tell him a lie?"

"How do you know it's a lie? Maybe Josh would bring him bad luck. All you've said was you *fear* he may be the bringer of ill fortune."

Hunter laughed. "Spoken like a true diplomat."

Sarre nodded contentedly. "Chanters were once the diplomats in Tallis," she said.

This time, as they crossed the courtyard of the castle, there was a full complement of guards. A servant took them to the dining hall where Lord and Lady Tredore stood to receive them in front of a vast, blazing log fire. The two tiny pigs, Pidger and Podger, lay curled upon the hearth, snoring contentedly. Josh, weary from the day's excitement, curled up with them.

Drinking horns were handed to the guests and filled with a sweetish liquid. They all drank a toast to the High King of Tallis.

"My own beer," said Lord Tredore. "We brew it on the estate." He looked up to the gallery where a group of minstrels were playing softly on stringed instruments and flutes.

"Ah, Ellath," said Tredore when a new guest entered.

Four servants carried a sedan chair, bearing a very old woman. They carefully descended the wide staircase and brought the chair to the fireside. To Tim's surprise, the old woman hopped out of it in quite a lively fashion and accepted a horn of beer, which she drank with relish. As she was introduced, she said, "Sarre and I already know each other. Our minds have met."

She then subjected Hunter and Tim in turn to a piercing gaze, her flickering eyes changing through various shades of green. Finally, she gave a nod of satisfaction, as if they had already told her things she was interested to know.

"Ellath is my great aunt," said Tredore. "The Duke Galeth would like to do away with her, but she's safe here on my estate."

"Is there anywhere else a Chanter can be safe?" asked Hunter.

Tredore shook his head. "No. These days, apart from me, only the High King has a Chanter. She is called Illya. The Duke wouldn't dare touch Illya, and the rest have been killed or are in hiding."

Hunter was puzzled. "It's been many years since I was last in Tallis," he said. "How did all this come about?"

"The misfortunes of the kingdom?" sighed Tredore. "Sit down, we'll eat while I tell you."

As servants brought in great platters of meat, game, vegetables, and fruit, Lord Tredore began.

"All would have been well if the High King's son, Prince

Briarre, had lived. His unexpected death plunged the kingdom into chaos. And we all thought the High King's daughter, the Lady of Tallis, was dead, too. That was when the King became unwell —"

"*Mad*, you mean," Lady Tredore interrupted sharply.

"*Unwell!*" roared Tredore. "The grief was enough to turn any man's head. But, one day, he will be restored to us."

Hunter leaned forward intently. "You say you all *thought* the Lady of Tallis was dead?"

Tredore nodded sadly. "She vanished for two years after her brother was killed. The King was inconsolable. Then she surprised us all by returning to nurse him."

Lady Tredore squeezed her husband's hand. "The High King thinks his daughter is still a child and the Prince is merely away on vacation, hunting for a Kanarki bloom on the Northern Rim."

Lord Tredore took a long drink from his horn and continued.

"It's Duke Galeth's fault. He's destroyed all the old ways of the kingdom. It was he who started this obsession for the New Blooms of Kanarki."

Lady Tredore saw the confusion on Hunter's face. "How long is it since you were in Tallis?" she asked.

"More than twelve years," he replied.

"So you don't know about the trouble the New Blooms of Kanarki have caused?" she asked.

Hunter shook his head. "I remember about the old blooms. They were very rare flower-shaped crystals that were only found in dark rock hollows on the Northern Rim of Tallis. It was the custom of young nobles to hunt for them as a proof of manhood."

"I don't understand," said Tim. "What's the difference between old blooms and new blooms?"

Ellath, the old Chanter, placed a hand on one of Tim's, and said, "After the High King, the Great Duke has the biggest estate in the kingdom. The Duke's lands, in the far north, stretch from east to west from one sea to the other and as far north as the Rim. There are terrible mountains there and strange wild beasts. It was once considered brave to hunt for the blooms but they were rarely found. When they were, they were considered rare and a special curiosity."

"Why did that change?" asked Tim.

Lady Tredore began to explain. "The Duke discovered a great cave in the mountains where crystal blooms were formed in great numbers."

"How were they discovered?" asked Tim.

"An extraordinary business, so the story goes. The descendants of one of Joseph Mossop's servants sold a map to the Great Duke. It showed the location of the cavern. The Duke opened a mine and now uses slaves to harvest the blooms, which look like flowers made of spun glass. They are so very beautiful and are prized even more than real flowers."

Lord Tredore took up the story. "A terrible madness descended on the nobles. They traded their estates with the Great Duke to obtain a single bloom. And wars broke out between the Lords, who had become obsessed with trying to steal one another's collections."

Ellath spoke again. "Finally, the High King managed to restore some kind of peace by inviting all of the nobles to live in the palace, where they could establish one great collection of the blooms. All but one of the nobles did go to live at the palace. Only Lord Tredore stayed on his own estate as the High King wanted him here to keep the peace across the Midlands."

"So, does the High King still rule?" said Hunter, puzzled. "I thought all power now lies in the hands of Great Duke Galeth."

"The High King rules only in name," answered Lord Tredore. "The Duke governs as Regent. He wants to become the legitimate heir by marrying the High King's daughter. But the Lady of Tallis has refused him. She says she cannot be wed without the King's permission."

"And, of course, the King thinks she is still a child," said Ellath. "So he won't give his permission for them to marry."

Lady Tredore looked wistful. "I wonder how the High King and the other members of the court are? I miss seeing our old friends."

"Well, I have a surprise and a treat for you, my dear," said Tredore. "I'm going to offer as a great tournament prize the flowers our guests have brought us. We shall invite the High King and all of the Tallis nobility to Tredore. We shall have a great ball and battle games for the knights and an archery contest for their squires, just as we used to in the old days."

Lady Tredore beamed at her husband. "That will be quite wonderful, my dear. I cannot thank you enough for such a kind thought."

Lord Tredore spoke to his Chanter. "Lady Ellath, will you issue the proper invitations? You know the protocol."

Ellath nodded. "I shall contact Illya tonight, My Lord. She will tell everyone at the High King's palace." Then, looking at Sarre, she said, "And I shall introduce you to Illya, child. I know your minds have not yet met, although Bethen was always a great friend to us both."

"Is the High King's Chanter well?" asked Sarre, who had been listening in silence.

Ellath nodded to her. "Illya has been renewing for a long time."

Tim leaned toward Sarre and whispered, "What's renewing?"

"I'm not sure," Sarre whispered back. "But it sounds hopeful."

"I'll need a few days to prepare," said Lady Tredore with even more enthusiasm. "It will be a huge undertaking to play host to all the aristocracy of Tallis."

Lord Tredore nodded, becoming even more excited by the prospect. "We'll have a fair for all the people on the estate. It's a good thing the Gurneys are here. They'll liven things up."

"Are you sure the Lords will come?" asked Tim.

"To a tournament? They'll come," answered Hunter. "It's a matter of honor."

"Now, young Tim," said Lord Tredore, "let us see more tricks from your amazing creature."

Tim called Josh, who after his nap had been gnawing contentedly on a huge bone provided by Lord Tredore. Reluctantly, the little dog came out from under the table and Tim put him through his paces. Lord and Lady Tredore and their entourage applauded happily.

After the meal, Hunter, Sarre, Tim, and Josh all strolled back to the Gurney camp. The fires were blazing and music filled the air. Tim remembered Lord Tredore's comment and thought how right he was. The Gurneys did liven things up.

Charto was delighted when they told him the news. "What a fine chance for trade!" he exclaimed.

"Can you get me a decent mount for the battle games?" Hunter said. "I intend to take part."

Charto snapped his fingers. "Consider it done. The finest mount of the tournament shall be yours."

The Arrival of the High King

Being the honored guests of Lord Tredore, Tim, Sarre, and Josh were able to roam anywhere about the castle during the preparations for the tournament's battle games. On the great meadow outside the walls, Charto and the other Gurneys prepared the fair for the families of the tenant farmers and their workers. In the yard, Lord Tredore was supervising the men who were attempting to repair the mechanical elevators. And the stout old soldier, called Captain Lunduf, was drilling troops for the guard of honor.

Inside the castle, Lady Tredore commanded an army of footmen and maids who were cleaning, washing, and dusting every room, making chambers ready for the many distinguished guests who were expected. The steward sat in his velvet robe at a high desk, writing on sheets of parchment with a goose-feather quill.

"Protocol," he sighed, when Sarre asked him what he was doing. "It's vital we put the right people in the right chambers or much offense will be given."

Sarre and Tim returned to the yard. The elevators were still stuck. Sections of the rampart wall had been removed, revealing a bewildering array of cogs and wheels.

"Nothing works," Lord Tredore said gloomily. "And these fools are never going to get it going. The battle games will be a fiasco. I shall have to cancel and be disgraced."

Shielding his eyes from the sun, Tim studied a windmill set on the top of the ramparts. Despite the strong breeze, the sails were not turning.

"What does that windmill do, My Lord?" he asked.

"When the wind blows it turns the sails that are supposed to make the clock in the great hall work, but it seems to be broken. Although the wind keeps blowing, the clock has stopped," Lord Tredore answered.

"And what powers the mechanics for the elevators?"

Lord Tredore shrugged. "I really don't know. It was all made by a chap called Mossop who stayed here with my great-grandfather more than a hundred years ago."

"Has the windmill ever gone wrong before?"

Lord Tredore shook his head.

"I could climb up and look," said Sarre.

"No need," said Tim, "I think I can see the trouble."

He loaded his slingshot, took careful aim, and let fly. The emerald he fired struck something white jammed between two large cogs of the windmill. His next shot dislodged it completely. It fell, bouncing off balconies, to land in the courtyard. Josh retrieved it and dropped it at Lord Tredore's feet. Immediately, the sails of the windmill began to turn and the cogs of the elevator mechanisms began to wind up.

"What an amazing shot," said Lord Tredore, looking down at the human skull Josh had dropped. "Now, how could that have got up there?"

"The Duke's prisoner balloons," said Captain Lunduf, who had finished drilling the guard of honor and come to join them. "They pass over the castle sometimes. One of the poor wretches must have lost his head."

"Take it to the great hall and place it on the mantel," Tredore instructed the Captain. "After the games we will give it a proper funeral."

Tim and Sarre were invited by their host to look at the Royal Box. They rode one of the clockwork elevators to halfway up the wall where they stepped into a wide corridor. On one side of it were positions for manning the walls in times of attack. On the other side, Tredore led them to one of the tiers of boxes that overlooked the old castle and its courtyard. The Royal Box contained a throne upholstered in purple velvet and flanked by lower benches.

Tredore gazed proudly about him. "This is the best bat-

tle games arena in Tallis," he said. "Even the one in the
royal palace has endless stairs to climb."

Tim pondered over the height of the viewing boxes.
How could spectators get a decent view of the games?
Surely, from up here, all they would see would be the tops
of the contestants' heads far below. But not wanting to
offend Lord Tredore he refrained from asking him about
it. But a sudden beating of wings, louder than the gusting
wind, gave Tim his answer. A vast plumed cockerel as big
as a Gurney pack pig had swooped into the arena and was
hovering level with the Royal Box. The gigantic bird was a
fearsome sight. Its great curved beak looked deadly as it
fixed one glittering eye, the size of a saucer, on the occu-
pants of the box, shook its great comb, and crowed.

Mounted on its back, just above the wings, was an
armored figure. Both rider and bird looked magnificent.
The cockerel's cockscomb and spurs glittered with gold.
Its feathers were chestnut and blue with a great tail of
curved white plumes. The rider, dressed in jewel-studded
silver armor, raised a hand in salute and tipped open the
visor of his helmet.

"Good morning, Lord Tredore," he called out. "Am I
the first to arrive?"

"My Lord Moora," Tredore called back. "Welcome.
Where is your retinue?"

"Up there," he answered, pointing to a dozen enormous sparrows, ridden by men at arms wearing the same
livery as his own and circling above the windmill. "My

wife will arrive in her own time. She prefers to travel in a carriage these days."

Tredore nodded and told him, "There are Gurneys working for me in the meadow below. They will direct your retinue to where they and their mounts may camp. You and your wife have an apartment in the castle. My apologies for this informal greeting. I will make amends when we meet below."

Lord Moora waved and soared away over the ramparts.

"I must get below and greet the others as they arrive," said Lord Tredore.

Tim and Sarre descended with him and while Lord Tredore hurried off to alert Lady Tredore and the castle staff, they went to the meadow to tell Hunter the guests had begun to arrive.

A wondrous scene greeted them. Flocks of giant birds were landing, led by the Lords of Tallis, each of whom was mounted on a fabulous fighting cockerel. Ladies of the court, dressed in medieval splendor, rode in carriages borne fore and aft by pairs of giant doves. They landed gently on the meadow where Gurneys marshaled each flight to keep a wide landing strip open for further arrivals. Armed with bows and arrows, youths, some not much older than Tim and mounted on bantam cocks, accompanied the Lords.

"They're the squires," explained Hunter. "In war, it's their job to guard their Lord's back in battle."

"Look," said Sarre, pointing.

A great chariot was approaching, supported in flight by four mighty magpies. Archers guarded the single figure who stepped out of it, clad in black-and-white armor. Immediately, a retinue of black-clad police guards flanked him as he strolled toward the castle.

"Who is that?" asked Tim.

"Galeth, the Great Duke," replied Hunter shortly.

Tim and Sarre pressed forward to see his face but their view was blocked by his escort. They turned back to the landing strip where all were now watching an ornate golden carriage held aloft by four enormous swans. This one landed to a welcoming fanfare of Gurney trumpets.

In the carriage, a tall, silver-bearded figure, clad in golden robes, was accompanied by the most beautiful woman Tim had ever seen. The figure in gold stepped from the carriage and held out a hand to help his companion alight. The woman's hair was the color of ripe wheat and hung to her waist in thick plaits. Her skin was golden and her eyes were blue as cornflowers. She walked with her head held high, and the shape of her white silk dress reminded Tim of a statue of a Greek goddess he'd once seen. But there was no emotion in her face. It was a lovely but expressionless mask.

"The High King and his daughter, the Lady of Tallis," said Hunter softly.

CHAPTER 17

Tim Hears a Secret

That night there was a ball and banquet in the great hall of Lord Tredore's castle. Tim watched, dazzled, as the aristocrats of Tallis assembled in all their glory.

The Ladies wore long, close-fitting velvet gowns in dark tones of purple, red, or laurel green. Their fair-skinned shoulders and arms were bare to show off contrasting bejeweled necklaces and bangles. In the candlelight, their diamonds, rubies, and emeralds shone like the changing patterns in a giant kaleidoscope.

With one exception, the Ladies wore their hair piled high and fashioned in complicated arrangements of curls glittering with tiny jewels. Only the Lady of Tallis, seated on a raised dais beside the High King, wore a plain white silk dress with her hair in a long plait unadorned by any jewels.

The Lords were dressed in black court uniforms of close-fitting velvet coats that reached halfway to the knee, tight breeches, and high boots. Each bore his coat of arms on his right breast. All wore swords. Like the Ladies, their hair had also been carefully arranged in elaborate curls. Many of them sported long mustaches and pointed beards.

Lord Tredore had loaned Hunter one of his own court costumes for the occasion. It fit well. On the breast it bore, in place of the Tredore coat of arms, the gold symbol of the Companion of Dragons. As Hunter's squire, Tim was dressed in similar clothes with the same emblem. Six Gurney wives had made the costume for him that afternoon.

The orchestra struck up and Tim listened, wondering at its familiarity. He looked up at Hunter, who smiled faintly and nodded. "It's 'Greensleeves,'" he said. "A lot of the old songs from Earth are played in Tallis."

Even more surprising was the first dance. Each Lord drew his sword with one hand and with the other held the hand of his partner as they formed two lines with Lords and Ladies facing one another. As the music played they began a sort of skipping hop, the Lords clashing swords with one another as they passed.

"That looks a bit dangerous," said Tim.

Hunter nodded, smiling. "There have been fatalities on some occasions."

Sarre entered with Ellath and Illya. Like them, she was wearing a long white silk Chanter's robe. She looked a bit nervous but managed to nod graciously to Tim when he waved.

After the sword dance, the musicians struck up a tune rather like a polka. The men sheathed their weapons and couples skipped together up and down the hall, dancing in a less dangerous fashion. Tim could see Sarre tapping her foot to the rhythm of the music and eventually she beckoned him over.

"Why don't you ask me to dance, Tim Swift?" she asked.

Tim blushed. "But you're dressed as a Chanter," he protested.

"Chanters like to dance, too," said Sarre, and held out her arms, inviting him to join her. "Or are you still too shy?"

Tim realized he didn't feel at all self-conscious. Boldly, he took Sarre's hand and they joined the others on the dance floor. They finished the polka quite well. The next tune was slower and they could talk.

"Why did you think Chanters don't dance?" Sarre asked.

"I thought you were like nuns," said Tim. "You don't see many nuns dancing where I come from."

"What are nuns?" asked Sarre.

"Religious women who all live together in places called convents and don't get married," Tim explained. "Instead, they do other good works."

Sarre laughed. "Chanters get married." And when Tim looked surprised, she added, "Well, not all of us, but most do."

"So being a Chanter is not like being religious?" asked Tim.

Sarre nodded. "It is in some ways. We try to be kind."

"But there aren't any churches or priests," said Tim.

"The Chanters do have a temple," replied Sarre. "But we only go there once, and when we are small children we're taught what is right and wrong."

"So, if Chanters aren't religious, what are they?"

"It's more a way of life. We teach and we look after the sick and we try to use our powers to help people," she said as the music came to an end.

After the dancing, footmen carried in tables that were swiftly decorated with silverware, candlesticks, vast bowls of fruit, cutlery, and glassware. Lady Tredore gave a nod of satisfaction to the chief steward. When the High King and the Lady of Tallis took their place at the head of the table the banquet began. Tim counted more than a hundred Lords, accompanied by their Ladies and senior members of their entourages.

Seated to the right of the High King were Lord and Lady Tredore, and on his left the Great Duke sat beside the Lady of Tallis.

As Ellath's guest, Sarre was seated with her quite high at the table. Beside them was the High King's Chanter,

Illya. She was tall, slender, and very old. Her eyes were hooded but Tim could see they, too, constantly changed color as she glanced about the room.

Close to the them was an ugly-looking man, a cadaverous figure with a straggling forked beard and an unhealthy complexion. During the meal he never once looked up, made no conversation, and hardly touched the delicious food set before him. The Lady seated next to Tim told him the man was the Duke's Warlock, Stryker.

Tim had accompanied Hunter to the banquet as his squire, but they were farther down the table, among the lesser Lords and Ladies of Tallis. Even so, Tim was close enough to watch the Great Duke Galeth. He was a powerful man, and handsome, in a self-indulgent-looking way.

Cosmetics had been applied to his large, fleshy features to make him look fierce. His eyebrows had been thickened and lines drawn to accentuate the downturning of his mouth. He tugged at his small, pointed beard. It drew attention to his hands, which were thick, ugly, and powerful. When he spoke to the Lady of Tallis he tried to cover his mouth with a fluttering motion, but Tim could see that his large teeth, although very white, were jagged like a shark's.

Music came from the minstrels' gallery and the fire, banked high with logs, was blazing. The hall was foggy with the smoke from thousands of candles and was very hot. Tim feared that the flowers, concealed in the great room awaiting their unveiling, might wilt in the heat.

When the feasting finished, Lord Tredore's steward mounted a rostrum to make an announcement.

"Your Majesties, Great Duke, My Lords and Ladies of Tallis. I am commanded by Lord Tredore to announce that the first event of the battle games tomorrow will be the squires' archery contest, and the prize will be a thoroughbred fighting cockerel."

A sigh of appreciation passed through the crowd and they drummed on the tables to show their approval.

Hunter whispered to Tim, "Fighting cockerels cost almost as much as a living flower on Tallis."

"Why?" asked Tim.

But before Hunter could answer, the steward continued. "The list of contenders for the battle games has been drawn up by lottery and is posted in the meadow. The final survivor shall win this prize!" The steward swept his hand toward a huge curtain hanging from the gallery.

Gurney trumpets sounded and the curtain was drawn aside to reveal the mighty mass of fresh blooms. There were gasps of admiration from the assembly, and several of the Lords stood up and shouted compliments to Lord and Lady Tredore, who smiled and rose to bow their acknowledgment. The thunderous applause continued until the curtain was drawn again and the steward announced an interval, so people could leave the table to stretch their legs.

"I'd better go and check that the flowers are being looked after properly," Tim said to Hunter. He was worried that the men who were to carry them outside would not treat them gently. Slipping behind the curtain, he found footmen handling the plants and one curious youth squeezing a petal.

"Get them outside carefully," Tim hissed crossly. "And put them where you were shown earlier. If any of these flowers are damaged I'll have Lord Tredore boil your ears in beer."

The threat seemed to be effective. The men scurried away, bearing the flowers as instructed, and Tim followed them to the cool of the meadow, where the flowers were placed in the prize tent. Although it was dark inside, Tim could still make out the blooms. He took a jug and sprinkled them with water. While at his silent task he heard two men talking outside the tent, their shadows thrown against the canvas by the light from hundreds of campfires.

Speaking with aristocratic accents the voices sounded young.

"How does it feel to get the better of a Gurney in a trade?" asked one, chuckling.

The other laughed. "Not even a Gurney could spot what was wrong with that bird."

"What did he give you for it?" asked the first.

"Enough to pay my debts, buy new armor — and this." He held up a dagger. The shadow was quite clear. It was the snake-shaped blade Charto had made.

Tim waited until the pair had moved away, then hurried back to the banquet hall. Before he could speak,

Hunter seized his elbow and muttered, "Why were you so long? Lord Tredore wants to introduce us to the High King."

He propelled Tim toward the top table, where the High King's chair was now empty. The Lady of Tallis sat, staring into the smoky depths of the hall, apparently not interested in what was taking place all around her.

Lord Tredore, rather embarrassed, bent to look under the table and called, "Your Majesty."

The old man with the crown now knocked askew on his head clambered out. "Caught them!" he said, grinning triumphantly. Pidger and Podger were wriggling in his hands.

"Your Majesty, may I present Hunter, Knight Companion of the Order of the Dragon, and his squire, Tim Swift."

The High King paid no heed to the introduction. Instead he exclaimed, "What is that?"

All eyes followed the High King's pointing finger.

It was Josh. He had followed Tim back from the flower tent and now sat at his master's heels, apparently paying rapt attention to the proceedings.

"My dog, Josh, Your Majesty," said Tim.

"A *pog*, you say?" replied the High King.

Tim was about to correct him when he saw Sarre shaking her head and he remembered her lesson.

"If you wish, Your Majesty. But I, foolishly, call it a dog."

"Yes," said the King, nodding. "I think I prefer dog.

From now on, the Josh creature shall always be a dog. Does he know any tricks?"

"He can walk like a man, Your Majesty," said Tim.

"Ha!" said the old man. "But can he walk like a king?"

Tim called out, "Walk, Josh."

The little dog rose on his hind legs and walked in a circle.

The High King clapped his hands in delight. "I must have a dog for my son, Prince Briarre, he will be back from his vacation soon, you know."

A silence fell. The King peered at Hunter and, for a moment, it seemed as if there was a gleam of recognition, but it died away. "So, you are a Dragon Knight, Sir Hunter. I can't say I remember investing you. Why have we not seen you at court with your clever squire?"

"I have been away, Your Majesty," Hunter replied.

When Hunter spoke, Tim saw the Lady of Tallis look up for the first time, startled by the sound of his voice, and was now staring at him. She continued to gaze intently at Hunter but he kept his eyes on the High King.

"So, do you intend to fight in the tournament tomorrow, Sir Hunter?" the High King asked.

"I do, Your Majesty."

"Do you hear that, my dear Duke?" said the King. "Here's a new opponent for you. You've beaten everyone else in the kingdom."

Tim looked at the Duke, who had scarcely paid attention during the previous conversation. The Duke was leaning across the table talking to Warlock Stryker. Hardly bothering to look at Hunter, he broke off to say, "I doubt if he will take long to deal with, Your Majesty."

"And what about you, young man?" said the King. "Will you be entering the squires' archery contest?"

"I have never used a bow and arrow, Your Majesty," replied Tim.

"And you are a squire?" said the High King, puzzled.

"He's a fine shot with his own weapon, Sire," said Lord Tredore. "Show him, Tim," he called out and threw his drinking horn high into the air.

Tim swept his slingshot from beneath his coat and had it aimed at the spinning horn as it was about to touch the vaulted ceiling. His shot knocked it down the hall. All but the Duke and Stryker applauded.

"Not a gentleman's weapon," said the Duke dismissively. "Did the Gurneys teach you to do that, boy?" he asked.

Lord Tredore strode a few paces to the fireplace and found the skull placed on the mantel. He tossed it into the Duke's lap.

"I suppose this was done with a gentleman's weapon," he said coldly. "It fell from one of your death balloons."

Not for a moment had the Lady of Tallis taken her eyes off Hunter. She no longer looked cold and aloof. Something more like yearning showed in her face, while Hunter acted as though she did not exist.

"I'm tired of you two squabbling," said the High King

angrily, sounding like a petulant little boy. "I'm going up to my rooms to play with Pidger and Podger." With that he swept from the hall. Everyone but the Lady of Tallis hastily rose to bow at his exit.

Hunter and Tim withdrew and as they crossed the great hall, Tim said, "Do you know the Lady of Tallis? She kept looking at you."

"Did she?" replied Hunter, sounding disinterested. But Tim could see that the knuckles of his left hand were white as he tightened his grip on the hilt of his sword.

Walking back to the Gurney camp, Tim told Hunter of the conversation he'd overheard when he'd been watering the flowers.

"You're sure it was Charto's knife?" said Hunter.

"Quite sure," answered Tim.

When they reached the camp, they found Charto in excellent spirits.

"Did you trade your knife for a fighting bird?" asked Hunter.

"Among other things," replied the Gurney. "It was worth it. You've never seen such a fine creature."

Tim told him of the conversation he'd overheard and Charto looked worried. "I should know never to trust an aristocrat," he snarled. "The boy was so blue-blooded, if I'd held him up to a clear sky he would have vanished."

"Let's look at what he sold you," said Hunter.

They walked across the meadow to where great lines of

fighting birds rested on perches inside the vast cages the Gurney's had made from spider-yarn nets.

"This is the one," said Charto.

They stopped before a magnificent creature that looked as noble and bold as any emperor.

"I examined him thoroughly," said Charto. "He seems faultless."

"Saddle him," said Hunter. "There's only one way to find out."

Cooing and chuckling to calm the bird, Charto approached and threw a saddle over the creature's neck. Hunter mounted the great cockerel and ordered Charto to open the cage. With a few beats of its powerful wings the bird soared into the air.

"What's he going to do?" asked Tim. As he spoke, Sarre joined them. She had stayed on at the banquet, talking to her fellow Chanters.

"See if it will fight shadows, I expect," Charto replied.

"Fight shadows?" echoed Sarre and Tim.

"A way of testing a bird's courage," replied Charto.

The many huge cooking fires, where the men at arms had pitched their camps in the meadow, lit the walls of the castle in a golden glow. Hunter circled his mount high above them, then came swooping down to fly the bird low, directly at the castle wall. As soon as the cockerel saw its own shadow caused by the campfires it shied away in terror.

Hunter made several further attempts to urge the bird

nearer the wall, but each time it saw its own shadow looming, it swerved away in fear. Finally, Hunter gave up and landed. They returned the bird to its cage, and Hunter shook his head as they watched it strut about for a moment before hopping back onto the huge tree branch it used as a perch.

"Battle shy," Hunter said.

"My friend, I am desolate," said Charto bitterly.

"But it seemed to do most of what you wanted," said Tim. "Surely you can't expect it to kill itself."

"A real fighting bird would have flown into the wall," said Hunter. "They're not intelligent, but they are the most courageous creatures I've ever encountered. This is a fine bird to fly for pleasure, but it's useless for warfare."

"Then where will you get a fighting bird good enough for you to ride in your battle with the Duke?" Tim asked.

After a brief silence Sarre answered. "That's simple, Tim," she said. "*You* will have to win the prize cockerel in the archery contest, which is first thing tomorrow."

CHAPTER 18

The Power of a Gurney Bow

A strong wind blew across the great meadow, snapping the banners that lined the archery range. A grandstand had been erected behind the shooting line. When nobility had taken their seats to watch the contest, footmen served them with Tredore beer and oatcakes. Crowds of estate workers and their families surrounded the range, enjoying the refreshments that Lord Tredore had also provided for them.

Tim was nervous. He took his place behind the line and glanced at his fellow contestants. Most were taller than he was and all appeared to be supremely confident. Dressed in tall boots and long, white, belted surcoats emblazoned with the coat of arms of the Lord they served, the squires chatted together as they tested their weapons, pulling on the strings of their bows, which were superbly crafted from horn and precious metals. Even their quivers were decorated with jewels and the feathered flights of their arrows dyed in bright colors.

Tim heard a voice he recognized. It was one of those he'd overheard outside the tent the night before. The youth was the tallest of the squires and his coat of arms showed two magpies. Tim remembered seeing him seated near the Duke's party at the dining table.

"What do you think of my next battle bird, Nevalt?" he asked the squire standing beside him and pointed at the first prize: the magnificent cockerel strutting up and down inside a long spider-net cage in front of the grandstand.

"A splendid mount, but you haven't won it yet, Urlica," his companion replied.

"And who's going to beat me?" said Urlica, nodding dismissively at Tim. "That Gurney boy, with his peasant's walking stick?"

Tim gripped his weapon. Charto had been up with him since dawn, shaving down a Gurney hunting bow so that Tim could manage to pull it. Tim knew his plain weapon didn't look very impressive.

"It's made of yew," Charto had explained earlier, when he handed Tim the length of hard wood that he'd trimmed to Tim's height. "Yew is perfect for bows. You see how it is darker on this side?"

"Yes," replied Tim doubtfully.

"That's the secret of its power," said Charto. "The inside is heartwood. It contracts when the bow is bent. The outside wood stretches and has amazing power to spring back. Bow makers for the aristocracy think they can achieve the same effect with metal and horn, but they never do."

Charto had strapped Tim's left forearm with a wide band of leather to protect it from the slap of the bowstring.

"Remember the wind," Charto said. "The arrow is long and light. A strong gust will catch a shaft and blow it an arm's length from where you aimed."

"I wish I could use my slingshot," said Tim.

"You'll manage," replied Charto. "I can see the way you hold the bow, it's been bred into you."

Suddenly, Tim recalled the words of old Eli: *"There must be bowman's blood in you."*

Tim stepped up to the shooting line with a new confidence, remembering all of Charto's instructions. The strong wind blew directly into his face. Twenty squires stood in line. Their targets, fifty paces away, were a row of life-sized wooden men brandishing swords.

"First round," shouted the umpire. "Three arrows. All must strike the target."

Tim notched his arrow, leaned forward, and pushing the bow with all his weight behind the thrust of his left arm, he drew the arrow back so far that the feathered flight brushed his lips. He turned his head to sight the target, the flight touching his ear — and let fly. The arrow hummed away and struck the head of the wooden figure.

Before the first arrow had sunk home, Tim had notched and shot his second, quickly followed by his third. All three of his shafts bristled from the target no more than a thumb's width apart. He'd finished an arrow faster than his nearest rival.

Half the contestants failed to hit the mark with all three of their arrows. They dropped out and the targets were moved another twenty-five paces farther away. Tim felt confident now. Not in a boastful sense, but with the certainty that he knew exactly what to do. The bow felt comfortable in his hand, almost as if it were a natural extension of his body.

Charto's voice reached Tim above the noisy chatter of the crowd. "Wind, Tim, remember the wind."

This time the umpire called to shoot just as Tim felt an even stronger gust of wind. He made a slight adjustment to his aim and once more all his arrows struck the head of his target.

For the next round, there were only five squires left.

"Ten more paces," called the umpire.

The target distance was adjusted as the wind continued to blow in gusting fits.

Tim judged his shots as he had before, and they all struck true. Finally, only he and the strutting Urlica remained in the contest.

"Ten more paces," called the umpire.

But Urlica now held up his arm. "I appeal to the stewards," he called out.

Three Lords strolled forward to join the umpire.

"This Gurney boy is using a bewitched bow," Urlica complained. "Some Chanter spell has been used so it shoots straighter than mine."

Hesitantly, the umpire reached out, fearing the bow might actually be magical. "Let me see your bow, boy."

Tim handed it to him and the stewards watched intently as he examined its length.

"It seems all right," said the umpire.

"Do you doubt the word of the Great Duke's squire?" demanded Urlica.

Tim ended the dispute. "If he thinks it's bewitched, let him use it and I'll shoot with his bow," he offered.

"Accepted," said Urlica, snatching the bow from the umpire and tossing his own at Tim's feet. Tim picked up the squire's weapon and pulled it experimentally.

He took aim, silently assessing the bow, took a deep breath and hoped luck was with him.

"Ready?" shouted the umpire.

"Ready," Tim and Urlica responded.

Both of their first and second shots hit their targets and a sigh went up from the crowd. Tim paused a fraction of a second with his third shot and Urlica's bowstring hummed. The squire's last arrow missed, but Tim's struck home, dead center on the wooden figure.

Throwing Tim's Gurney bow aside, Urlica stalked away

as Charto, Hunter, and Sarre hurried to congratulate the winner of the fabulous battle bird.

"You were right, Charto," said Tim. "I watched the flags down the course so I could tell when a stronger gust of wind was coming. I had to aim higher with his weapon. His bow wasn't as powerful as the one you made for me."

"By my left leg, what a gamble to take!" said Charto, impressed. "You could be a Gurney."

Tim was escorted by the steward to stand before the High King to be presented with a symbolic, golden arrow. As he took his place, he saw the Lady of Tallis was again watching Hunter in the crowd.

"Fine shooting, my boy, you certainly earned your prize cockerel," the High King congratulated Tim, at the same time bending down to stroke Josh. "This afternoon, you must bring the dog and watch the tournament from the Royal Box."

Tim bowed and thanked the High King before retreating back into the crowd.

The steward announced that the battle games would commence after lunch, when a fanfare would be sounded. Until then, all were invited to enjoy the Gurney fair.

Tim and Sarre wandered through the rides and games, watching the fun. Farmers sat facing one another on greased logs, each one attempting to knock the other off. Children rode a merry-go-round, its great silk sails driven by the wind, and the Gurneys gave rides to ladies and gentlemen on the swaying pack pigs that had been specially washed and scented for the occasion.

The bravest among the revelers climbed a high wooden tower and slid to the ground on a great chute of silk. There were sideshows of jugglers, knife-throwing contests, rope-climbing amusements, and a ring where Luxo challenged farm lads to wrestle with him. Most were bigger and broader than he was but Luxo had techniques that sent each of them sailing about the ring.

Tim and Sarre ate spiced fruit and grilled meat on sticks for their lunch. When the fanfare sounded, Sarre went off to take her place in the viewing box she was to share with Ellath and Illya.

Tim hurried to attend Hunter who was in the saddling enclosure, preparing to ride Tim's prize cockerel. Charto had already helped him into most of his leather armor.

"I can finish here," Tim said to Charto. "You go into the arena so you can watch the games."

Tim helped Hunter don a wide leather belt with straps dangling from it that had to be attached to the saddle to prevent Hunter from falling off the bird's back. When Tim had secured them all to Hunter's satisfaction, Hunter nodded his thanks and smiled. "Take my sword, Tim. We don't use them in the games."

"Good luck, Hunter," said Tim, picking up the weapon and hurrying off with Josh toward the elevator that would take them up to the Royal Box.

The High King waved a greeting.

"How do you like your new fighting bird?" asked the High King. "What have you done with him?"

"Hunter is riding him, Your Majesty," said Tim proudly.

"Well, I hope he brings him luck," replied the King, stroking Josh. "I'm tired of the Duke always winning."

The fanfare sounded for the first bout to commence and Tim sat forward, fascinated. Strutting proudly and flashing glances at each other, the fighting birds were led into the ring of the old castle's courtyard. Another fanfare gave the order to begin and the birds rose into the air slashing at each other with their spurs.

"The spurs can't do any harm," the High King told Tim. "They're bound so they can't wound one another. It would be different in a real battle."

Nonetheless, it looked dangerous enough to Tim.

Each contestant carried a long, light lance with a pad on the end dipped in brightly colored paint.

"And, of course, their lances would be unpadded in a real battle," continued the King. "In this game, the first knight who marks three hits on his opponent wins."

The first few bouts often ended quite quickly, but as the less skillful men were eliminated the battles became more interesting. Hunter was an expert at the game. He dispatched all his opponents within minutes of rising into the air. So did the Great Duke. It was obvious that they were going to be matched for the final battle of the games. Eventually, their contest was announced.

"This should be worth watching," said the High King,

who had Josh on his lap and was scratching him behind the ears.

As the bout began, each rider urged his bird to gain the higher position. They had risen level with the top of the castle walls before the Duke swerved his bird to jab at his opponent, but Hunter reined away, turned in a tight circle, and struck the Duke on the shoulder, marking it with yellow paint. The Duke retaliated swiftly and marked Hunter's arm with a bright splash of scarlet.

Both men became more wary, keeping their birds gliding and soaring about each other just out of lance range, until the Duke suddenly swooped under Hunter and marked his thigh with another jab. Tim saw Hunter wince; the padded lance must be harder than he'd imagined. Then they closed in for a head-to-head attack. The Duke's nerve broke first; he broke to the right, and Hunter's lance hit his midriff just as they broke away.

"The last blow decides," exclaimed the King.

"Hunter is wounded!" the Lady of Tallis suddenly cried out in distress. "Stop the fight, Father!"

But the roar of the crowd was too great for the King's command to be heard. Tim realized it wasn't scarlet paint but *blood* running from the two places where the Duke's lance had made hits. Hunter's leather armor had been pierced. The razor-sharp blade had not been removed from the Duke's lance, merely wrapped in the paint-soaked cloth.

Hunter was swaying in his saddle. It seemed to Tim that only the saddle straps were preventing Hunter from plunging down into the courtyard. The Duke was now so confident, he had raised the visor of his helmet and waved a salute to his supporters. Then he urged his fighting bird into a dive to finish off Hunter.

It was a mistake.

Just before the impact, Hunter caused his bird to suddenly spread its wings and loop over backward to realign itself behind the Duke's tail. Effortlessly, Hunter leaned forward and jabbed the Duke in the small of his back to finish the game.

The rage on the Duke's face was clear to everyone as the cheers for Hunter's victory followed him from the arena.

Both Tim and the Lady of Tallis were leaning anxiously over the rail of the Royal Box, when Sarre called out from the next box, "Don't worry, Tim, Hunter is not badly wounded." Gesturing with her hand to include Ellath and Illya, she added, "We *all* feel he is all right."

The Lady of Tallis recovered her composure and once more took her seat.

The steward announced that the award ceremony would take place in the great hall of the castle. Tim waited for Sarre and when she met him he could see she was troubled.

"There's still something dangerous about," she told him. "Ellath and Illya feel it, too."

"What sort of thing?" asked Tim.

Sarre shook her head. "Just a sense of danger. It's come and gone ever since we first left the Tregger camp in the forest. I wish my powers were stronger."

When they entered the great hall it was already crowded with the noblemen and their retinues. The High King and the Lady of Tallis were seated on a platform before the fabulous display of flowers.

"Great sport," chuckled the High King. "Great sport." Then he looked concerned as Hunter limped forward, his face drawn and white from the wounds he had received.

The King looked at the Duke who was standing at the foot of the platform with his companions. Stryker was whispering urgently to him, and the Duke only looked up when the Lady of Tallis said, "I see you were careless with your lance, Your Grace. Had you faced a lesser man you might have killed him."

The High King stood up and laid his hand on Hunter's shoulder as he came and stood before him. Tim could see the High King had tears in his eyes. "My son fights like you at the battle games, Sir Hunter. Maybe you saw him once?"

"I did, Your Majesty," replied Hunter.

The High King nodded. "The prize is yours. You have won all that you brought with you. With these rare blooms you could buy much in this kingdom."

Hunter looked at the High King's daughter and bowed. "The flowers are for the Lady of Tallis —" He had more to say, but the Duke interrupted.

"Your Majesty," he shouted. "I have just learned that the man you honor here is an escaped criminal." The Duke strode onto the platform and jabbed his finger at Hunter, who was leaning against a chair for support.

The Duke continued. "He is the fugitive better known as Robert Quester."

A roar of consternation went up among the nobles, until the High King stood and held up his hand for silence.

"How do you know this?" said the High King. "I see little resemblance to Robert Quester, and I knew him well."

"Men change, Your Majesty," replied the Duke.

The High King shook his head. "Quester had an open face, and he was broader. This man is thin, and his hair streaked with gray."

"Stryker," said the Duke turning to his Warlock. "Tell the High King what you know."

The cadaverous figure with the forked beard stepped forward, banged his staff on the stone floor, and announced, "I, too, knew the criminal Quester, long ago, Your Majesty. Then I saw him again recently. I was journeying in the Forest of the Southern Rim. I did not recognize him immediately — but my spirit servant did."

Stryker shook his staff and a black-and-brown–patterned snake slithered from the end and curled on the floor beside him.

There was a murmur of apprehension all around as the Lords and Ladies stepped back in alarm, many of them clutching at a broach or some other charm and muttering incantations.

"What are they doing?" Tim whispered to Sarre.

"They are afraid of Stryker's creature," she replied.

"It's only a grass snake," said Tim.

Sarre shook her head. "It is a spirit snake," she whispered. "Stryker can control its ghost — and read its thoughts."

"Snakes don't have thoughts," said Tim. "Neither do ghosts, for that matter," he added.

"Perhaps not in your world, Tim, but in Tallis, some do," Sarre assured him.

Stryker continued, "My spirit snake has followed Robert Quester from the south ever since I saw that he had returned to Tallis. It recognized him. He may seem changed to us — but not to my creature."

"How did it recognize him?" asked Lord Tredore.

Stryker smiled, revealing his yellow teeth. "Long ago, at the palace of the High King, Robert Quester was swimming in a lake. He disturbed my spirit snake and it bit him. Look on the prisoner's left arm — below the elbow."

A guard removed the armor and pulled back the sleeve of Hunter's shirt. Two purple scars, close together, were quite clearly visible.

Stryker held up his staff. "My creature has tasted Robert Quester's blood. Let it drink again, and if Hunter is Robert Quester, the snake will change color."

"But that's not proof," whispered Tim. "It could just be a trick."

"It's enough proof for the noblemen of Tallis," replied Sarre softly. "They're simple people."

Stryker gestured with his staff, and the snake slithered across the floor and darted its tongue into a drop of blood that had dripped onto the floor from Hunter's wounded thigh.

Slowly, its jagged stripes turned from dull brown and black to livid yellows and greens. In doing so, it swelled to twice its previous size. Then it curled up and raised its head with its fangs ready to strike at Hunter.

No one moved; all were transfixed by the hideous malevolence of the creature.

Tim shouted, "*Josh! Go for it!*"

The little dog leaped across the floor and seized the hissing snake behind its head. With one vigorous shake he killed the creature. Holding it in his mouth he trotted back to Tim and laid it at his feet.

A gasp of astonishment went up from the onlookers.

Apoplectic with rage, Stryker raised his staff to strike Tim but the Duke held out a restraining hand. Stepping forward he said, "Robert Quester, many years ago you were sentenced to death by the High Court of Tallis for the murder of Prince Briarre."

"That is a lie," cried the Lady of Tallis angrily.

"How do you know, My Lady?" replied the Duke softly. "At the time of the trial, you were not available to give evidence."

The Lady of Tallis shook her head. "Like my father, I, too, was unwell and have no memory of the events that took place immediately after my brother's death."

The Duke raised his hands to the crowd. "We sympathize with your feelings, My Lady, but others who were actually there told us of Quester's treachery."

The Duke pointed at Hunter. "You escaped your fate on that occasion, Robert Quester, but Providence has returned you to us. And since then a greater punishment than execution has become available in this kingdom. What might best be described as a *living death*. You shall spend the rest of your life in the Mines of Kanarki."

The Duke snapped his fingers. "Guards, tend his wounds well. I don't want him to die for a long time yet. He has his sentence to fulfill."

The Lady of Tallis did not speak but continued to watch Hunter, her face drained with grief. Hunter gave a half shrug and looked into the Duke's face. "I came here to kill you," he said in a voice so quiet the crowd had to strain to hear his words. "I thank you for the sentence, as I fully intend to keep the promise I made myself."

The Duke laughed lightly. "You shall have many years to plan my end, Robert Quester. But it will all be a fantasy. There really is no escape from the mines."

"I did not pass this judgment!" protested the High King.

"You did, Your Majesty. Many years ago," the Duke replied dismissively. "Like most other things, you have forgotten the occasion."

Noticing Tim and Sarre, the Duke casually added, "And take the children, too."

An angry murmur passed through the crowd, and Lord

Tredore stepped forward. "They are my guests here!" he shouted. "They have committed no crime."

The Duke's eyes flared for a moment. "I say what is a crime in Tallis," he said softly.

The crowd fell silent. All that could be heard was the loud ticking of the great hall's clock, which had been working again ever since Tim had knocked down the skull obstructing the driving mechanism.

Suddenly, the ticking stopped. Lord Tredore understood the significance; he clutched his wife's hand and looked up fearfully. The wind always stopped blowing for a few brief minutes whenever it was about to change direction. Puzzled, people glanced about them, sensing some impending danger.

At last, Lady Tredore, in a voice full of dread, shouted, "The Killing Wind is coming!"

When the Clock Stopped

With Lady Tredore's alarm still echoing around the great hall, the crowd surged forward in panic, almost knocking over the High King's raised platform. Despite their reputation for courage in battle, the noble Lords were filled with dread when it came to the hideous danger of the Killing Wind.

"To the cellars," shouted Lord Tredore. "There are enough silk masks there to protect all of you."

Hunter, still held captive by the Duke's men, was too weakened by his wounds to take advantage of the panic and escape, but the guards had not yet seized Sarre and Tim.

"Come with me," Charto shouted to them as he darted out of the bustle and grabbed their arms. Still clutching Hunter's sword, Tim scooped up Josh as he and Sarre followed Charto, forcing their way against the tide of panicking nobles.

Once outside they saw more people streaming toward the castle. Heading in the opposite direction, they ran across the courtyard, over the drawbridge, and into the great meadow.

Racing toward the Gurney encampment, they encountered crowds of fairgoers also running for the protection of the castle cellars. Overcoming their own terror, some squires and soldiers were covering the last of the giant birdcages with silk. Then they, too, ran for the castle as the storm struck and the wind blew like a tornado.

"Won't the bird tents tear away?" shouted Tim.

Charto shook his head. "The silk is secured with spider yarn."

The wind raged through the fairground amusements, tearing up tents and setting the windmill ride turning at fantastic speed. A sail broke free and hurtled like a kite toward the last running figure, knocking him from his feet. It was Urlica, the Duke's squire, trying to reach the castle.

Sarre looked toward the north. A line of billowing black clouds was unfolding in the sky, blown toward them by the full force of the Killing Wind.

"Come with us, Urlica, or you'll die!" Charto bellowed, seizing the squire by his surcoat as he struggled to his feet.

"I must get to the castle cellars!" Urlica shouted as he tried to wriggle free.

The Gurney chief saw there was no time to argue. He punched Urlica on the jaw, scooped up his body, threw him over his shoulder, and kept running.

Close to the Gurney camp, the great pack pigs were already tearing long trenches into the ground with their hooves and snouts. The Gurneys worked fast but without panic. They had done this many times before. Tim and Sarre covered their faces with silk masks and waited for Charto's instructions.

"What about the pigs?" shouted Tim above the roaring storm.

"They are not affected by the Killing Wind — no animals are, only birds and people," he shouted back, gesturing to a trench that lay close to the landing ground. "Get into this trench and don't come out before I tell you to."

They leaped in and dragged silk sheets over themselves while the pigs kicked earth and turf over them. Charto had thrown Urlica in the trench beside them as if he were a sack of grain. Tim lay on his side in the darkness and made a space for Josh close to his body. The little dog began to wriggle violently in the confined space.

"Let me touch his head," said Sarre. "I can put him to sleep."

She reached out and Tim could feel Josh go limp. He took Sarre's hand and she squeezed it tightly.

The noise of the storm was slightly muffled by the layers of silk and earth covering them, but they could still hear it raging overhead.

* * *

After a long time the roaring wind died down and in the pitch darkness they could feel Urlica beginning to stir. Tim felt Sarre's fingers slip from his own and in the confined space he saw a faint white glow. It grew stronger and Tim could see that it came from Sarre's hands, which she was holding over Urlica's forehead.

"What are you doing?" Tim asked.

"Finding out if there is a better person inside," Sarre answered.

"Is there?" asked Tim.

"We shall see," she answered.

After what seemed like half a day, they heard Charto's voice coming from outside the trench.

"Tim, Sarre, the Killing Wind has passed but it's best if you stay hidden. The Duke's soldiers will be searching for you. How's the squire?"

"He won't cause any trouble," replied Sarre.

"Is it safe to breath the air outside?" asked Tim.

"Yes," answered Charto.

Tim set about working a narrow gap with his hands so they could see out from where they were buried.

"You're sure it's safe now?" he asked, still nervous about the unseen threat.

"I am," replied Sarre, removing her mask. "The black spores carried by the wind become harmless when they touch the earth. They only kill if you breathe them in while they are still airborne."

While they remained hidden, Charto passed them water and remained close by. The rest of the Gurneys dug themselves out of their shelter, leaving Sarre, Tim, Josh, and the Duke's squire still concealed beneath the turf.

Gradually, people returned to the grounds around the castle. A contingent of the Duke's guards arrived to search the camp for Sarre and Tim. They crashed about, deliberately breaking whatever they could. The Gurney men watched sullenly, wanting to fight them but held in check by Charto. Sometimes, soldiers passed so close to their hiding place, Tim and Sarre could have reached out and touched their boots.

Eventually, the soldiers were called away by their captain. Still, Tim and Sarre waited for Charto to give the all-clear. They remained hidden but could see the court of the High King preparing to leave Lord Tredore's castle.

Once more, the carriages and fighting birds soared into the air. The last to leave was the Great Duke and his entourage. He stood by his carriage watching as a prisoner was led onto the landing ground in chains. Even though the man's head was covered in a sinister leather hood, Tim knew it was Hunter.

"Can't we help him?" said Tim desperately.

"Stryker's powers are too strong for me," said Sarre unhappily. "I can do nothing against them."

Even with Hunter's sword, Tim knew he would be no match for the Duke's men. Miserably, he watched Hunter stumble blindly into the transport carriage, which then lifted into the air, held aloft by giant blackbirds, and flew away to the north.

When all was finally clear, Charto dug them out, and woken by Sarre's touch, Josh ran about barking cheerfully. But Urlica seemed to be in a trance. He accepted water from Charto but said nothing.

"We need to question him," said Charto.

"He will answer me," said Sarre, once again placing her hand on Urlica's forehead.

"Why was Hunter wearing that leather hood?" she asked.

"It will protect him from the killing spores in the Duke's mine," replied Urlica. "I'm told the only light in the Mines of Kanarki is a faint glow that comes from the giant mushrooms growing there. The mask will also accustom Hunter's eyes to the gloom."

"Did you say the spores come from the mines?" said Charto, surprised.

The squire nodded. "When the mushrooms die they crumble into a cloud of killing spores, and as these are released the Blooms of Kanarki are revealed."

"Are you quite sure?" asked Charto. "You're saying the mushrooms in the Kanarki caves are the reason the north wind kills."

"Quite sure. I've been there — to visit the garrison of soldiers who guard the mines — I've seen it with my own eyes."

"So the Duke causes the Killing Wind?" asked Charto, astonished.

Urlica nodded. "When he saw how much the nobles desired the blooms he cared nothing for how many lives would be destroyed to obtain them, as long as it made him richer and more powerful. All the chaos he has caused in Tallis has been to his advantage," said the squire. "The mushrooms used to be buried, sealed in the great caves, until the Duke opened the mines at Kanarki. The wind is natural, of course. But now it sucks out the spores that used to remain trapped and rains them down on us."

"How many people work in the mines?" asked Tim.

"Hundreds. But they do not survive for long. We never see them again after they go into the caves. Except for the ones who come out to collect the food from the guards."

"Don't they try to escape?"

Urlica shook his head. "Warlock Stryker takes away their minds and their willpower."

"We must rescue Hunter," said Tim desperately.

"Against the power of the Duke?" said Charto, shaking his head. "It would take an army. Stay with us, lad. You should be planning to go home."

"I do want to go home," Tim answered honestly. "But I can't abandon Hunter."

"Why?" asked Charto. "Did you give him your word?"

Tim shook his head. "I don't know why," he murmured. "It's just something inside me."

"It is called honor," said Urlica. He stood up and looked about himself as though he had woken from a long sleep. He pulled off the surcoat bearing the Duke's coat of arms and tossed it aside. "I am from the Clan of Dagar. My ancestors lived by our code of honor. Then I was taken into the Duke's service. Gradually, I became accustomed to doing things my father had always taught me were wrong. Bit by bit, I lost my sense of duty to the High King. It was as if a sickness had swept over me — but I think I may have been cured."

Charto suddenly smiled and slapped Tim on the shoulder. "We Gurneys also have our honor. We shall come with you to free Hunter."

This time, Sarre shook her head. "No, Charto," she said firmly. "This must be done with stealth. Somehow, Tim and I must find a way to do it alone."

"Gurneys can be stealthy," Charto persisted. "There are none stealthier."

Sarre smiled and took his hand. "Your pigs would not like it in the mountains of the north, Charto. Their feet were made for softer roads."

Just then, Ellath and Illya, who had not returned to the palace with the High King, walked into the camp. When Charto began to tell the old Chanters of the conversation they'd just been having, Ellath held up her hand. "We know what Sarre and Tim intend to do," she said.

"Do you agree?" asked Charto.

"We must contemplate before we decide," said Illya. "We shall return in the morning with our verdict."

"Whatever you decide, I'm going after Hunter," said Tim.

"We shall give our verdict to Sarre in the *morning*," said Illya firmly.

Tim slept uneasily that night. He kept dreaming he could see Hunter in the leather mask and he was calling Tim's name. Eventually, he got up and left his tent. He was sitting by the embers of the campfire scratching Josh behind the ears, when Sarre came to join him. The first streaks of dawn were lighting the dark sky.

"The Chanters are coming," she said.

"Do you know what they have decided?" Tim asked.

Sarre shook her head. "They don't want me to know yet."

"Then it will be bad news," said Tim bitterly.

Sarre and Tim stood up as Ellath and Illya approached, then wasted no time preparing them for their decision.

"Sarre is not yet ready for the tasks she would have to undertake," said Ellath flatly.

"When will she be ready?" Tim asked angrily. "In a year? Two years? By that time Hunter will be dead!"

The Chanters didn't react to his anger. Illya spoke briskly. "It depends how fast Sarre learns the next part of her training. But learn she must, or you will both be killed. There is much confusion and danger in both your futures. We can see that much. If you are to survive, you must be better prepared. Unless you would simply prefer pointless deaths?"

Tim shook his head. Despite his earlier impatience, he realized that what the Chanter said made sense. Just then, Urlica came from his tent and Charto emerged from his. They stood silently beside the group already gathered around the fire.

"What must I do?" asked Sarre.

"Both of you must go to The Crack and prepare yourselves for the future."

"I will come with you," offered Urlica.

The Chanters shook their heads. "Stay with Lord Tredore, Urlica. Someday you will be needed here," said Illya.

"Where's The Crack?" asked Tim, puzzled. "What is it?"

Charto waved. "Far to the north and east, fairly close to the sea, I'm told. I have never been there. We Gurneys keep away from that part of the country."

"Is it dangerous?" asked Tim.

"Your life is dangerous, Tim," said Illya, smiling now. "The Crack is only another part of your story."

Journey to the Crack

The landscape began to change again. For several days Sarre, Tim, and Josh had journeyed north, leaving the rich farmland of Tredore far behind them. At first there were wide windswept grasslands with no sign of habitation, then the grass gave way to lichen-covered rock as they encountered a vast moorland stretching before them like an ocean of gorse and heather.

It was a bleak, lifeless place, with occasional outcrops of granite and areas of treacherous quicksand. Tim was worried they might blunder into the bogs but the pack pig Charto had given them was surefooted and smelled danger whenever they approached soft ground. The wind blew hard but the sky was so overcast it was impossible to work out directions from the position of the sun.

The Gurneys had also made them presents of the binoculars and compass that Hunter had traded with them. But the compass didn't seem able to find north. The needle jumped and swung wildly, never pointing in any direction for more than a few seconds at a time. Finally, Tim confessed he thought they were lost.

Sarre stopped the pig and dismounted to stand on a rock. She closed her eyes and Tim sat watching her in the wind.

After a long time she opened her eyes and walked briskly back and remounted the pig.

"That way," she pointed.

"I think we've just come from there," said Tim doubtfully.

"Ellath and Illya have directed me," said Sarre. "We have been led astray."

"By Stryker," said Tim anxiously.

Sarre shook her head. "No, nothing evil. It seems the Chanters make the way to The Crack confusing, so as to protect it."

Eventually, the moor ended and they came upon a wall of grass so tall that they could only just see over it from the top of the pig.

Sarre consulted the map Charto had given them.

"What does it say?" asked Tim.

"Very little," replied Sarre. "Charto has never visited this part of Tallis. All the map shows is a wide stretch of nothing with the words *Land of Birds*, then another big gap and the words *The Crack*."

"Here be dragons," muttered Tim.

"Dragons?" repeated Sarre. "What do you mean?"

"Nothing," said Tim. "It's what old mapmakers on Earth used to put on charts in places that hadn't yet been explored. If they didn't know what the land was like beyond a certain point they wrote *Here be Dragons* on the map, just in case."

All day, Tim and Sarre rode the pack pig as it swayed forward through the tall grass. The stalks were as thick as bamboo and looked to Tim like giant-sized stalks of wild wheat. As usual throughout their journeys, Josh dozed on Tim's lap, although occasionally he'd get a burst of energy and jump down to run about the pack pig's feet, yapping with an excess of high spirits.

As the afternoon wore on they were approaching a forest of vast trees. Suddenly, they came upon a clearing in the grass where three gigantic eggs lay in a nest.

"Here, indeed, be dragons!" Tim muttered.

"Hey, clear off from there," a voice shouted.

They looked up to see that an enormously fat man had appeared in the clearing, mounted on a huge bird with legs like stilts and a long, thin, curved beak. The bird stood several feet taller than their pack pig.

"We're sorry," replied Sarre. "We didn't know there'd be a nest here."

"That's all right," the man said cheerfully. "Follow me, I know where all the nests are, and I don't want you disturbing them."

The man took a zigzagging route through the long grass until they reached the forest, where he stopped in a glade and dismounted. Sarre and Tim slid down gratefully from the pack pig.

The man wasn't actually as fat as he had first appeared. He was wearing a padded leather suit and thick gauntlets that made him look very stout.

"Could you tell us where we are, please?" asked Tim.

"Birdland," the man answered. "My name is Lightfoot. My family breeds the toughest battle birds, the swiftest robins, the most elegant swans, the jauntiest magpies."

Sarre and Tim exchanged amused glances.

"Why don't the Gurneys know about this place?" asked Tim.

The man laughed. "Do you think we want the Gurneys coming and taking over our family business? When we've trained the birds, we take them to the fairs. We've always kept this place a secret. You're the first outsiders to cross the moor in a hundred years or more. The last person to come who wasn't a Chanter was Joseph Mossop."

"Mossop!" said Tim. "We've heard of him."

"A remarkable man," said Lightfoot. "He made the great clockwork mechanisms of Tredore Castle."

"We know that," said Tim.

"Oh, yes," said Lightfoot. "And he did some work on the Great Palace of the High Kings."

"How did you prevent the Gurneys from finding this place?" asked Tim.

"A family gift," said Lightfoot. "We can sense people coming across the great moor. We confuse them with our thoughts so they get lost and have to turn back." He looked shrewdly at Sarre. "It doesn't always work with Chanters, though."

As he spoke, a vast robin fluttered down from a tree and hopped over to Lightfoot. He took a handful of massive seeds, the size of walnuts, from his pocket and threw one to the bird. Then, although the robin was huge, it was still quite young and pecked greedily at Lightfoot's gauntleted hand.

"You can see why I dress like this," he chuckled.

"Are we far from The Crack?" Sarre asked.

Lightfoot shook his head. "Two days away. Once you've passed through the forest and the stones, then you'll be there. At least that's what they say, I've never visited it myself."

With surprising agility, he leaped up onto the back of the tall bird and turned into the forest. "Good luck," he called.

"What are the stones?" Tim shouted after him.

"You'll know when you see them," replied Lightfoot, his voice already quite distant.

Tim and Sarre continued through the forest until nightfall, when they camped by a stream. They erected their silk tent and lit a cooking fire. It was Tim's turn to prepare the evening meal and he made a tasty stew out of dried fish, wild herbs, and vegetables.

Tim had brought Hunter's sword and pack with them when they'd left the Gurney camp. Lightfoot's reference to Joseph Mossop had reminded him of Anne Mossop's diary and he looked for it in Hunter's haversack. It was right at the bottom, wrapped together with Hunter's own journal in the large parchment document Hunter had taken from the concealed cupboard in the Enton Arms at Milchen.

The parchment was a map showing a curving range of rocks that seemed to connect with a route through a range of mountains. An inscription on the map explained how to reach the caves of Kanarki. What wasn't clear was where the curving rocks leading to the route actually were.

Sarre and Tim puzzled over the map.

"Look for the white peaks from the tower by moonlight," Sarre read the inscription aloud. *"They cannot be seen in the heat of the day but they will lead you to where you must climb the great wall."*

Tim noted the curving row of peaks. Two tall and three short. The last one was notched at the top. But there was absolutely no clue as to their location. Baffled, they put the map aside, and Tim picked up Hunter's journal. He'd intended to look at Anne Mossop's diary first, but his curiosity about Hunter proved too great.

"Read it to me," said Sarre, piling more dry wood onto the fire so Tim would be able to make out the handwriting. Sparks burst from the burning branches and flickered up through the vast trees, the flames providing Tim with enough light to read by.

"I do not write this journal for fame or gain but to give a true account of the extraordinary events that happened after I found my way to the land of Tallis and the reason why I must find my way there again — and kill a man.

"My name is Hunter now, but once I was known as Robert Quester. The extraordinary series of events that led me to the village of Enton and the House on Falling Star Hill began more than twelve years ago, when I was a medical student. I had been raised by an uncle who was comfortably rich but he died during the year I began to study medicine.

"During the summer vacation of my fifth year, I went climbing in the Lake District with a friend. After three days, my friend developed a cold and urged me to make some easy climbs alone as he would be indisposed for a few days.

"It is unwise to climb without companions but I was not going to be far from our hotel and they knew when to expect me home for supper. I reassured my friend I would take no more than a stiff walk and set out with a knapsack and rope. I hardly noted my route, letting events happen as they would.

"After I had reached a decent height and enjoyed a magnificent but lonely view, I decided to start down. It was a glorious day of blazing heat. As I glanced up at the sun, I heard a sudden roaring noise like a train coming toward me through a tunnel. Blinking into the sun, I saw a blazing ball of fire hurtling from the sky.

"I thought at first it would strike me. It came so close I felt the heat of its friction burning through the atmosphere. But it crashed with a thunderous roar into the rock face below.

"The mountainside shuddered and a fair amount of cascading shingle caused me to lose my footing. I tumbled down and instead of striking the rock face I found myself in blackness with the sensation of being swallowed by some great animal.

"I was in darkness for a short time, then found myself lying on softish lichen-covered ground. It was the strangest place I had ever seen — so odd I thought at first I must be dreaming. Light in all the colors of the spectrum flickered about me and the sky appeared to be enclosed in an intense, darkened dome. The ground was ragged, uneven, and scattered randomly with objects covered with lichen. It seemed so desolate, I shouted for some kind of human contact.

"I heard a pitifully weak voice calling in return. After a search, I found a young man lying half-concealed in a depression between the trunks of two lichen-covered trees. Even in the strange, flickering light I could see he was close to death. Four arrows protruded from the blood-soaked garment he wore. Although he was weak as a kitten, as I knelt over him he attempted to raise the sword he held.

"'Are you another assassin?' he asked defiantly.

"'I'm no assassin,' I replied, but he fainted as I answered. I removed the arrows, and after a hasty examination of his wounds, realized luck had been on his side. The thick padded coat he wore had saved his life. The arrow closest to his heart had barely pierced the skin, inflicting no more than a bad chest wound. Nonetheless, he had lost a great deal of blood. I removed the padded coat and in so doing caused a stream of precious jewels to pour from the holes made by the arrows. After binding him with bandages from the first-aid kit I always carried, I was in a quandary.

"Although everything felt real I was still half-convinced I was dreaming. But what was certain was that I had to get the young man to a place of safety. He began to come around and I asked him which way we should go.

"'Where is the bloom?' he asked anxiously.

"'I don't know what you mean,' I answered.

"He felt around him and as he did so, I saw that apart from the precious stones that had spilled from his coat, the ground was thick with them. But the object he located was quite different. Shaped like an exquisite flower, it was formed from crystalline compounds of many hues that gave it astonishing beauty and perfect form.

"'I must guard this — it's very fragile,' he said intensely.

"In my knapsack was a Thermos flask of coffee. I gave him a cup, drank some myself, then wrapped the flowerlike object in a handkerchief and slipped it into the flask.

"'I'm going to have to carry you,' I told him. 'It will be painful.'

"He smiled and nodded but gave no indication of discomfort as I got him onto my back. Following his directions I staggered through the weird landscape, too involved in my immediate task to question the oddity of my circumstances.

"Eventually, we came to rougher ground. I realized we were on a high plateau and that the ground fell away into the peaks of a mountainside.

"'Where on earth are we?' I asked.

"'This is not your Earth,' my companion answered. 'We are on the Northern Rim of Tallis.'"

Although they were fascinated by Hunter's journal, Tim and Sarre were so tired they could barely keep their eyes open. Sarre suggested they sleep and read more of the journal in the morning. Marking the place in the book, Tim laid it aside, and almost numb with exhaustion, he piled more logs on the fire and checked the pack pig. It was munching contentedly on huge acorns that had fallen from a giant oak tree.

Like a sleepwalker, Tim entered the silk tent, where Sarre was already asleep. He lay in the darkness, listening to the wind sighing through the trees but within minutes he, too, had fallen into a deep sleep.

A Reunion

When they set out the following morning, Sarre steered the swaying pack pig while Tim, with Josh on his lap, continued to read Hunter's journal aloud to her as they rode through the forest.

"We made the long and treacherous descent of the mountainside with me having to lower my companion down the sheerest parts before climbing down myself. By the time we reached the foothills, I was so exhausted I barely managed to notice my surroundings. I gained the impression of a rocky wild place before fainting into a deep sleep.

"I awoke to the sound of shouting. A search party had located us. Still dazed by our ordeal, we were placed into a sort of carriage and to my astonishment, I realized we were lifted into the air by four gigantic pigeons!

"That is how I came to the Kingdom of Tallis. My rational mind told me such a place was impossible but now it seemed I existed in another dimension — in some kind of parallel world. I was taken in the flying carriage to an immense palace of staggering beauty.

"Set among lakes and mountains, its tall spires rose above buildings that would have taken weeks to explore. People inhabited it as they would a city.

"The ruler was the High King and the youth I had saved from death was his son, Prince Briarre. Briarre's younger sister, Almea, was known by her title as the Lady of Tallis, because the King's wife was dead.

"At first, I thought Tallis was a paradise. But I soon learned that dark currents ran beneath its placid surface. The kingdom was similar in some aspects to a European state in the Middle Ages. There was no semblance of democracy, the High King ruled through a council, the members of which he appointed. Some were aristocrats but the majority were selected from the merchants and yeoman farmers.

"Most aristocrats stayed on their estates, hunting, farming, and occasionally fighting their neighbors. There was a system of schools throughout the kingdom in which clever boys and girls were watched for and advanced if they were capable.

"But the most astonishing thing for me to accept about Tallis were the Chanters and the Warlocks. At first, I thought they were simply superstitious manifestations of a previous primitive culture, but I was quite wrong.

"Both the Chanters and Warlocks proved to have similar extraordinary abilities. Neither used their powers to gain influence for *themselves. They preferred to serve those who reflected their personal codes of behavior. All aristocrats had either a Chanter or Warlock as part of their entourage.*

"The Chanters were all female and by inclination peaceful, unless faced by danger. They were able to communicate telepathically over vast distances, as were the Warlocks. Their other powers were more mysterious and they kept them secret.

"It was instantly possible to tell the nature of an aristocrat by their choice of Warlock or Chanter. Those with Warlocks were invariably proud, vicious, quarrelsome, and completely without intellectual interests. Aristocrats with Chanters were equally proud and warlike but usually kinder, less quarrelsome, and some were even artistic.

"There was some gold coinage in use but also a great deal of barter took place. I never saw the southern part of the country but I understand it was mostly good farmland. The oddest aspect was the total absence of flowers. They just didn't grow anywhere in Tallis. Consequently, flowers were prized above jewels when they were brought into Tallis by a people called Treggers, who were able to cross back and forth between Tallis and Earth.

"There is a Rim all around Tallis and at the very edge of it a strange gray mist where the air ceases. In the north and south there is land and in the east and west there are seas. I never visited the Rim in the south, but by all accounts it is similar to the one in the north. Meteorites and falling stars punch holes through Earth to Tallis. These passages, called starways, seal themselves again and only become passable on anniversaries such as at the full moon.

"I discovered that Chanters and Warlocks have the ability to 'see' the starways, and with the aid of Time Maps are able to appear on Earth more or less when they choose. Tallis has always had visitors from Earth but not all people make a successful transition. Some are quite normal, but passing through the passages can affect some things or people in quite another way. Some creatures don't seem to make the journey at all. There are no horses or dogs. Birds are transmuted to gigantic proportions, as are certain plants. Maybe minds are also altered. I do not know.

"At first, I wanted to return to Earth as soon as possible. But the High King was so grateful that I had saved his son's life, he insisted I stay in the great palace. He even made me a member of the aristocracy in Tallis. I became the best of friends with Prince Briarre, who was a fine man and would have made a great High King.

"I soon fell in love with the Lady of Tallis, and she returned my feelings. The first months in Tallis were the happiest of my life, but I was foolish and naive. I didn't realize I had offended the second most powerful man in the kingdom, Galeth, the Great Duke.

"It was his ambition to marry the Lady of Tallis, but my presence caused his plans to go awry. Cynically, he engineered a war between the great Lords in the south of the kingdom as a way of getting the High King out of the way.

"The High King departed to knock the heads of the warring Lords together and left the Great Duke in charge as Regent of Tallis. In the High King's absence, Illya, the High King's Chanter, told Prince Briarre that she'd learned of a plot to murder him and the High King, and that it was Galeth's men who had attempted the previous assassination of the Prince. Ultimately, the Great Duke's plan was to marry the Lady of Tallis, thus making himself the new High King.

"Prince Briarre set about thwarting the Duke's plans. First, he insisted the Lady of Tallis marry me immediately, something that needed no encouragement as we were deeply in love. Then, all three of us would go to the High King and reveal the Duke's plot. The day after our secret marriage, we set off.

"We made our way to the sea where we were to take fast boats of the Royal Fleet to a port near to where the King was trying to bring an end to civil war.

"But the Duke heard of our plan through his Warlock, Stryker, and pursued us. I transferred to a different boat to give the Prince and Almea a chance to go on while I fought a rearguard action. But within my sight, the Duke's men boarded the ship that carried the Prince and my new wife. I attempted a rescue by boarding their boat but encountered the Duke himself. I was no match for him as a swordsman but before he could finish me off I fell into the sea, leaving Prince Briarre and Almea to be hacked to death.

"I sank to the ocean bed, and when I struggled to the surface having almost drowned due to the weight of my padded armor, I was picked up by a fishing boat. It was out of Falmouth in England. I was back on Earth and the woman I loved and my dearest friend were dead—killed in another dimension.

"From that day on, I swore vengeance on the Great Duke, no matter what it would take. I would find my way back to Tallis. I became fabulously rich because my surcoat was stuffed with precious jewels. I took a new name and roamed the world preparing for my return.

"In Japan, I learned the art of swordsmanship. I trained for three years and had my weapon forged by a master. Then I began to seek a way back to Tallis. It took me many years. I searched every centimeter of the area where I had first entered the kingdom but with no luck. Then I remembered stories I'd heard in Tallis of a visitor from Earth called Mossop who was something of a legend. I employed agents to conduct research. Finally, one day I came upon the diary of Anne Mossop, and that led me to the house on Falling Star Hill."

Tim stopped reading the journal. He knew the rest of the story.

"So Hunter is married to the Lady of Tallis," said Sarre, astonished.

"I knew she'd recognized him at Lord Tredore's castle," answered Tim.

"But the Duke obviously doesn't know they're married," said Sarre. "Or he would have had him killed rather than banished to the mines."

"Why doesn't the Duke just kill the High King and seize power?" asked Tim. "He seems to run things, anyway."

Sarre shook her head. "The aristocrats still believe they must be ruled by someone of royal blood. If the Duke usurped the throne they would unite against him."

"What about the Chanters?" asked Tim. "Was there no way they could fight back?"

Sarre shook her head. "When Stryker and the Duke

murdered all the Warlocks, Stryker found a way to take their powers into himself. Suddenly, he could intercept the Chanters' messages and detect where they originated. With this power he hunted down the Chanters, too, and killed them. That is why many of the sisterhood fled to the Forest of the Southern Rim."

"So is that the only place where Chanters are safe now?" asked Tim.

"That and The Crack, which is the most important part of Tallis for the Chanters. But the elders feared that if The Crack were used as a place of refuge, Stryker with his extra powers might find a way to enter."

Tim had a lot to think about, and as the great pig plodded on they remained silent until Josh, refreshed from his sleep, demanded attention. Tim slipped down from the pig's back and, for a time, threw giant acorns for Josh to retrieve.

They were traveling on an ancient pathway through the forest and there were now patches of gigantic brambles growing beneath the trees. Occasionally, they saw worn-looking stones and soon left the forest behind. But the brambles grew thicker and higher, towering above their heads, their tangled stems heavier and the spikes more threatening. The path continued between two dense walls of bramble so thick and high that the pack pig was scarcely able to pass. The wind blew hard and the pathway became gloomier as the brambles entwined overhead to form a long dark tunnel.

Eventually, they emerged into a shaft of bright sunlight that lit a wide semicircle of grass. The high brambles curved around on either side of them as they faced an enormous obstruction of stones that stood as high as a ten-story building. There was something familiar about its formation.

"You know what this is like?" asked Sarre as they gazed at the mighty columns.

Tim nodded. "The maze in the barn on Falling Star Hill."

Sarre guided the pig forward and they saw there was an inscription carved in the base of the first great stone. It read:

JOSEPH MOSSOP

From the entrance of the maze stepped the figure of a woman dressed in the robes of a Chanter. Joyfully, Sarre slipped down from the back of the pack pig and ran forward to embrace her. Josh also dashed forward, leaping up and down in his excitement.

It was Bethen.

"We thought you were dead," cried Sarre.

Bethen laughed. "It takes a great deal to kill an old Chanter like me, child," she replied. "I have been resting to renew my powers and waiting for you both."

"You knew we would come?" asked Tim.

"The sisterhood of Chanters hoped it would be so," she answered. "We were not sure."

Carrying Josh, Bethen climbed aboard the pack pig without much effort and Sarre scrambled up after her.

"Take us into The Crack, Sarre," said Bethen. "If you still know the secret of Mossop's maze."

Sarre did remember the way through the baffling twists and turns. It was exactly the same as the one on Falling Star Hill but on a gigantic scale. Eventually, they emerged into a mighty valley where the ground fell away in front of them. The great thickets of brambles continued to grow all along the cliff tops, concealing the valley and effectively cutting it off from the rest of Tallis.

The ancient, overgrown road into The Crack descended steeply into another kind of forest. They were soon deep in surroundings that were stranger than anything Tim had yet seen in this kingdom of surprises.

The Strange Tooth

No wind blew through The Crack, but passed high above the great valley, leaving the land below untouched. The warm air was heavy with moisture, and mists gathered in the canopies of the towering trees. Heat rose from the dark red earth that nourished the plants growing all around them. Great curling fronds of ferns stretched out above their heads; vines, thick as Tim's forearm, entwined and hung from the massive trees that were heavy with fruit and fleshy leaves.

They journeyed along the remains of the ancient road for half a day, the pack pig happily snatching fruit from the overhanging trees without having to alter his easy pace.

Finally, in the late afternoon, Bethen instructed them

to turn from the road, and after a short time on a narrow trail they reached a sunlit clearing. They were at the foot of an immense outcrop of granite that rose from the valley, higher than the tallest trees. At the base was a wide cave mouth where a warm spring bubbled from the earth.

Other caves, lit by lanterns, led off the main cavern. All were comfortably furnished.

"Who made all this, Bethen?" asked Tim, puzzled by the carpets, chairs, tables, and beds.

"There are others living here in The Crack, people hiding from the Duke's police," said the Chanter. "They bring me food and help me in other ways. You'll find it's very comfortable here."

"I have to move on very soon, Bethen," Tim said anxiously. "Hunter has been captured by the Duke and taken to work in his mine. I *must* find a way to rescue him."

"I know," replied Bethen. "I have been in contact with Illya. And I have also managed to touch Hunter's mind."

"I thought Stryker had taken it from him," said Tim.

"Not completely, Hunter is too strong. His mind is clouded with suffering — but he is surviving."

"But for how long?" asked Tim. "We must get to him as soon as we can!"

"You must learn patience, Tim," Bethen answered firmly. Then she said, "And tomorrow, Sarre, we begin the last part of your training as a Chanter. You will need all your strength. We will eat, then you must get some sleep."

* * *

Early the next morning, Tim and Josh explored their new surroundings. They found a pathway that led to another network of caves. Staying out of sight, Tim watched the people who lived in them. He could tell from their clothes they had been townspeople, and included entire families. But he kept himself out of sight, thinking it would be better for Bethen to make introductions.

When he returned to Bethen's cave he ate some fruit and a sweetish bread and watched while Bethen prepared herself for Sarre's lessons.

"Would you prefer me to leave you alone?" he asked.

"You may watch if you wish to," replied Bethen. "Providing you remain very quiet. But I think you'll find it very dull."

She was right. When Sarre joined her all they did was sit facing each other cross-legged on a carpet at the mouth of the cave, with their eyes closed and their hands touching each other's palms. Tim had very quickly had enough. He was about to leave to explore more of The Crack when an idea occurred to him. He found some parchment and a hard crayon and slipped them inside his jerkin, then he searched through Hunter's haversack and retrieved the compass and binoculars.

Telling Josh to wait by the hot spring, Tim found a tree with a wide base near the clearing and began a steady climb. Although the tree was enormously tall, the thick vines curling about its trunk made the task fairly easy. Even so, it still took him a few hours to reach the uppermost branches. He discovered his choice had been a good one, because it rose much higher than the other trees. He sat down to rest in bright sunlight amid the canopy of great fleshy leaves and looked out over the mighty valley. Overhead, he could hear the moaning of the wind blowing across The Crack, but where he sat, all was still.

He scanned his surroundings through the binoculars and took a compass reading. Then, slowly and carefully, he began to sketch a map on the parchment. He was more or less in the middle of the valley, which was at least twenty-five kilometers wide and ran from north to south. Sheer cliffs dropped from the fringe of giant brambles. To the north, details of the landscape vanished into the mist.

Most of The Crack was filled with the wild junglelike forest, but he could see that there were some open stretches of savannah to the north and a large lake.

A wide river flowed from the east and curved to head south, passing quite close to Bethen's clearing. Other large rock formations, almost mountains and covered with vegetation, rose from the floor of the valley. The outcrop hiding Bethen's cavern was close by and a few meters higher than the tree he occupied.

In the far north there was another puzzling feature, blurred and difficult to see in the misty heat haze. It was as tall as one of the mountains but much paler in color. Tim wondered if it could be the curving rocks mentioned on Mossop's map. The inscription had said the heat of the day made it impossible to see them clearly.

When Tim's map was as complete as he could make it he started the climb back to the ground. It was much quicker to get down but it still took him nearly two hours.

At the clearing, he found Sarre playing with Josh while Bethen washed clothes in the warm spring. There was a delicious smell of cooking but it wasn't coming from their camp clearing.

"The people who live nearby have invited us to supper," said Sarre. "They're making us a special meal."

Although Tim was hungry, he was more interested in telling Sarre what he had seen.

Sarre was very impressed by Tim's map.

"And the wind passes high above the length of the valley," said Tim. "You can't even feel it in the treetops."

"That's right," said Bethen. "There is no Killing Wind in The Crack. The heat from the earth constantly takes the air upward, so the spores pass harmlessly high overhead."

Tim pointed to the north. "What's up here, Bethen?" he asked. "There are shapes I couldn't make out, even with the binoculars."

"Oh, you'll find out eventually," Bethen said, continuing with her washing.

"Maybe the villagers can tell us what's there," Sarre whispered to Tim. "Bethen can be very mysterious sometimes."

* * *

Tim had hardly been able to contain his curiosity until they visited the other caves that evening. But the three families living there didn't know what lay to the far north.

"And we don't want to know," said Elan, who had been elected their leader because he was the eldest.

"Why not?" asked Tim, puzzled by his attitude. It reminded him of his grandfather, who had never thought to ask why no one would grow flowers in Enton.

"This is a wild, unnatural place," Elan answered. "I know we're safe from the Duke's police, but I miss my business. I'm a cabinetmaker. It isn't enough for me to just reach out and take fruit from a tree or empty game traps a few times a day. Or to live in a cave. Besides —" He stopped, thinking better of what he was about to say.

"Besides what?" asked Sarre.

"Nothing," Elan answered evasively.

"There *is* something, Elan," said Bethen. "Why don't you tell us what it is?"

"If you must know, it's the giant, beyond the river," blurted out his wife, Marta.

"Giant!" said Bethen. "You've never mentioned a giant before!"

"It's bad luck," said Elan. "If we talk about him, he'll hear and come to kill us."

"How could he possibly hear you?" asked Tim. "If he lives beyond the river it would take him days to get here, never mind hearing what you say."

"He's a giant, isn't he?" demanded Marta. "So he'll have giant ears — stands to reason."

"My people have known The Crack for generations," said Bethen gently. "The Chanters have no stories that tell of giants."

"Before you came here, Bethen, there hadn't been a Chanter living in The Crack for more than twelve years," said Elan stubbornly. "The giant has come since then."

"Are you sure?" said Bethen. "Maybe someone dreamed it all."

Elan stood up and went to the back of the cave. When he returned he laid something on the table. White and the size of a loaf of bread, it was unquestionably a human tooth!

"Borun found that when he was fishing in the great river last year. Since then, none of us have gone anywhere near the north," he said flatly.

"I'm sorry for doubting you," said Bethen, gazing down at the extraordinary object.

"Did you ever see anything like that on Earth, Tim?" Borun's daughter asked. An attractive, dark-haired girl of about Sarre's age, she'd made sure she'd sat next to him at the table.

Tim shook his head and, sensing that he was about to blush, quickly imagined he was talking to Sarre as he said, "We do have lots of real flowers, though."

"Flowers," gasped the girl. "How many?"

Tim shrugged. "Thousands and thousands. Millions!"

"And you can see them every day?"

"Oh, yes, and touch them," he said, then thought to add, "I'm sorry, I don't know your name."

"It's Dalcima," she answered, smiling and tossing her long hair away from her face.

"Dalcima," repeated Tim. "That's pretty. It sounds like a musical instrument, doesn't it, Sarre?"

"I'm sorry," said Sarre with a very bright smile. She was sitting opposite Tim and the girl. "I didn't hear what you said."

"I said, isn't *Dalcima* a pretty name?"

"Hmmm," murmured Sarre and turned away to join a different conversation.

Tim talked easily to Dalcima and quickly found he could make her laugh; they chatted away happily for the rest of the evening. Tim was quite sorry when it was time to return to Bethen's cave.

Sarre remained quiet as they strolled back.

"Did you see I didn't have any problem talking to that girl?" Tim asked.

"Yes, I noticed," Sarre answered coolly.

"I did what you said," enthused Tim. "I just imagined she was you."

"That must have been difficult," said Sarre sharply as they reached the entrance to Bethen's cave. "She isn't anything like me." And, with that, she swept inside without saying good night.

Tim, baffled by her sudden moodiness, raised his hands questioningly. "What have I done?"

Bethen, with a dozing Josh in her arms, shrugged and shook her head. "You'll have to figure that one out for yourself, Tim."

Tim took Josh and sat outside by the fire, stroking the little dog and puzzling over Sarre's odd behavior. Some time later, he was still none the wiser, so he made up his mind to think about something else: that is, how he would occupy his time while Sarre took instruction from Bethen over the following days. As soon as he'd seen the giant's tooth earlier in the evening, he'd known what he would have to do.

CHAPTER 23

Tim Explores the Crack

"I still don't think you should go on your own, Tim," said Sarre, obviously in a better mood the following morning.

Tim was loading the pack pig with a tent, supplies, his map, and Hunter's sword and haversack. "I'll be safe enough," he replied. "I'm only going to look. I'll do all I can to avoid danger, I assure you. Besides, it'll keep me from worrying so much about Hunter."

"We've told you he's all right for the moment. Please, won't you wait?" said Sarre, making one last plea. "Bethen says my training will be finished in a few more days. Then I can come with you."

Tim laughed, "I'll be back by then."

Although Sarre was concerned, Bethen didn't object to

his exploration at all. "Sometimes it's right to follow your instincts," she said, handing him a saddlebag packed with plenty of food for the journey, including a generous supply of tocca, a thick sweet confection that tasted rather like chocolate.

With Josh seated in a leather bucket hanging from the saddle horn he set off into the forest. By midmorning Tim was at the bank of the river and heading north. He stopped for a time to stretch his legs and let Josh paddle in the shallows. Twice he came to wide swathes of grassland where wild cattle grazed, and saw columns of smoke rising in the distance above the trees. He assumed they were the cooking fires of other people taking refuge in The Crack but didn't bother to seek out their camps.

When night fell, he chose to pitch his tent in a thick part of the forest so that the flames of his campfire wouldn't attract unwelcome visitors.

For three days Tim headed north. The speed of his progress varied because a passage through the jungle had to twist and turn around trees and other obstructions. The pack pig made better time through the savannah, pushing its way through the tall grass like a fat-bottomed ship on a sea. Josh occasionally leaped down to dart about in the undergrowth. Although Tim was riding, the journey tired him and each night he slept soundly, not even bothering after the first night to pitch his tent or light a fire. The ground was warm enough.

On the third evening of his journey he was crossing

some wide grassland meadows that rose and fell through a series of small valleys. From the crests of the hills Tim could see the strange, distant, shimmering landmark but still could not make out its true form.

Suddenly, four suntanned men, bearded and long-haired, rose up ahead of him in the long grass. Their clothes were made of soft animal hide, and they were armed with spears and bows. Two of them carried a pole with a deer they'd killed hanging from it.

"You're frightening the game, boy," said an elderly man. His hair hung to his shoulders and he wore an eye patch made of leather, but he sounded more amused than threatening.

"I'm sorry," Tim replied warily. "I have some tocca with me. If you'd like to share it."

"How much?" asked another of the hunting party. Tim showed them he had half a saddlebagful, and the men seemed pleased. Just then Josh raised his head over the edge of his leather bucket. The men looked startled, then apprehensive.

After Tim had managed to convince them that the little dog was tame, the men dared to stroke Josh, and the one-eyed man asked Tim if he'd like to spend the night in their village. "Our people would like to see your creature."

Tim accepted and followed the hunting party to their camp, which was on a ridge of high ground shaded by trees and inside a bend of the wide river. The settlement consisted of a dozen huts with reed-thatched roofs and mud walls set around a village green that, although open on all sides, was protected by a thatched roof. In the center of the green was a long communal table. Under the same roof was a brick-built roasting fire that already had small game and vegetables grilling over the charcoals. The villagers gathered around to watch Josh — who reveled in being a curiosity — doing his tricks and barking appreciatively at the applause they earned.

When Tim asked the villagers if they had any waste food to spare for his pack pig, they led the huge animal to a tip where she could graze contentedly on hay, discarded vegetables, and fruit.

Heavy rain began to fall as Tim returned to the sheltered communal table.

"Will your pig be all right?" asked Laita, wife of the one-eyed man, Fargo.

"She's fine," said Tim, laughing. "She likes rain."

While they ate, the villagers told Tim of how they had to leave their lands when their Lords had exchanged them for Blooms of Kanarki, and how they had fled from the Duke's police to avoid being forced into slavery. They'd made their way down the river to The Crack and after a time they'd encountered others who had also fled from the Duke's punishment.

"We decided to live in small groups," explained Fargo. "So if the Duke's police do ever get into The Crack it will be harder for them to find us all and those they don't find can hide in the jungle and ambush them."

"Why don't the Duke's men follow those who escape down the river?" asked Tim.

"They've tried, but it's an incredibly hard journey," said

Fargo. "First, it takes two days to pass through the rapids. Only the best boatmen survive. Then, there are sheer precipices on each side from which we can drop rocks or fire arrows down on them. Finally, the river feeds into a long tunnel that we've sealed off with spider nets. The fish can get through but not the Duke's police. We have watchers all along the rapids to sound the alarm, and others stationed on the precipices. All the villagers of The Crack give the watchers food and clothes so all they have to do is guard us. They only raise the nets if the people coming through are of no danger to us."

Tim had come a long way and still wanted to find out more about the land to the north. He produced his map and asked Fargo what lay ahead and did he know the nature of the strange shimmering object on the horizon?

"Is it a set of curving rocks?" Tim asked.

Fargo shook his head. "I don't know. We don't go farther north than this," he answered.

"Why not?" Tim asked, thinking he probably knew what their answer would be.

"The giant, that's why not," Fargo answered shortly.

"Is he dangerous?" asked Tim.

"Not if you keep out of his way," Laita replied. "That's what we do. If you take our advice, you'll go back. What's the point of stirring up trouble?"

"I've got to find out what that pale-colored object is," Tim answered.

"Why?" asked Fargo. "It's bound to be trouble, too."

Tim sighed. "I have a friend called Hunter who is in terrible danger. I have a strange feeling that I might find something there that will help him."

Laita looked at him closely. "Have you been near a Chanter recently?" she asked.

"Yes," replied Tim. "Why do you ask?"

Laita nodded knowingly. "She wants you to go there."

"Do you think so?" said Tim.

"She probably put the curiosity in your head."

"Be careful, boy, curiosity can get us all into strife," said Fargo. But he smiled. "On the other hand it makes us what we are."

The rain stopped and Fargo offered Tim a bed for the night. Tim thanked him but refused, saying he would camp near the bend in the river, having already established that his pack pig would be able to ford the stream at that point early the next morning.

As Fargo's settlement was so close to his camp, Tim built a big fire, more for light than heat. He'd remembered Anne Mossop's diary and dug it out from the bottom of Hunter's haversack.

The entries were written in a neat copperplate script and Tim quickly realized it wasn't a diary at all, not in the sense of having daily entries. It was more like a story of Anne's life with Joseph Mossop. It began when Mossop came to work as an apprentice for her father, a prosperous stonemason, called Edward Blewitt.

Anne had inherited the business when her father died, and soon after that she married Joseph Mossop. Although Joseph was a skilled mason, his heart was really in his experiments as an inventor. They moved to Falling Star Hill so he could build a house and a barn big enough to carry out his trade and still have space for a workshop to conduct his experiments.

Not long after they'd built the house, the Mossops returned from a visit to some of Anne's relatives to find the villagers of Enton full of news about a star that had fallen on the hill, but they thought little of it.

At the time, Mossop was working on a pair of spectacles that he hoped would allow the wearer to see through clouds. He called them prismascopes. A few days later, Anne Mossop told her husband that the flowers had begun to disappear from around the house, and she thought she'd seen some odd flickering shadows, but Joseph was too involved in his research to pay much attention.

Then one day he rushed into the kitchen, so excited he could hardly speak. "Look, look!" he said, thrusting the spectacles toward his wife and pointing to the meadow in front of the house.

Bewildered, she put them on and was astonished to see little men gathering the wildflowers and placing them in the knapsacks they wore on their backs. When Anne removed the prismascopes she could no longer see the intruders, but she could still see flowers moving through the air.

Mossop put the prismascopes on again and called out, "Friends, may I offer you some refreshments?"

At first, the little men were cautious but Joseph eventually won them over, and to his utter astonishment, the Treggers showed him the place in the barn where the starway to their world was. Swearing his wife to secrecy, Joseph Mossop journeyed to Tallis with the Treggers. When he returned, it was as if no time at all had passed on Earth. Hurriedly, he built the maze to conceal the starway, and that was the beginning of Anne and Joseph's extraordinary adventures.

Tim was gripped. All this was making sense. And not for the first time he thought what a remarkable man Mossop must have been. He read on.

Mossop soon discovered that many of the inventions he'd struggled with on Earth worked easily in Tallis. The endless problems he'd encountered with his universal clockwork motor caused no difficulties there. By winding up a small spring, the device caused a series of flywheels and ratchets to turn with massively increased power. Enough to drive mighty engines.

His excavating Mole, a machine that could bore through the earth at surprising speed, transformed the sanitation on Tallis. Even the smallest household could afford plumbing.

By taking the floating leaves from the petrified trees and incorporating their lifting power into machines he was able to undertake extraordinary building projects. The most spectacular of them were reputed to be the two great water cascades he'd built in the Palace of the High King and the Temple of the Chanters.

No wonder the Mossops were almost worshipped, thought Tim, thinking of the Treggers' bowing to Mossop's top hat.

Anne and Joseph Mossop could have become rich just by taking jewels from the Southern Rim but they grew to love Tallis. They set up as merchants in Milchen and lived quite modestly, while continuing to come and go from the house on Falling Star Hill. After he had built Lord Tredore's battle games castle, Mossop's fame spread and he was invited to carry out various works at the Palace of the High King.

The High King showed him the royal collection of Blooms of Kanarki. These exquisite jeweled flowers were found only on the Northern Rim of Tallis, and were so rare and difficult to find that seeking them became one of the great quests that young nobles had to fulfill to prove their manhood.

The Northern Rim was part of the mountainous lands of the Great Duke. No crops or livestock were farmed on his vast estate but he was wealthy because he controlled the precious jewel trade in the north. He also prospered from a great tax that he levied on any Bloom of Kanarki found by the young noblemen.

One day, while Mossop was working on improvements to the High King's castle, a strange man he suspected of being a Warlock sold him an ancient map with curious script on it. Mossop deciphered the writing, which told of a great sealed cave in the Kanarki Mountains and warned that, although the cave contained great treasure, breathing the air in it could cause death.

When Mossop finished the work on the High King's castle he immediately left on a journey back to Earth. Some months later, he returned to Tallis with cases full of equipment and, leaving Anne Mossop at the High King's castle, took three servants with him on a secret expedition to the Kanarki Mountains. There, he located the cave that was sealed by a slab of white stone.

Mossop's equipment for the expedition consisted of a mechanical clockwork Mole, a deep-sea diver's helmet, and a portable pump. The Mole bored through the wall and Mossop entered, wearing the diver's helmet.

What he found was astonishing — great caverns filled with Kanarki blooms and huge mushroomlike fungi that emitted a faint purple glow. As he explored, one of the mushrooms exploded in a dense black cloud, which was immediately drawn out of the cave by the wind, revealing a Bloom of Kanarki.

Just then, Mossop's clean air supply stopped. He stumbled to the entrance and found two of the servants were dead. They had inhaled the mushroom spores from the black cloud as it was sucked out of the cave by the wind. The third servant was alive but paralyzed with fear. He had survived because he'd wrapped a scarf made of spider-yarn silk around his mouth. Mossop operated the pump himself to restore his air supply and the helmet kept him alive until the spores had dispersed.

After swearing the surviving servant to secrecy with

the promise of a generous reward, Joseph Mossop resealed the cave and eventually returned to the High King's palace.

When he confided in his wife the secret of the Kanarki caves, they decided it was too dangerous to reveal the new source of blooms to the people of Tallis. Anne urged Joseph to make a map and hide it separately from the rest of his original papers, which were to be stored in the Temple of the Chanters.

They eventually returned to Milchen and Joseph concealed his map in the secret panel above the fireplace in the Enton Arms. Anne and Joseph Mossop continued their lives, moving as they wished between Tallis and Earth.

Anne's journal also revealed that her husband had completed an incredible project for his friends, the Treggers. But he had kept the work absolutely secret, even from the Treggers themselves.

When the Mossops first went to Tallis, the then Great Duke was called Marka, and he sounded just as unpleasant as his descendant, Galeth. He hunted Treggers in the southern forest to sell them as slaves. He also built a great road to reach the stone trees so he could more easily harvest their red-and-gold leaves.

As Tim read on he discovered what was probably Mossop's most amazing accomplishment: He had constructed a ghost army of automatons, which he concealed in the Forest of the Southern Rim. Whenever the Duke led an expedition to capture Treggers, he went equipped with heavy fighting pigs and armored troops. The pressure from their massive weight triggered the mechanisms and caused the mechanical ghost army to spring from their hiding places and attack with a deadly storm of arrows.

Being small and light, the Treggers themselves didn't trigger the mechanism that caused the ghost army to appear. Mossop never told the Treggers about the hidden army of mechanical men, as he feared the Duke might learn the secret by torturing the little people. The only other visitors who entered the forest on heavy animals were the Gurneys, so Mossop gave them maps of safe pathways. Being as superstitious as the aristocrats, the Gurneys always stuck to the Mossop pathways.

Tim lay Anne Mossop's diary aside and let out a long low whistle. "Wow!" he exclaimed. At last he understood the mystery of the ghost army. And, Tim realized, Hunter had read all this, too — he had known about it all along.

Tim had been so absorbed in the story, he hadn't noticed the first signs of dawn. He stood up by the white ash of his fire, stretched, and looked around him. Above, a great pink sky edged with pale lemon and washed blue lay over The Crack, its reflection turning the river into a wide curving rainbow of color where it passed through the emerald forest.

Despite reading all night, Tim didn't feel in the least tired and wanted to resume his journey immediately. He saddled the pack pig, loaded Josh into his traveling bucket, and they waded across the river into the jungle that lay to the north.

The Giant's Secret

About noon, the jungle gradually thinned out and the pig carried them into another wide expanse of grassland. After a time, they skirted a chain of small lakes, where Tim allowed Josh and the pack pig to splash and wallow in the shallows. Then they continued through the tall grass, which whispered gently as the pack pig thrust aside its golden mass.

Tim began to feel very tired. Missing a night's sleep was finally catching up with him, so he leaned back comfortably in the pig's chairlike saddle. A warm sun beat down from a dazzling blue sky. Tim pulled down the brim of his leather hat to shade his face and soon drifted into a deep and dreamless sleep as the pig trudged on. Twilight came and still Tim slept.

The savannah ended and the jungle began again. It was cooler when darkness fell and eventually the pack pig stopped unbidden by its sleeping rider. In a clearing, lit by the moon, stood a tree heavy with ripe, dark red fruit. The pig grazed and Tim slept on until Josh gave a sudden sharp bark.

Tim awoke with a start, uncertain of his surroundings. Josh was growling quietly and looking to the north. Tim could hear noises. Something was crashing through the undergrowth toward them. Unsheathing Hunter's sword, Tim slid to the ground, and Josh leaped down after him.

The noise grew steadily louder, until a gigantic figure burst into the clearing. Silhouetted against the moon, it stood vast, squat, and terrifying. The pig gave a loud snuffling snort and the huge figure let out a squeak of surprise. Then it leaned forward, reaching out a massive hand.

Tim couldn't help closing his eyes, fully expecting to be plucked into the air and crushed, but the hand merely patted the pack pig.

"Hey, piggie, piggie," a voice said gently. The pack pig grunted and rubbed his shoulder against the outstretched hand.

Tim could see the figure more clearly now in the bright moonlight. To his astonishment, it was a very young boy! Albeit, one of enormous proportions. The boy's chubby body was dressed in rags and the giant shoes he wore were cracked and holed but Tim could see they'd been made on

Earth, not Tallis. His blond curly hair hung down to his shoulders.

"Who are you, little boy?" the giant asked Tim. "Why didn't you run away when I came? Everybody else does."

He put his hand down on the ground, palm upward, and Josh fearlessly ran onto it. The giant lifted Josh gently and smiled.

"That's my dog. He's called Josh," said Tim nervously, still brandishing Hunter's sword. "And I'm Tim. Who are you?"

"My name is Tom Tagg. I live in Enton. I've been lost for ages and I want to go home!" said the giant child, with a great rumbling sniff.

"Tagg!" gasped Tim, lowering the sword. He'd heard that name before. "Enton!" Could this huge creature be the little boy who had gone missing?

"Is your mother's name Megan, Tom?"

"Do you know my mother?" said the boy eagerly, almost dropping Josh to the ground. "Is she here?"

"No, Tom," said Tim. "But she's been looking for you ever since you went missing."

"Can you take me home?" Tom asked, so hopefully that Tim almost forgot his own troubles.

"I'll do my best," he said. "But it may take a bit of time. I have to rescue another friend first."

"I want to go home *now*," said Tom petulantly, and he shook the tree so hard its red fruits were flung off like missiles from its branches.

"I know you're lonely," said Tim sternly. "But I can only do one thing at a time. The more you help me, the quicker we'll be able to get you home."

"Promise?" said Tom.

"I promise," answered Tim. "Tell me, how did you get here, so far north?"

"I followed the little men on Falling Star Hill," said Tom, "and suddenly I came to a strange place where I was much bigger than anyone else. Then I saw a great big balloon land and I hid. A lot of wild children got out, but I didn't like the man who was in charge. He had a long beard and a big stick. I was frightened of him even though he was much smaller than me."

"Stryker the Warlock," Tim murmured.

Tom continued, "I waited until they were a bit farther away, then I got into the balloon and pulled up the rope. It sailed away. I flew in it for a long time. There was a storm, lightning struck the balloon, and it came down. And I've been here ever since."

"Why do you go about at night?"

Tom shrugged sadly. "All the people are afraid of me and run away. No one wants to play with me, so I come out only at night. I'm used to being on my own now."

"Well, it won't be for much longer," Tim said, trying to sound reassuring. Then he asked, "Where are you living now?"

"In the big white house," said Tom.

"Where's the white house?" asked Tim.

"This way," said Tom, beckoning Tim to come with him. The pig followed easily along the path the giant boy had trampled through the jungle. As Tom Tagg walked ahead, Tim calculated how tall he was. At least three times taller than Hunter, he decided. Then he remembered Hunter once telling him that some things alter as they come through the starways and tried not to think about the possibility of meeting some giant-sized insect, like a wasp or centipede.

Tom led them to an ancient overgrown road of the sort Tim had traveled along before. It took them to what Tim had been trying for so long to discern through the heat haze, but it looked nothing like the curving rocks shown on Mossop's map. In the cool of the night the air no longer shimmered. Standing sharp and clear in the moonlight was a vast white building topped with a spired tower. A flight of steps led up to a portico that was supported by six marble statues dressed in the costumes of Chanters.

More than half the building and tower was covered in thick curling ivy. Although in good repair the building looked as though it had been abandoned for many years.

Carved into the lintel supported by the statues were the words:

TEMPLE OF THE CHANTERS

As Tim stood, taking it all in, Tom told him, "This is where I live. No one bothers me here."

Great golden doors stood open and they stepped inside the massive white interior. In a corner near the doorway,

Tim found the remains of the balloon in which Tom had escaped from the Rim. It was still soft and buoyant with a few of the floating leaves that hadn't escaped.

At first glance, the vast temple appeared to consist of just one vaulted marble hall, lit by bright moonlight streaming in through the high windows of the tower. There was no decoration on the walls or ceiling to detract from the simplicity of the structure. Tim sensed an overwhelming serenity within the walls of this temple.

"There's more up the stairs," said Tom. "And there's another room at the end of the hall."

Tim found the room and read the inscription carved above the door.

THE WORKS OF JOSEPH MOSSOP

PRESENTED TO THE CHANTERS FOR SAFEKEEPING

Inside, the room was lined with shelves, all crammed with familiar-looking scrolls. But these were the originals of the ones he'd seen in the tavern in Milchen. He examined one and noted the wax seal. Then he ran down to the pack pig and fetched Hunter's haversack. Inside, he took out the map Hunter had found hidden in Mossop's rooms in Milchen and reread the inscription.

"Where are the stairs to the tower?" Tim asked the giant boy.

"Over there," said Tom, pointing and yawning as he lay down to sleep on his balloon, with Josh nestling down beside him.

Tim found a small doorway made of white stone and as

he pushed the door open, he, too, felt suddenly overcome with weariness. But he was determined to carry on. Trudging up the seemingly endless flights of stairs inside the great tower, Tim soon felt as if his legs were on fire but he gritted his teeth and forced himself to keep climbing. Finally, he emerged into a tiny room. The windows all around it overlooked the whole of The Crack.

Tim felt a strange tingling sensation, as if his body were charged with electricity. The room seemed to be filled with it. He took his binoculars and slowly scanned the horizon in all directions. All the while, his entire body was tingling with tiny shocks.

Then, to the north, he saw two large and three small peaks in the far distance. He checked them against the map Hunter had found in the Enton Arms and saw that they matched exactly. "Yes!" Tim murmured, jubilant to have found them. But then, suddenly overcome by his exertions, he slid to the floor, oblivious to the hardness of the stones, and fell into a deep sleep.

Tom Tagg was still slumbering on the remains of the balloon when Tim came downstairs the next morning. Rather than wake him, Tim occupied himself by looking through more of the scrolls. They were records of all the things Joseph Mossop had made and built in Tallis. Bridges, harbors, viaducts, paddleboats, elevators, fountains, improved chimneys, cooking stoves, dust extractors, windmills — there were endless inventions and innovations that had made life better for the people of the kingdom. One scroll contained yet another secret that Joseph Mossop had never disclosed. Tim carefully rolled this scroll up together with the map showing the way to the caves of Kanarki.

Tom began to stir as Tim stood by him.

"You are real!" said the boy, raising his head and blinking happily. "I thought you might have been a dream."

"No, I'm real enough, Tom," said Tim, smiling at him. "How would you like to come with me?"

"Oh, I'd like that," said the boy. "I'm fed up with being on my own. I'll just get my things." He felt under the balloon and produced a large bundle wrapped in a grubby red handkerchief.

On a sudden impulse, Tim filled a sack with some of the floating leaves from the balloon.

"It's a long walk," Tim warned as he loaded the pack pig.

"Not for me," said Tom, grinning. "I've got longer legs."

They set off together, retracing their way along the ancient road from the temple, through the jungle to the clearing where they'd first met, then back along the track the pack pig had previously forged through the dense undergrowth when Tim had been asleep on her back. The journey was uneventful but did take a bit longer than Tim had done on his way to the temple. Although the giant boy easily kept pace with the pig and plucked fruits to eat along the way, sometimes he grew weary of the endless walking and wanted to stop and play with Josh. And Tim thought it better to give Fargo's camp a wide berth in case Tom's gigantic presence frightened the villagers.

Something was puzzling Tim on the journey back to Bethen's cavern. Sarre had told him she would be able to return him to the exact moment when he had vanished from Earth. Did that mean he wouldn't be any older? If that were so, how was it that some people aged while they were in Tallis? Obviously Joseph and Anne Mossop had grown old there. But Tom Tagg was still a young boy, although years had passed since his disappearance. Maybe Bethen would know the answer.

At last, as twilight fell on the fourth day with the sky over The Crack turning gold, Tim recognized the peak of the little mountain that contained Bethen's cavern. Sarre was at the warm spring and there was a large fire burning at the mouth of the cave. Tim guessed it was to make it look more welcoming, as the evening was quite warm.

He slid down off the pack pig and Sarre ran to hug him. There was something different about her. Although she looked exactly the same, she had a new air of confidence.

"We were expecting you," she said. Then she looked up at Tim's companion who stood shyly clutching his bundle of possessions by the hot spring until Tim introduced him.

"Hello, Tom," she said, smiling sweetly. "I'm very glad you could come with Tim."

"Where's Bethen?" asked Tim. "There's something I must ask her."

"I'm here, Tim," a voice answered, and he saw a radiant figure emerge from the cavern. It was Bethen, transformed. Her movements as she hurried forward were those of a young woman.

"What's happened to you?" asked Tim, bewildered.

"I have entered my last life as a Chanter, Tim," she said. "I successfully passed on my knowledge to Sarre. It was a sort of examination for me as well."

She spoke then to Tom, totally unsurprised by the presence of the giant boy. "Are you hungry, Tom?"

He nodded, still too shy to speak.

"If you would care to take a bath in the spring, when you come out we have new clothes for you and some supper."

Tim looked down at the table, mystified. There was a set of clothes and a meal for each of them on it. But the clothes were for a normal-sized child and the food only the usual modestly sized servings. Tim had become accustomed to seeing Tom consume vast quantities of fruit each day. The whole amount on the table would be less than a mouthful for him.

While Bethen led Tom to the spring, Tim said to Sarre, "Do you think Bethen knows why some people from Earth grow older in Tallis, while others, like Tom and me, remain the same age?"

"I know why, Tim," she replied. "Those who come to Tallis by accident do not grow older. But if you come here to seek something for yourself, you do."

"Why?"

Sarre laughed. "That I don't know. Nor does Bethen. No one can know everything."

Bethen and Tom returned from the spring with Josh yapping excitedly about the boy's feet. To Tim's astonishment, Tom was now the size of a normal boy.

"Look!" said Tom excitedly. "I'm my proper size again. The spring must have shrunk me."

Bethen smiled but said nothing.

Tim was almost getting accustomed to the extraordinary powers of the Chanters but now he had a question.

"Bethen, you knew I would go to the Temple of the Chanters, didn't you?"

"I hoped you would," she replied.

"Do you know everything that is going to happen to us in the future?"

Bethen smiled and shook her head. "Chanters can see what *might* happen in the future. Sometimes, we can nudge people in a particular direction but we can't be certain of the eventual outcome. By going to the Temple you discovered a shorter and secret route to the caves of Kanarki. A way even the Duke and Stryker do not know."

"I'm sorry I was impatient about finding Hunter," said Tim. "I'm beginning to understand that you trust me to find my own way and that I will when the time is right."

While they ate supper, Tim began to describe what he had learned on his journey. But, seeing that Tom wanted to play, Sarre searched for something to amuse him. In her pouch she found the seed packets Tim had given her when they'd first met, and she went off with Tom, scattering seeds about the camp. Tim laughed, glad to see that Josh was inadvertently covering the seeds with earth as he leaped up and down trying to catch them in his jaws.

When their game was over, Tim told Sarre what he had learned from Anne Mossop's diary.

"So the Duke has caused the Killing Winds by reopening the sealed caves of Kanarki to get at the blooms?" said Sarre.

"It looks that way," said Tim. "But more important, we now know where Hunter is held captive, and I'm going to try to rescue him."

"You will have to prepare," said Bethen.

"How? I want to leave first thing tomorrow."

"You will have to climb the great precipice," said Bethen. "And when you get to the caves, how will you breathe among the killing spores?"

"We will have silk masks."

"The spores there will be too highly concentrated to rely on silk masks alone."

Tim nodded in frustration. "I see what you mean," he replied. "Perhaps I don't know enough about the dangers involved."

"There are things Sarre and I can teach you," said Bethen. "We will start tomorrow."

Little Tom was so tired he had already fallen asleep at

the table. Bethen carried him to a bed in the cave and returned with his giant-sized bundle. She unwrapped it and they saw the things he had kept throughout his time alone in Tallis.

A huge rusty penknife with a broken blade, three massive seashells, and five enormous fireworks.

"What are these?" asked Bethen, holding one of the fireworks.

Tim explained.

"They won't work in Tallis, then," said Sarre. "We know about the gunpowder on Earth. But it doesn't work in Tallis. People have often brought guns here but they've always failed to shoot."

Tim smiled and gazed at the seashells.

CHAPTER 25

Teaching Tim

The following morning, Sarre began Tim's training. "Right, I am going to teach you a series of exercises," Sarre said briskly. "They are both mental and physical."

"How long will this take?" Tim asked.

"That depends on you," said Sarre. "It has nothing to do with intelligence or the part of your mind that is rational. It is all to do with trust and belief in yourself."

"Then what will I be able to do?"

Sarre smiled. "Hold your breath for over an hour."

"That's impossible!" protested Tim.

"All sorts of things are possible in Tallis," Sarre reminded him.

By the afternoon, after long and patient instruction from

Sarre, Tim was astonished to find that he was able to slow down his heart rate so that it hardly beat at all. At the end of the day, he could hold his breath for nearly an hour and a half. Bethen and Sarre were delighted with his progress.

"Now, if you were to lie down and close your eyes people would think you were dead," explained Sarre. "Your breathing has stopped and your heartbeat and pulse are so faint, only a Chanter would know you were alive."

"Which means you will be able to enter the caves of the killing spores without inhaling them," added Bethen.

"And now I'll teach you to climb like a Tregger," said Sarre.

They loaded the pack pig with supplies, and leaving Bethen, Josh, and Tom Tagg at the cavern, they journeyed to the nearest part of the precipice at the side of The Crack.

When they'd made camp, Sarre and Tim inspected the wall that rose far above the forest canopy. Sarre told him to stand against the cliff face and feel the surface of it with his fingertips for the slightest cracks and indentations.

"Tregger climbing must be done with an unbroken rhythm," she said, showing how she could move nimbly across the rocky surface by taking her weight for a moment on the slightest holds her fingertips could grasp.

They worked just above ground-level because Tim fell many times, but with each attempt he got a bit higher. Eventually, Sarre thought he was ready for the next stage. She climbed higher and banged spikes into the surface,

then she secured Tim with the spider yarn and he continued to practice.

Tim soon realized that he no longer needed to look for
hand- and toeholds. His movements became more instinc-
tive and graceful as he learned to change his weight from
hand to foot and move across the surface of the rock in the
same dancing motion as Sarre.

"This is great! I didn't think I'd be able to climb like this
so soon," Tim called to Sarre as they moved up the cliff face.

"Well, Bethen has helped a bit by giving you confidence," Sarre replied. "She always says the ability to do
things happens mostly in the mind."

Finally, Sarre said she'd taught him all she knew and
that they'd make one last ascent. This time, with Tim taking the lead, they climbed the whole height of the precipice, right up to the great bramble barrier at the top. Sarre
showed him how to hook spider yarns into the thicket to
make an intricate cat's cradle, and they cheerfully sat in it,
dangling their feet into the abyss below and eating the fruit
they'd brought in a knapsack.

Tim scanned the horizon with the binoculars but couldn't
make out the jagged peaks that were marked on Joseph
Mossop's map. All he could see through the heat haze above
the jungle was the shimmering Temple of the Chanters.

"The caves of Kanarki are about there," he said, pointing
as Sarre looked through the binoculars. "But you can only
see the peaks from the top of the tower in the Temple."

Before they started their climb back down the precipice, they had a grim reminder of the Duke's punishments. Overhead, a prisoner balloon was drifting north in the wind stream above The Crack. It was close enough for them to see the lifeless bodies chained to the airborne bag.

When Tim and Sarre returned to Bethen's cavern they immediately began their preparations for the journey to the caves of Kanarki.

"Don't you want to come with us to the Temple, Bethen?" asked Tim, the evening before they left.

"I go there whenever I want to," Bethen answered lightly, without looking up from the board game she was playing with Tom.

"You've been there?" said Tim. "It looks as if no one has visited it for years."

"My mind goes there," she said, moving a diamond across the board.

"I win!" Tom whooped, gleefully snatching her diamond from the square and substituting one of his rubies.

"You're too good for me, young man," Bethen said. Then she looked up at Tim who was laying out the equipment they would take.

"Your *mind* goes there?" asked Tim.

Bethen smiled. "Chanters make only one physical journey to the Temple, as a pilgrimage. From then on, it's our minds that visit, and we guard the Temple with our thoughts. All Chanters take it in turn to be on guard for part of each day."

"Was that what I could feel when I was in the tower?" asked Tim.

"Yes," answered Bethen. "And that's why the Duke's men never come to The Crack. They can't find it. Even when they fly above it in balloons, to them it just looks like the ordinary fields of Tallis."

"So there's really no need for the people here to watch the river for intruders?"

Bethen shook her head. "No, but it's good for people to think they are responsible for their own protection."

"And what about the bird man who told me his tribe confuses the Gurneys with their thoughts?"

"It is we Chanters who are confusing the bird men."

"Incredible!" said Tim, wondering if he would ever get used to the strange way things worked in Tallis.

Bethen smiled at Tim, then as Sarre emerged from the cavern with saddlebags packed with food, she rose and put an arm around her.

"This will be a very special journey for Sarre — the best kind for a Chanter. She is making her pilgrimage to the Temple and helping to right a great wrong."

She scooped Tom Tagg up from the table where he was making patterns with precious stones. "Time for bed, young Tom; more games tomorrow."

Sarre also went to bed but Tim had something to do before he slept. He took a large smooth rock and placed it near enough to the fire for him to see what he was doing by the flickering flames. Then, he wrapped one of Tom's seashells in silk and pounded it with another stone until the shell was reduced to fine-grained powder. He worked on for another hour before slipping into his own bed.

Sarre, Tim, and Josh set off at dawn mounted on the pig whose saddlebags were packed with plenty of supplies for their journey. With Hunter's sword always slung across his back, Tim spent much of the time practicing the breathing exercises Sarre had taught him. And while Tim was occupied, Josh was happy to run about alongside them, barking to get up into his leather bucket and ride with Tim again whenever he grew tired.

They made good time, and by evening of the third day they were approaching the Temple on the ancient road when, suddenly, three massive cracks of thunder rumbled overhead and heavy rain began to pound down. Ignoring the rain, Sarre told Tim she would return the following morning, then dismounted to approach the Temple of Chanters on foot.

Tim understood she wanted to be alone at the sacred place, so he made camp a fair distance away under a vast sheltering tree. He fed Josh and the pig, then toasted some bread and cheese on his campfire and ate it while listening to the rain beating down on the canopy of leaves above.

CHAPTER 26

Sarre at the Temple of the Chanters

It was still raining heavily the following morning when Sarre came stepping through the misty pools that had formed on the jungle floor overnight. Tim had already loaded up the pig, so they quickly remounted and moved off to pass the Temple and head due north toward the caves of Kanarki. There were no more clearings or grasslands but fresh streams were gushing through the dense undergrowth, their bubbling torrents dark red from the soil they washed over.

The rain continued nonstop, and only Josh was thoroughly enjoying it. The little dog ran barking through the streams or dozed contentedly under his leather bucket, which Tim had turned upside down to make a dry bed for him. That evening they sheltered on high ground under a tree and managed to light a fire. The jungle seemed endless.

The next morning, Tim took the map, binoculars, and compass and climbed a high tree. When he came down he was more cheerful. "I can see the rocks straight ahead, despite the rain," he told Sarre. "It's extraordinary. When I moved a few feet to one side they seemed to disappear."

"How far away are they?" asked Sarre.

"About half a day's march, I'd guess."

Tim was right. After a few hours, they came to the first of the range of white rock peaks, each one set in a curve about an arm's length apart. When they reached the last one, there were more signs of the ancient overgrown road — just an occasional smooth length of oblong stone, half obscured by moss and glittering in the rain. It led them on, still following the curve of the rocks, through the dripping jungle toward the immense, precipitous side of The Crack.

At long last, the rain stopped and bright sunshine blazed down, causing steam to rise through the jungle like mist on an autumn morning. With Tim regularly consulting the compass, they pressed on until they reached the cliff face. Tim dismounted with Josh and put out his hand to feel the rock, which was smooth and still warm from the sun. Apart from the clearing in which they'd stopped, the jungle grew thickly against the face of the precipice, making it impossible to explore far in either direction. Tim checked Joseph Mossop's map again.

"It says to follow the curve of the white rocks to the point on the cliff face where we must start our climb," Tim said. "Sounds like we're very close to where we go up."

"Good," said Sarre briskly. "We'll start in the morning. I'm hungry, thirsty, and ready for a bath."

"Food and drink is easy enough," said Tim. "But where on earth — Tallis, I mean — are you going to find a bath?"

"Don't you worry about that. You make camp and get the fire going and I'll see about the washing arrangements," Sarre answered with a grin.

Tim made a fire using some of the dry kindling he always kept in one of the saddlebags as Charto had taught him. The tinderbox he'd brought required him to strike a flint on a rasp of metal until the sparks ignited a patch of dry cotton. However, he also still had the boxes of matches he'd taken from Mossop's secret cupboard in the Enton Arms at Milchen and used one now to save time. When the fire was going, Sarre returned looking refreshed.

"So, where did you find a bath?" Tim asked.

"Come and see," she said, beckoning him a little way into the forest where there was a squat tree with a wide trunk and enormous low branches thick with vast leaves, each one as large as Tim. The leaves cupped upward. Sarre had attached a length of spider yarn to a branch and, when she pulled it, fresh, warm rainwater cascaded down like a mountain stream.

By the time Tim had showered and washed out his clothes, Sarre had wrapped a fish in large leaves and had it cooking in the embers at the edge of the fire. Josh sat close by, watching the fish intently.

"Where did you catch this?" Tim asked as Sarre divided the catch among the three of them.

"The stream coming out through the rock face is teeming with fish," she answered cheerfully.

The fresh fish was sweet, succulent, and slightly smoky tasting; certainly the best Tim had ever eaten. He leaned back against a tree savoring every mouthful and thought about the adventures to come.

At daybreak the next morning, Tim was already up preparing for their climb. He packed the leather bucket and knapsack. First, came a layer of the floating leaves he'd taken from Tom's balloon, then his silk sleeping bag with his water canteen, food, the binoculars and compass, maps, and a hammer and spikes all packed around it so as to leave a space for Josh. Lashed together and attached with spider yarn to his belt, the bucket floated comfortably beside him, and with Hunter's sword strapped across his back he would be free to climb unhindered.

Sarre woke a little later than Tim and quickly bundled her possessions into her silk sleeping bag, but before starting the climb they ate breakfast, watching the early pink-tinged light throw the shadows of trees on the wall of the precipice. A ray of sunlight suddenly showed them they'd found the right spot, for just a few meters away was the name JOSEPH MOSSOP, carved into the rock at the base of the precipice. And higher up, beneath a large iron spike, another inscription read:

AFTER THIS YOU ARE ON YOUR OWN.

"Oh, very funny!" said Tim, grinning as he looked up at the sheer smooth wall that towered to giddying heights above them. "Shame we'll never get to meet this Joseph Mossop, I like the sound of him."

Then with mock gallantry he bowed to Sarre, and with a rolling flourish of his hand he indicated the spike. "After you."

And Sarre began the ascent.

Concentrating totally on the rock face, Tim detached his mind from the passage of time. Sarre had taught him that a collapse of willpower can occur if climbers allow themselves to think they are nearing the end of a daunting climb, only to discover that it has hardly begun.

It was hot on the rock face and this part of the precipice was far, far higher than where they had practiced. The sun beat down on Tim's back and only his changing shadow marked the passing of time. Every few hours he would bang spikes into the wall and rope himself with spider yarn to the cliff face so he could give Josh a drink of water from the canteen.

Twilight was falling over The Crack when he heard Sarre call to him from above.

"We've made it, Tim — and there's a way under the brambles."

After a few more minutes of climbing he found her sitting, legs dangling over the edge of the crag at the dark mouth of a small tunnel. He scrambled to sit beside her and pulled in the floating bucket. Josh immediately leaped out and trotted around, sniffing all the new smells. Just above their heads, thick tendrils of the bramble dangled down to overlap the cliff face. Carved above the tunnel another message from Joseph Mossop read:

WELL DONE!

A sudden wave of weariness washed over Tim; he swayed unsteadily and Sarre had to quickly pull him backward into the tunnel. A moment or two in the cool revived him, and they crawled through the smooth passage to emerge eventually on the rocky ground that rose beyond the thickets of bramble. The last glimmer of light faded and they were in darkness. A hard wind, cold enough to make Tim shiver, blew to the north. They climbed into their silk sleeping bags and, too tired to eat, slept where they lay.

The Dreadful Valley

They woke before dawn to find the blue-black sky was awash with swirling pale green, pink, blue, and yellow color.

"We're near the Northern Rim," said Sarre. "That's why the sky is different." As she spoke, the first darting rays of the morning sun touched the mountain range that lay ahead of them. Jagged, snowcapped peaks stretched on farther than they could see.

Joseph Mossop's map showed the route they had to take but the way was hard. The ground was rocky and uneven, or thick with broken shale that slipped treacherously beneath their feet at every step.

The only vegetation was patches of thick moss interrupted by clumps of low scrubby bushes. No bright colors relieved the monotony of the landscape. Everything was blackish gray, dreary shades of brown or dark green. Even the sky was no longer full of color, just an even grayness that hardly cast a shadow.

"What a miserable place," said Tim when they stopped to eat after walking all morning. "I've never seen anything so depressing."

Josh, however, was in excellent spirits and was wagging his tail furiously as he growled amongst a clump of bushes.

"At least he seems to be happy," said Tim, plodding on.

Sarre suddenly stood up and laughed, embarrassed. "I'm so sorry, Tim," she said. "I quite forgot to do something for you."

"What?" he asked suspiciously.

"Close your eyes," she said, and she placed the palms of her hands on his temples.

"You may look now," she said.

Tim blinked about him, amazed. The dreary landscape was transformed. The sky was now a pale eggshell blue and sunlight sparkled on the snowcapped mountains. There, high meadows of emerald grass and tumbling streams, foaming white, cascaded around them. Immediately, Tim felt his spirits lift.

"I'm afraid the dreariness you saw before was an illusion. The work of the Chanters," Sarre explained. "It's all part of the way unwelcome visitors are kept from The Crack. Anyone who approached from this direction would be affected as you were and want to turn back. Josh saw things as they really are, that's why he's been so cheerful."

They walked on, all the time moving to higher and higher ground. Each peak they crossed led to a taller mountain. By the third day the landscape really did become grimmer. Finally, they came to a terrible place. A mountainside scattered with human bones, rusting chains, and torn fragments of cloth.

This was obviously where the wind blew the punishment balloons. This range of mountains would be too high for the balloons to cross. They must have been dashed against the jagged rocks and their grisly cargoes scattered across the mountainside.

Filled with pity for the fate of the victims, Tim and Sarre looked around them at the horrifying result of the Duke's cruelty and ambition.

"Hunter is right," said Tim softly. "The Duke *must* be destroyed."

Sarre did not speak, but held Josh tight in her arms and they hurried on through the dreadful place.

When they had passed to the next valley, Tim once more consulted Mossop's map. From the shape of the landscape ahead he knew they were almost at the caves of Kanarki. As they climbed higher, the harsh wind blew constantly to the north and the weather grew bleak and cold. No vegetation could grow here. When they reached the high ground between two peaks, they saw they had at last arrived.

*   *   *

Concealing themselves among overhanging rocks they peered down. Tim glanced at the map again, puzzled, until he realized that details of the landscape must have altered since Mossop had made his map. It showed a sheer mountainside and — on an opposing rock face, across a wide chasm and set back from an outcrop of rock — the eye-shaped mouth of the cave Mossop had explored.

Now, just below them, cut into the mountain they were on, was an immense ledge overlooking the deep abyss. The ledge was at least a hundred paces wide and another fifty paces deep. The abyss could be bridged only by lowering a narrow drawbridge that was presently raised at an angle of forty-five degrees. The winding gear was guarded by two soldiers standing next to charcoal braziers. The eye-shaped cavern opposite the ledge was overhung by a vast rocky brow.

On the great ledge beneath Tim and Sarre, so close they could almost reach out and touch the roof, was a stone building. As they took all this in, six of the Duke's guards, escorted by a company of archers, emerged from the building carrying three cauldrons of steaming food. As they placed the cauldrons on the ground near the narrow bridge, another guard was using a large windlass he'd brought with him to operate the winding gear that lowered the drawbridge. He then sounded a horn, and all the guards retreated several paces while the archers stood with their bows at the ready.

From the mouth of the cave opposite, six filthy, half-naked figures emerged to cross the narrow drawbridge. These men wore sinister-looking leather masks and the ragged remnants of clothes. They seemed to be in fairly good physical condition but they shuffled forward as if their spirits had been broken.

Each pair carried between them an empty cauldron that they placed on the ground on the soldiers' side of the bridge. They then picked up the filled cauldrons of food and returned with them to the cave. The guards raised the drawbridge again before taking the empty cauldrons and the windlass back to the guardhouse.

"I must get close to one of the guards so I can look into his mind," Sarre whispered to Tim.

He looked up into the sky. It was already growing dark and the first faint glimmers of the pastel-colored lights were beginning to swirl.

"Wait until nightfall," he replied.

Thankfully, Josh behaved well. Sensing that Tim and Sarre wanted him to stay silent, he lay between them on the rocky ground, his head between his paws, and remained still.

After a few hours of darkness the voices in the guardhouse died away. The two men standing guard by the bridge were illuminated by the flickering light of their braziers.

Tim touched Josh's head, whispering, "Stay, boy," then he and Sarre crept down to the great flat ledge below and tiptoed forward to stand in the darkness just outside the circles of light made by the glowing braziers.

Out of the gloom, Tim fired his slingshot. One of the guards, struck full on the forehead by a large ruby, collapsed unconscious like a puppet with its strings suddenly cut. The other guard took a step toward his fallen companion and was about to blow the alarm horn when Sarre darted forward, curtsied, and smiled up at him. No sight could have been more unlikely in this desolate place. Startled, the man stood stock-still, staring in silence as Sarre reached up and gently touched his forehead.

At Sarre's touch, he, too, fell to the ground. Tim quickly retrieved his ruby so as to leave no evidence, then helped Sarre drag him into the darkness. Sarre held her hands to the guard's temple for about a minute, then went back to touch the head of the guard Tim had felled.

"All done," she whispered. "I have the information we need."

They climbed swiftly and silently back to where Josh was waiting and watched as the two guards roused themselves, shook their heads, and continued their vigil as if nothing had happened.

Once they'd moved out of earshot, Sarre told Tim what she had learned from the guards' minds.

"There are twenty of them here," she began. "They all hate doing this guard duty. It is seen as a punishment, and despite the elaborate precautions they take, they live in constant terror of the Killing Wind."

"I thought the Killing Wind didn't blow very often."

"It does up here. They have small changes of wind all the time. Almost every day, usually in the early morning, but it doesn't affect the rest of Tallis. That's why the slaves have to live in their special masks and only take them off to eat. Their masks have to provide a lot stronger protection than ordinary silk ones because of the high concentration of spores when a mushroom bursts; also, the prisoners have hardly any warning of a wind change because they're inside the caverns. The guardhouse below is specially built to protect the guards. It can be completely sealed. But they're still terrified they might get caught in the open with the door locked before they can get inside, so they never stray far from its protection."

"How long does the danger last?"

"Fifteen minutes — half an hour — but much longer, of course, when it's a wind that affects the whole of Tallis."

"Did you find out why the ledge is so big?" asked Tim.

"So that transport carriages can land here. The Great Duke sends a bird transport once a month to deliver supplies and collect the blooms that have been taken from the mine. There's a transport due tomorrow."

"What time?"

"Late morning."

A plan was already forming in Tim's mind but its success would depend on the unpredictable wind. When he explained it to Sarre, she nodded her agreement and immediately began tying one end of a length of spider yarn into a loop. They put on their knapsacks, and Tim hung Hunter's sword over his back. Now all they could do was wait, crouched among the rocks, hoping for a moment of luck.

"Can you put Josh to sleep until we get back from the cavern?" Tim whispered. "If he sees us fighting or in danger he'll want to join in."

"Yes, of course," replied Sarre, laying her hands on the little dog's head. Instantly, Josh fell asleep among the rocks.

The luck they needed came just after dawn. The wind died, and in the sudden calm the two guards ran toward the guardhouse shouting for the other sentries to keep the door ajar.

The moment it slammed behind the guards, Tim and Sarre raced down to the wide platform and ran for the drawbridge. As they reached it, they felt the wind begin to blow south.

An eerie howling came from the cave opposite as Sarre began to climb the raised drawbridge. Tim was holding his breath as Sarre had taught him. He watched as a dense black cloud of spores was drawn out from the mouth of the cave and caught up by the now soaring wind.

Tim could just see Sarre tying the spider yarn to the top of the bridge. As soon as it was secure, they both seized the loop and swung across the chasm to land on the ledge beneath the cave's entrance. Tim slashed through the yarn with Hunter's sword, and holding their arms in front of their eyes for protection, they battled forward to enter the caves of Kanarki.

CHAPTER 28

The Prisoners of Kanarki

Inside the cave a short tunnel the height of a tall man led to a large jagged hole. Around the base were fragments of the stone slab that had once acted as a seal, and beyond it was darkness.

"Face me for a moment," Sarre said to Tim, and she placed her hands over his eyes. "Now you will be able to see inside."

Passing through the rough-hewn gap they entered a vast chamber so high that the faint purple glow coming from the lower rock surfaces was only just enough to reveal its roof. Tim imagined a cathedral could easily fit into the space. A strong wind was still whirling thick clouds of the black spores out through the tunnel they'd just come through and gradually dispersing them.

The walls of the cavern rose in terraces. At first glance, they appeared to have been man-made, but in fact they had been shaped by the water that seeped constantly down the cavern walls. Each tier contained clusters of huge grayish green mushrooms that emitted the faint purple glow and filled the air with a dank, musty odor. From the base of each mushroom grew tendrils that immersed themselves in the trickling water that gathered in shallow pools on the uneven floor.

In a mighty space at the center of the cavern, piled one upon another, were large open cages built of rough wooden stakes. The cages were interconnected with ladders and walkways. And inside them, swinging in the wind, were at least a hundred hammocks, occupied by hooded and raggedly clothed figures. They appeared to be asleep or perhaps just waiting for the wind to abate.

"I'm going to try and contact them with my mind first," Tim heard Sarre say.

Tim nodded, amazed that she could speak at the same time as holding her breath. He didn't dare attempt it himself, despite his training, and nor did he want to risk swallowing any of the spores. Every minute or so he had to fight off a rising sense of panic as he remembered it was only his willpower keeping him from instant death.

After a few minutes, Sarre told him, "They are like the living dead. They have no thoughts, but they do have just enough control to perform simple tasks. And in part of their minds they are aware of being in this nightm —"

Her voice stopped. "It's Hunter!" she said. "I've found him. I think I can call him to us."

Tim watched the cages and saw one masked figure rise slowly from his hammock and begin to make his way down through the cages. As he shuffled toward them, Sarre concentrated with all her power, fighting to free his mind. Gradually, his shambling steps changed to a more normal walking pace.

As Hunter came to them through the purple gloom, Tim could hear Sarre's calm voice saying, "It's Sarre and Tim, Hunter. We've come to rescue you."

"Can you help the others, too?" Hunter croaked through his mask as he reached out to grip their shoulders.

"I think so," said Sarre, immediately turning her attention to the minds of the listless bodies swinging in the hammocks. Again concentrating the power of her mind, Sarre reawakened the men and, one by one, they left the cages to crowd before Tim, Hunter, and Sarre.

In the meantime, Tim had unslung the sword he'd been wearing for so long and silently handed it back to Hunter. Tim sensed that Hunter seemed to gain strength as his hand fastened gratefully on its hilt.

"Thank you, Tim," he croaked.

At Hunter's words, muffled by the mask he wore, Tim had to suppress a smile of relief and force himself to keep holding his breath.

"Lords of Tallis," Sarre addressed the prisoners. "We're going to show you how to escape from this vile place."

Fortunately, at that moment the wind died down and the whirling spores began to fall to the ground. A few minutes later, Tim finally dared to breathe again.

"One of the Duke's bird transports is coming today," Sarre continued. "When it arrives we're going to overpower the guards and seize it. As many of us as possible will escape on the transporter. For the rest of you we have a map showing how to get over the mountains to The Crack."

"Won't Stryker know we have escaped?" asked a prisoner.

"It will be some time before he realizes," answered Sarre. "And, anyway, the minds of the Chanters will protect you — so do not be afraid."

"Can you help us remove these masks?" called one of the ragged Lords.

"Yes, but not until we've overcome the guards," said Tim. "We don't want them put on the alert."

"What about the archers?" asked a tall man. "How will we deal with them?"

"You'll see when the guards bring your morning food," Tim answered and went on to explain the rest of his plan, hoping Hunter would approve.

"Are you sure it will work?" asked another of the prisoners.

"According to Joseph Mossop," Tim answered cautiously.

"Well, if it doesn't, at least we'll die fighting," said the tall prisoner grimly.

* * *

CHAPTER 30

An Encounter with the Great Duke

As they entered the palace grounds, the road divided into three separate wide carriageways. The two outer lanes, bearing the supply wagons for distant parts of the estate, swung away sharply to the left and right and descended into tunnels. Charto, Hunter, and the Prince kept up a show of Gurney merriment as the pack pigs swayed along among the other traffic on the main road, which was paved with golden stone. They passed through a magnificent avenue of mighty trees from which hung thousands of colored lamps to emerge into a vast, artificially created landscape.

Great lawns rolled away from them, dotted all the way

After the wind had returned to blowing from the south and the last of the spores had drifted down to the ground, the soldiers on duty cautiously emerged from the guard-house and returned to their positions by the drawbridge.

Tim, Hunter, and the tall prisoner stood concealed in the shadows close to the cave mouth. All of the Lords were now armed with thick wooden stakes that they'd taken from the cages and sharpened with Hunter's sword.

When the horn sounded, signifying the cauldrons of food were waiting, six of the prisoners shuffled out of the cave as usual and the drawbridge was lowered.

Under the watchful eyes of the archers, the six prisoners shuffled across the drawbridge to the opposite ledge. All of a sudden they moved fast, thrusting their empty cauldrons among the full ones and crouching down behind the makeshift barrier they created. The guards, momentarily puzzled, merely stood there trying to assess what was going on.

Then Tim emerged out of the cave holding what appeared to be a burning stick the size of a rolling pin. Fire fizzed from one end of it as he hurled it through the air across the abyss. The archers reeled back as it exploded like a thunderclap at their feet, blasting them with rock and gravel.

As the missile left Tim's hand, the strongest of the remaining prisoners were already rushing across the lowered drawbridge, roaring their defiance, and within moments the dazed guards were overpowered. A few tried to put up a fight but Hunter and the tall prisoner made short work of them.

"Quickly," Sarre called out, "I can feel the bird transport is on its way."

"How long have we got?" asked Hunter.

"No more than an hour," Sarre answered.

The freed prisoners worked fast. They dragged the guards into the stone guardhouse and removed their uniforms before tying them up. In all this melee Josh suddenly turned up, barking happily to see Hunter again. Sarre must have released him from his sleep among the rocks.

The smell of the unwashed prisoners was overpowering but there were plenty of showers in the guardhouse, which were fed by a waterfall. Using anything sharp they could find, the men hurriedly cut off their leather masks, revealing the beards and hair that had grown to extraordinary lengths inside them. Racing against time, they roughly lopped off the matted hairs, hurried through the showers, and set about shaving.

Relatively clean and dressed in a guard's uniform, Hunter joined Tim and Sarre at the window where they were anxiously scanning the sky for the expected bird transport. Suddenly, the three became aware of a complete silence behind them. Turning, they saw all the men were kneeling, heads bowed before the tall man.

Hunter stared at him in astonishment. Then the two men were laughing and embracing each other. As Hunter stepped back, Tim was surprised to see there were tears in his eyes.

Now Hunter bowed before the tall figure, saying, "Your Imperial Highness, Duke Briarre, Prince of Tallis, may I present to you our gallant rescuers, the Chanter Sarre and Tim Swift."

A roar of cheering now rose from the other men. Free of their masks and with their minds unclouded, they were finally recognizing one another. They were the Lords who had been accused of treason by the Great Duke. The joyful reunion continued, until Josh barked a warning.

Looking from the window, Tim called out urgently, "The transporter is about to land!"

Two of the Lords dressed in captured uniforms ran from the guardhouse to stand by the bridge. Hunter led a group of similarly uniformed men outside to welcome the transporter.

It was a vast carriage, so heavy it took eight gigantic pigeons to land it close to the edge of the chasm. But there were only two men on board, and the rest of the space was filled with stores packed in wooden crates and huge, sealed pottery vases.

The drivers were easily overpowered, and while the cargo was being unloaded, Prince Briarre and Hunter were eager to question Tim about the explosion he had made.

"I found Joseph Mossop's document archives at the Temple of the Chanters," he explained. "He had discovered how to make gunpowder work in Tallis but wisely thought it would be better not to reveal it to the people."

"So what is the secret?" asked Hunter.

"You just add a small amount of calcium to it," said Tim. He told them briefly about the giant boy who had been living at the Temple and ended by saying, "Tom Tagg had some seashells in his bundle, so I ground up one and added it to the gunpowder in his fireworks."

"*Fireworks*? You have more?" asked Prince Briarre.

Tim showed them the others he had in his knapsack. "I thought we might be able to seal off the cave again," he said.

"That would be the finest work you could do on Tallis," said the Prince grimly.

"How did you know how much to add?" asked Hunter.

"I just guessed," said Tim, grinning.

Hunter and Prince Briarre surveyed the transporter critically.

"I think we can get everyone in. There's less than a hundred of us, and these carriages are built to transport the Duke's soldiers," said the Prince scratching his chin in a not very regal manner. "But will the birds be able to get it off the ground?"

"We don't fear the danger, Your Majesty," shouted several of the freed Lords.

"We'll take the risk, Your Highness," called others. "Nothing could be worse than being left here."

"Brave men, but foolish," the Prince muttered to

Hunter. "A problem we've always had with the noblemen of Tallis."

"Your Highness, Tim and I have a solution," said Sarre briskly.

Prince Briarre smiled. "I see the young Chanter has no fear of speaking her mind to royalty," he said.

"A Chanter's role is to advise, Your Highness," Sarre responded, smiling. "Flattery we leave to the courtiers."

"Then, let us hear your advice, Chanter."

But it was Tim who now spoke. "Your Highness, beyond this range of mountains there is a valley of bones and the remains of many of the Duke's punishment balloons, which still contain some of their floating leaves. If we can gather together enough leaves, the pigeons will lift our combined weight with ease."

One party of Lords was soon dispatched over the mountain to fetch the leaves, and another set to making a meal, while Tim and Hunter prepared to seal off the cave. They made a long silk fuse and dipped it in lantern oil from one of the pottery urns. After lodging the remaining fireworks in the overhanging brow of the cave, they attached the fuse to them and trailed it back across the bridge to the ledge. Then they went to eat while they waited for the Lords to return with the leaves.

Aided on their return trek by the buoyancy of the leaves they had gathered, the Lords were soon back, and many eager hands worked quickly to attach the leaves. Everyone crowded aboard the now-buoyant transporter, and as it was about to soar into the air, Tim lit the long fuse with one of his matches and dropped it to fizz its way across the bridge.

The pigeons quickly carried them well out of range and the transporter was already high above the peaks of the next mountain range by the time they heard the mighty thunderclap of the explosion. A great roaring cheer went up from the Lords.

Then the wind changed. Jubilation turned to panic. A sudden storm was hurtling after them from the north. The drivers urged the birds on but a huge dark cloud was about to overtake them.

"The Killing Wind is upon us," shouted a voice as choking clouds of dust engulfed them.

But after a few moments of terror, there were sudden shouts of laughter and relief. They were alive. There were no spores in this wind — just dust from the great explosion.

"It worked!" shouted Tim triumphantly. "The caves of Kanarki are sealed!" And they set course for The Crack.

Reading his map, Tim directed the drivers as the giant pigeons soared over the mountain ranges that he and Sarre had taken so long to cross on foot. Even so, the journey took nearly a day. Finally, marking their position on the map, Tim said, "We must go down now. The Crack should be directly beneath us."

"But there's nothing but mountain peaks," protested the drivers.

"They're only an illusion made by the Chanters," said Sarre. "There are no mountains really."

Still the drivers were reluctant to descend.

"Do as they say, My Lords," commanded the Prince quietly, and the drivers redirected the huge birds to take the transport down.

Apart from the rhythmic beating of the birds' wings, all was silent. Sarre looked relaxed, but Tim only managed to stay calm by stilling his heartbeat as she had taught him. What if he'd misread the map?

Even though all the Lords still believed they were about to be dashed onto the jagged rock peaks, they stood quiet and unflinching, awaiting their fate.

Passing effortlessly through the terrifying illusion, they found themselves hovering over the great open valley of The Crack.

A Plan of Battle

Tim and Sarre were sitting by the campfire in front of Bethen's cavern, listening to Hunter and the Prince talk about the past. The rescued Lords were nearby, making spears, clubs, and bows and arrows from a variety of wood they had cut in the jungle. Bethen and the other people living in the caves and nearby in the forest had managed to provide some clothes for the Lords and some leather and cloth for making more. But the Lords still felt underdressed without their traditional weapons.

"I thought you were dead —" Hunter was saying to the Prince, "you and Lady Almea — when I fell into the sea and through the starway back to Earth. Since that day I've lived only to find a way back into Tallis so I could destroy the Duke."

"How long have you been away?" asked Prince Briarre.

"More than twelve years," Hunter replied bitterly.

"I remember virtually nothing since the Duke and his men boarded our boat," said the Prince sadly. "It has been like living in the fog of a nightmare." He looked down at his arms and flexed them. "But I feel strong enough."

Sarre said, "That's because they gave you enough food and made you work hard, Your Highness. It was the Duke's orders."

"How do you know?"

"I was able to read the mind of one of the guards."

"It is a long time to have been more dead than alive," said the Prince sadly.

"Too long," said Hunter. "But the Duke is going to pay for what he's done. We must finalize our plans, he will know by now that we've escaped."

The Lords gathered closer around the two men, and one of them asked, "How will he know that? Sarre said the Chanters' minds would keep the knowledge from reaching him."

"Yes, but the transporter we captured didn't return to him. He would have sent scouts to find out why," the Prince explained.

"What do you think he'll do?" asked another.

Hunter threw a stick into the flames before he answered. "The Duke is determined to rule Tallis, but the only way its nobility will accept him is if Prince Briarre and the High King are out of the way and he can marry Almea, the Lady of Tallis. The Duke already has the High King and the Princess in his power. He doesn't know where Prince Briarre is, but he will know the Prince will try to rescue the royal family. I think he will just wait for Prince Briarre to come to him."

"Something I fully intend to do," said the Prince.

"You can't go alone," said Hunter. "To destroy the Duke we will need an army."

"My men will still be loyal to me," said one of the Lords.

"And mine," chorused the others.

Hunter shook his head. "That's good, and we may need to call on them, but your estates are scattered all over Tallis, it would take too long to rally your soldiers. The Duke's forces would destroy your small armies one by one before we could form them into one force strong enough to storm the High King's castle."

Bethen had come to the fire and stood listening to Hunter. Now she unfurled Tim's map on the table. "If you were to gather all your forces together in the Midlands," she said, pointing to the estate of Lord Tredore, "you could concentrate all your armies here and force the Duke to march south to attack you where you are well defended."

"But what would make him come out to attack us?" asked the Prince.

Bethen smiled. "No great army could take the High

King's palace. It was made impregnable by Joseph Mossop. But if a small group could rescue the High King and the Lady of Tallis and bring them to Tredore's castle, then the Duke would be forced to lay siege to Castle Tredore or see all his dreams come to nothing."

Hunter and Prince Briarre studied the map.

"It could work but getting into the High King's castle could be difficult," said Hunter.

"Treggers and Gurneys could get in," said Bethen. "You know how fond the nobles are of Tregger servants and Gurney musicians."

Hunter nodded thoughtfully. It was true, he remembered how highly the Lords and Ladies of Tallis prized Treggers and enjoyed dressing them up in fanciful costumes.

"Most of the Treggers are in the Forest of the Southern Rim," he said. "Even if we could get to them in time, it would be unfair to put them in so much danger."

"Bethen could make Tim and me into Treggers," said Sarre.

"*Make* you into Treggers!" repeated the Prince dubiously. "How?"

Sarre nodded. "She could easily reduce us to Tregger size in her shrinking pool."

"But only if she can make us bigger again!" said Tim, sounding alarmed.

"That is the least danger you will have to fear, Tim," said Bethen dryly.

"What about the Gurney musicians?" asked the Prince.

"I thought you and Hunter might do the job," said Bethen.

"I can't get used to that name for you, Robert," said the Prince.

Hunter smiled and said, "Robert will do, Your Highness." And then to Bethen, he added, "How could *we* pass ourselves off as Gurneys?" he said, gesturing to Prince Briarre.

"You're certainly pale enough from your long imprisonment in the cave," said Bethen. "I could dye your hair and give you singing voices as sweet as any Gurney's."

"But who could teach us to *act* like them?" said the Prince.

Just then they heard something approaching through the forest, crashing through undergrowth and snorting loudly. To everyone's astonishment, a pack pig swayed into the camp with Charto seated on it, fast asleep.

"I summoned him with a dream," said Bethen, smiling mischievously. "He has been asleep for many days."

Charto blinked awake and slid stiffly down from the pig's back as his friends leaped up, grinning to welcome him.

"Hunter!" he shouted in astonishment and clasped his hand, grinning with pleasure. "Tim! And Sarre! My dream has come true."

"Where are your people?" asked Hunter.

Charto snatched up some food and took a great swallow of juice from a gourd before he answered.

"The Duke's police have been making raids throughout Tallis," he said. "Something has obviously infuriated him.

All the Gurney bands have fled to the Forest of the Southern Rim. I was going with them but on the road I fell into a deep sleep and my pig seems to have brought me here."

He looked about him in wonderment. "Where exactly is *here?*" he asked.

"You are in The Crack," said Bethen.

Charto grew even paler than normal when he recognized who spoke.

"Bethen! And so young!" he gasped. "Impossible! You're *dead.*"

"The reports were greatly exaggerated," said Bethen, smiling. "It takes a great deal to kill a Chanter."

Another crashing in the undergrowth heralded the arrival of another pack pig. It was the one Tim and Sarre had ridden to The Crack and left grazing at the base of the precipice — she'd found her way back and was now thrusting her way into the camp, knocking aside any Lords who stood between her and Charto.

"Lucretia!" Charto shouted as he rushed to embrace the great creature, who nuzzled him affectionately in return.

"We need you to do us an important service, Charto," said Bethen.

"Anything, Great Lady," he replied.

"We need you to transform the Prince of Tallis and Hunter into Gurneys. Make them look like Gurneys, sound like Gurneys, sing and dance like Gurneys, *think* like Gurneys! Can you do that?"

Charto stroked his beard while he examined them critically. "A difficult task, but I'll see what I can do with them," he replied.

It took two days but with Bethen's help, Charto did transform the Prince and Hunter. Their hair and beards were dyed a fiery orange-red and hung in ringlets to their shoulders. Their pale skins were dusted with freckles. Both had learned the swaying walk of the Gurneys and to throw their heads back and laugh in Charto's bellowing fashion. Bethen's Chanter powers gave them the confidence to quickly acquire the skill of playing their stringed instruments, which looked rather like long-necked mandolins, and Charto taught them several songs.

But the Gurney chief was not yet happy with one aspect of the Prince's performance.

"Walk toward me as if you are about to pass by me," he instructed Prince Briarre.

As the Prince came level with Charto, the Gurney knocked him roughly aside with his shoulder. The Prince stiffened and automatically his hand reached for the dagger in his belt.

"No, no, no!" shouted Charto. "Remember you have to react like a Gurney, not the Prince of Tallis. Let's swap roles and I'll show you how a Gurney would behave."

This time, when the Prince's shoulder struck Charto, the Gurney bowed low with an ingratiating smile and said, "Forgive my stupidity, Great Lord. The path is yours."

Charto snapped up and said, "Now, *that* is how every

Gurney learns to act, right from childhood. As a Gurney, you must always keep your rage in your heart. We Gurneys survive by hiding our anger. We have a saying: *The price of pride is always too high*. If you go for your sword when a Lord insults you, then you'll soon find yourself dangling from a punishment balloon."

"I didn't know how it is for your people," said the Prince. "But I promise you, Charto, it will change."

"Beware, Your Highness," said Charto, laughing. "You may get to like the life of a Gurney so much you may never want to be a prince again."

When, at last, Charto said he could do no more with Hunter and the Prince, Bethen took first Sarre, then Tim to the hot spring. After which, she gave them the Tregger clothes she had made for them to wear, and when they were dressed she held up a long looking glass. They were amazed. They still looked like themselves but their ears, noses, and chins were sharper. They really did look like Treggers. And dressed in the Gurney clothes that Charto had made for them, Hunter and the Prince also looked the part and were especially impressed that Charto had modified their string instruments to provide a hiding place for their swords.

By this time, the freed Lords had already departed for their own lands with plans to secretly rally their men, merge them into two great armies, then rendezvous at Tredore Castle.

The following morning, when the pack pigs were fully loaded with supplies, Tim was putting Josh in his traveling bucket when Hunter asked, "Is it a good idea for the dog to accompany us, Tim? He'll attract attention."

"Let the dog come, he has his place in the scheme of things," said Bethen, who was climbing aboard the pig already mounted by Tim and Sarre.

"Are *you* coming with us?" asked Hunter, surprised.

"Of course I am," she replied. "They wouldn't dare keep a Chanter out of the High King's palace. Even with that poisonous toad, Galeth, the 'Great' Duke in charge. Besides, it's time I took another look at that creature, Stryker."

Once she'd made herself comfortable, Bethen asked the Prince and Hunter, "How do you intend to gain an appointment with the Great Steward?"

"I shall request it," said the Prince, puzzled.

Bethen shook her head. "And you think he will take time to see a *Gurney*?"

The two men looked thoughtful as Bethen reached inside her robes, saying, "But perhaps he'll see you if you offer him this."

She was holding up a Bloom of Kanarki.

The journey to the Palace of the High King took a little more than two weeks. The pack pigs plodded tirelessly over great moors, skirted huge lakes, trekked through mighty forests and seas of grass, and trotted contentedly along the hedgerowed lanes that divided the farmlands. All the while, Charto had Hunter and the Prince playing their instruments and loudly singing along with him.

"You'd never know they hadn't been singing Gurney songs all their lives," said Tim to Sarre one night as they sat around the campfire. "They're rather good."

The weather was becoming autumnal. As they passed the last of the farms, the land rolled on in each direction like a great park, its trees touched with russet and gold. Eventually, they came to one of the ancient overgrown roads.

"We're getting close to the High King's palace," said Charto. "I came here when I was a boy."

"Home," said the Prince. "But I have never seen it like this."

"How do you mean?" asked Hunter.

The Prince smiled. "I was always in a procession or riding in a royal carriage surrounded by guards. Nothing was ever this simple before. I never really saw how beautiful it was."

"Well, it's about to get ugly," said Charto in a low voice. "A party of the Duke's police is watching us. Remember to smile and be humble."

"I'll try," said the Prince softly, bowing to the black figures mounted on fighting boars as they passed.

Twilight was falling as other roads joined theirs and they found themselves traveling among a lot of other traffic. A regiment of lancers trotted past, mounted on lean, prancing pink pigs. Plow swine lumbered by, pulling huge carts filled with vegetables, fruit, grain, and barrels of fish. They mingled on the road with ladies and gentlemen, some riding hunting pigs and others bowling along in sporty carriages.

Tim even spotted an extraordinary machine that hummed by almost silently, driven by footmen.

"The pigless carriage," he called to Hunter.

"That's my father's Mossop wagon," said Prince Briarre, speaking quietly so as not to be overheard. "It was made for one of our ancestors; it's the only one in the kingdom. The grooms must be keeping it in working order."

They watched it effortlessly overtake the rest of the traffic and disappear into the throng ahead.

Night fell and the busy road stretching before them was soon bathed in moonlight. The wind was gentle and warm despite the lateness of the year. Ahead, the rolling landscape slowly began to slope up toward some mighty walls that looked as sheer and smooth as the precipice at The Crack. They were lit by flaming beacons, flaring in the wind.

"The Palace of the High King," Charto said to Tim and Sarre, who had been standing up in their stirrups to catch their first glimpse.

* * *

The road was leading them to a mighty gatehouse four stories high and set into the enormous walls that soared up from the rising ground ahead of them.

"What about Josh?" asked Tim. "We don't want him to draw attention to us."

"Pass him to me," said Bethen, reaching out to take the little dog. "Be still, Josh," she ordered, and resting him on her arm she deftly concealed him beneath the wide flowing sleeve of her silk robe.

Most of the traffic was allowed to pass through the gatehouse unhindered but the commander of a guard called them to one side to be examined. Tim fought to still his racing heartbeat and keep his eyes on the one real Gurney in their party.

Charto swept off his hat, saying, "We have traveled from the south, Master, bringing Tregger servants to offer to the Great Steward. We are also escorting a Chanter."

This seemed to be enough for the commander, for he immediately waved them through and they entered the grounds of the Palace of the High King.

Tim had half-expected to enter a courtyard, like the one at Lord Tredore's castle. Even though he had read the description in Hunter's journal, Tim was still astonished by the wonders that lay behind the mighty wall.

to the horizon with exquisite pavilions glowing with light. Each was artfully arranged within a bower of trees. It was clear that everything they saw, including the rise and fall of the landscape, had been fashioned by artists. The illuminated walls and spires of the castle lay ahead, greater in size than the town Tim lived in on Earth. Beyond it, the mountain peaks were bathed in moonlight.

Glancing into the nearest pavilions as they passed, they saw groups of people listening to orators or musicians. In others, people just sat reading. In one, a man stood at an easel painting a woman dressed in hunting costume and mounted on a slender, pedigree hunting pig. Deer roamed freely, grazing on the lawns. There were small fruit bushes in profusion, their crops cultivated in a variety of colors — to compensate for a lack of flowers, Tim guessed.

As they approached a great lake, a huge creature glided past them to flit to and fro across the surface of the water. For a moment, Tim thought it was a bird but then he saw it was a giant dragonfly, the shimmering color of its wings changing in the lantern light. A young man was seated on its back, and there were more of them darting and twisting just above the surface of the lake. The mounted youths were playing some sort of game in the darkness.

Lily pads floated like small boats on the surface of the water. Everything about the landscape inside the High King's castle, including the lake, was huge. It was almost as if it had all been built for giants.

As the two pack pigs swayed slowly around the lake,

laughter and music tinkled across the water from pleasure boats lit up with colored lanterns that sent long streams of rippling reflections across the surface. Some of the larger boats were even more brightly lit. On board, passengers were enjoying leisurely meals as they cruised the great lake. Smaller craft were filled with musicians who serenaded the larger boats. Everyone seemed to be dressed in white or the palest of yellows and blues.

"Is it some sort of festival?" asked Tim.

The Prince shook his head. "Every day is like this at the Palace of the High King," he replied.

Beyond the lake rose a gleaming wall of light illuminating the castle set on a high plateau above. Against the night sky Tim could see a dazzling array of battlements, towers, and numerous gilded spires.

"This is phenomenal!" said Tim. "Where does all the illumination come from?"

"Joseph Mossop installed gaslight everywhere," replied the Prince.

As they approached another mighty wall of glittering light, Tim realized it was in fact a gigantic man-made waterfall that cascaded hundreds of meters from the plateau down into the lake. To reach the castle level there were vast elevators, rather like the ones at Lord Tredore's castle, but these were much bigger and were set within the mighty torrent with the passengers kept dry under glass awnings.

To reach the elevators the pack pigs walked parallel with the waterfall along a wide stone jetty where the pleasure boats moored. All but Bethen dismounted to wait for one of the mighty lifts to come to rest beside the jetty. They boarded the elevator along with a host of white-clad revelers, who all seemed delighted to see the pack pigs.

The revelers were also friendly toward Tim and Sarre, whose Tregger heads they patted for luck. But they seemed a little more reserved with Hunter and the Prince who were cheerfully laughing and joking with Charto like true Gurneys. Bethen sat silently, ignoring everyone.

When they disembarked at the top, they saw that the roaring cascade was fed by a wide river that also served as a moat. The extent of the castle was clearer now. Prince Briarre explained that it was actually a vast collection of buildings that had been added to over the centuries in a variety of architectural styles, but as they were each constructed of the same pale gold stone they all blended together harmoniously.

Hunter pointed out that the connecting wings of the castle enclosed a seemingly endless complex of high-walled gardens, orchards, formal gardens, and gigantic conservatories covering hundreds of acres that were filled with fruit-bearing vines. There was even a hunting park.

As well as the High King and the Great Duke, who each occupied their own castle, thousands of people lived in the complex of buildings, including virtually all the noble families of Tallis, with their personal retinues comprised of battalions of soldiers and innumerable servants.

One aspect was new to Hunter and the Prince. Since they had last been here, the Duke had established a series of great barracks to house his personal army. They occupied an area of the estate that had once been parkland, and his guards patroled the area where all the nobles kept their battle birds.

Strumming their Gurney instruments and occasionally bursting into song, Hunter and the Prince led their party on through the strolling crowds until they came to a tall building with a great fountain jetting up water in front of it. Despite the lateness of the hour, lights blazed at every window. They could see into a large ground-floor room in which row upon row of men were sitting at high desks, dealing with tottering piles of paperwork. Other clerks hurried about the room collecting and distributing more documents.

Inside the marble-clad reception area about fifty haughty receptionists sat at desks in front of a long row of doors. Hundreds of elegantly dressed people sat on benches, patiently waiting for their name to be called.

The man with the biggest crowd waiting in front of him sat nonchalantly at his desk eating a large pie with a silver knife. He wore a powdered wig and his clothes were protected by a white napkin tied about his throat.

"Wait here," said Bethen.

Hunter was about to say something but Bethen fixed him with a stare and said, "Do as you're told, Gurney!"

Immediately, the Prince, Hunter, and Charto bowed deeply and stood back with Sarre and Tim. The people on the benches seemed so dispirited by the tedium of their waiting that none of them even noticed the little dog suddenly peer out from Bethen's sleeve before she quickly pushed him out of sight.

As she approached the man eating the pie he looked up and watched her warily. Chanters had lost a great deal of their status in recent years but they still commanded a certain respect.

"I wish to see the Great Steward immediately," said Bethen curtly.

"Impossible," he replied. "There is a wait of many days."

"He will want to see me and my companions," said Bethen and she produced the Kanarki bloom from her flowing silk robes.

The man sat upright, staring at the exquisite crystal flower. Most blooms were locked away and only viewed on special occasions. The pie on his plate was now forgotten as he reached out a greasy hand.

"This is not for the likes of you to touch," said Bethen. "Now, go and tell the Great Steward I have a present for him."

Impressed, the man scuttled away, and despite the enormity of the bribe they still had to wait more than an hour. Eventually, the bewigged receptionist returned with a splendidly dressed Tregger whose blue velvet costume glittered with jewels.

"The Tregger will take you to the Great Steward," said the man.

"This way," piped the Tregger and he led them into what appeared to be an endless corridor. Through some of the half-open doors they passed they saw more rows of toiling clerks. Clearly, not everyone at the High King's palace enjoyed a holiday every day.

"Why are you dressed as peasant Treggers?" asked their guide suddenly, without turning around.

"We *are* peasant Treggers," Sarre replied quickly.

"No," he said lightly, "You're *disguised* as Treggers. Allow me to know the difference."

"What is your name?" Bethen asked as they continued to walk.

"Erif," he replied.

"Stop, Erif," commanded Bethen, at a stretch of the corridor between open doors. The little man turned and Bethen lay a hand on his head. Then she smiled and told him quietly, "This is the Prince of Tallis. We have come to rescue his sister and the High King."

"Bethen! Are you mad?" Hunter hissed in alarm.

She shook her head. "Erif can be trusted."

The Tregger looked up at Briarre, his eyes shining with worshipful awe. "Are you *really* the Prince of Tallis?" he whispered.

"I am," said Briarre.

The Tregger knelt. "Your Highness, we have hoped a long time for just such a miracle."

"Tell him to rise!" hissed Charto, looking up and down the corridor in alarm. "At this rate, it'll be a *miracle* if we continue to live."

As they hurried on along the corridor, Erif told them,

"You can trust the Treggers in the palace but no one else. The Duke has spies everywhere. But we know even more than he does."

Tim was about to ask Erif what he meant but they had arrived at an impressive set of double doors, much larger than all the others they'd passed. Knocking lightly, the Tregger entered.

Inside was a huge but sparsely furnished room. There were no decorations on the paneled walls nor any carpets covering the wooden floorboards. But arranged in a circle were desks at which men, quills poised, bowed over sheets of paper. Striding up and down in the middle of them, hands clasped behind his back, was a short elderly man with a worried frown. He was dressed in a long velvet robe with an elaborate chain of office about his neck and was dictating to each of the secretaries in turn.

"Letter to Lord Beltha," he said, pointing at one of the secretaries and dictating in a sharp, commanding voice. "It has come to the attention of Lord Poller that you are allowing your tame fawns to graze in his garden. Please cease the practice immediately." He swung to face another clerk. "Letter to the Mayor of Gulla. Sir, Please supply the castle with one hundred tons of smoked fish by the end of the month. If smoked fish is not available in sufficient quantity you may substitute salted fish instead." He pointed to yet another of the men. "Letter to the High King's chief house-keeper. Madam, Once again, the High King's table linen has not been changed. This must be done promptly after every meal." His finger selected another scribe. "To the Captain of Squires. Lord Fulmin, The banned sport of cascade jumping has started again. Any squire caught taking part in this game will serve two terms of guard duty with the garrison at the Mines of Kanar —" He stopped dictating the moment he saw the group at the doorway.

"Go!" he commanded, and all of the secretaries leaped up and hurried from the room.

The moment they'd gone he slammed shut the doors and turned to kneel before Prince Briarre.

Hunter raised his eyes to the ceiling in exasperation. "So much for our Gurney disguises," he said.

"Your Highness!" said the Great Steward. Then he looked at Hunter. "I carried the Prince in my arms when he was a boy. I would recognize him if he were disguised in the body of the Great Duke. And I recognize you, too, Robert Quester."

"Rise, old friend," said Prince Briarre. "And for the sake of all our lives, you must behave toward me as if I were truly a Gurney."

The Prince turned to his companions and said, "This is Lord Weira, one of my father's most trusted friends."

Lord Weira held up a hand and spoke urgently. "Why did you bring him here, Bethen?"

"To save the High King and the Lady of Tallis, you old fool," Bethen told him affectionately.

"We have only a few minutes before the Duke's spies will be listening to us," he said. "What do you command, Your Highness?"

"Employ us as musicians and the two children as Tregger servants. We will tell you the rest when the time comes."

Lord Weira nodded, wasting no time with other questions.

He picked up a paper from his desk, muttering, "I may have just the thing." Then, glancing at the document, he said, "Excellent, this will do. The High King's Chamberlain has requested entertainers for tonight's banquet." He looked at Charto, "Can you play that thing?"

"I can, Master."

Lord Weira nodded. "As a Chanter, Bethen may come and go as she pleases, and I can appoint you Treggers to serve the Lady of Tallis. But once inside the High King's castle you will be trapped. It does not appear so, but the Duke has it sealed like a gigantic dungeon."

"Just get us inside," said Prince Briarre.

Lord Weira scribbled a note. "This will introduce you and act as a pass," he explained.

As he handed the parchment to Hunter there was the sound of marching feet in the corridor outside. The doors were flung open and the Great Duke strode into the room flanked by guards.

Everyone had the presence of mind to bow — with the exception of Bethen, who pointedly ignored the Duke.

"My Lord Weira," said the Duke, studying the figures

before him. "I was told you were entertaining unusual guests. Gurney scum, Treggers, and a Chanter. Your tastes never cease to astonish me."

Lord Weira gave another half bow. "This old Chanter, who I know from the past, brought them, Your Grace. She came to beg a favor."

"What favor?" asked the Duke, eyeing Bethen.

"Employment for her companions. It seems, life is growing harder beyond the estates of the High King."

"And you were prepared to see her on such a trivial matter?"

"I couldn't resist her bribe, Your Grace," replied Lord Weira, smiling as he pointed to the Bloom of Kanarki on the desk.

The Duke nodded, satisfied that corruption was the motive. He examined the bloom. "The value of this has recently increased dramatically," he said. "Did you know all the prisoners have escaped from the mines, and for the time being no more blooms are being gathered?"

"I heard a rumor, Your Grace," said Lord Weira.

The Duke nodded. "We could face a rebellion in the coming weeks. You must ensure the High King's estate has enough supplies to withstand a siege."

"I have already begun to do so," said Lord Weira.

The Duke nodded. "Always the efficient peasant, eh, Weira. What did your family do?"

"My father was a weaver, Your Grace. As you may remember, I was educated at the Royal School."

"And what a credit you have been to that splendid establishment," said the Duke, then he seemed to become bored by the conversation. "Well, I must press on," he added. "I am dining with the High King."

"I hope you have a pleasant evening, Your Grace."

The Duke swept out, and they straightened up from their bowing to listen to the receding sound of marching feet.

"Why did he call on you? Does he already suspect something?" Hunter asked.

Lord Weira shook his head. "I don't think so, Robert. This is the usual day of the week he inspects the administration building. The Great Duke has many faults but he is not lazy."

He looked at Bethen and raised his eyebrows. "You are to be congratulated on your timing, Chanter."

"I remember the way to the High King's quarters," said Hunter, tucking the pass Lord Weira had handed him into his jeweled leather jerkin.

"Give that note to Lord Aska, the High King's Chamberlain," said Weira. "He'll tell you your duties. But don't trust him, he's one of the Duke's appointments."

"If he can appoint his own people, why does the Duke allow you to survive?" asked Hunter.

Lord Weira smiled. "Putting modesty aside, I'm too useful. The working of the whole of the High King's palace would collapse if I were removed. He uses me, but he doesn't trust me."

"How many are loyal to the Duke?" asked the Prince.

Lord Weira shrugged. "I have no way of knowing. The nobles of Tallis can be fickle." He shrugged again. "Once you're inside I can be of little help. But if I can do anything — I am yours to command."

Hunter and Prince Briarre led the way to the High King's keep through a seemingly endless maze of gardens and pleasure grounds filled with strolling nobles and their servants. Many of them were accompanied by Treggers.

The grounds were brightly lit by the gas lamps that threw soft light over the ancient walls and were reflected from countless windows. There was an extraordinary variety of plants, ivy, vines, trees, and the air was heavy with the sweet smells of scented shrubs. Even at this late hour, gardeners were out tending the grounds.

As they strolled on, talking in low voices about happier times they'd spent here, Prince Briarre and Hunter unconsciously began to straighten their backs and look confident and determined, until Charto gave them a hearty slap on the back and reminded them they were supposed to be Gurneys.

Tim and Sarre were surprised to find that the High King's keep was comparatively modest: just five round towers set with battlements instead of spires. The walls were built of the same pale gold-colored stone as all the other buildings but were worn smoother by time.

It was by far the plainest building they had yet seen and was set within wide treeless lawns. Two large, curving wings supported by flying buttresses had been added to connect it to other buildings nearby. There was also a drawbridge and an old, drained, grassed-over moat.

Tethered on a short line above the five towers was a massive balloon, manned by the Duke's police. In front of the drawbridge was another, single slender tower as tall as the castle keep itself. Tim saw it was exactly the same shape as the tower on top of the Temple of the Chanters in The Crack.

"Illya lives here," said Bethen, surreptitiously passing Josh to Tim, who quickly thrust the little dog under his Tregger jerkin and buttoned it up.

"Over the centuries, the whole palace has gradually been built up around this one original building," explained Prince Briarre as they approached. "It was the fort of the first High King, my ancestor, Briarre the Bold."

Finally, they passed over the drawbridge and were confronted by more of the Duke's men, who examined the note from Lord Weira before allowing them to enter a small courtyard. Immediately in front of them loomed the central tower, which was supported by the other four towers built against it. A young man in a long surcoat descended an open staircase and approached them.

"Easy enough to get in," Hunter whispered.

"Getting out is the trick," replied the Prince.

Meeting the Lady of Tallis

"Are you the musicians?" the young man demanded petulantly. "I requested musicians for tonight."

"We are, Master," replied Charto quickly, with a sweeping gesture that included Hunter and the Prince.

"And these young Treggers are new servants for the Lady of Tallis," said Bethen. "I am here to visit the Chanter, Illya."

"I am Lord Aska, the High King's Chamberlain," said the young man, looking suspiciously at the bulge in Tim's jerkin.

"Why is this one so fat?" he asked.

Once more, Charto had the quickest wits; he was more accustomed to people questioning him in a superior manner. "He has eaten too much good Gurney food on the journey, Master. Treggers are not used to it," he said, bowing deeply.

Lord Aska nodded and snapped his fingers. Three footmen hurried forward from the shadows.

"Take these Treggers to the Lady of Tallis and the Gurneys to the minstrels' gallery," he instructed. Then he said to Charto, "Go directly to the great hall. You may begin to play immediately."

One of the footmen led Tim and Sarre off in a different direction from Hunter, Charto, and the Prince. They walked along corridors, up flights of stone stairs, and passed through chambers until they stopped before a great iron-bound door. The footman knocked and waited. A Lady-in-waiting answered.

"New Tregger servants for the Princess, Ma'am," said the footman, and departed.

"What is it, Ladia?" called a woman's voice.

The Lady-in-waiting ushered them into the chamber. It was a round stone-walled room with a pair of long windows leading to a balcony. The Lady of Tallis, wearing a pair of rimless spectacles, sat reading by candlelight at a high desk.

She looked up, removed the spectacles, and smiled when she saw Tim and Sarre. "Hello, Treggers. And to what do I owe the honor of this visit?" she asked gently.

Tim bowed and Sarre curtsied. "We are to be your new servants, Your Royal Highness," Sarre said.

The Princess frowned. "Did the Duke send you to spy on me?"

"No, Ma'am!" replied Tim hotly. "We were sent by Lord Weira. We wish only to serve you."

Now she looked concerned. "Come here," she said, holding out her hands. She took theirs and continued, "Listen to me carefully, Treggers. I am Princess Almea, the Lady of Tallis. You will be in grave danger if you serve me."

As she was speaking, Josh thrust his head out of Tim's jerkin.

"Oh!" Almea gasped. "I've seen that creature before," she said. "He is a dog from Earth. I saw him at Lord Tredore's castle. How did you come by him?"

Tim wasn't yet sure whether they were being spied on, so he took a quill pen from her desk and wrote on a sheet of parchment: *We have come with the man you call Robert Quester.*

For a moment, they thought the Princess was going to faint, but she quickly recovered and said to her Lady-in-waiting, "Play something, Ladia — make it loud."

Ladia sat at a small keyboard instrument similar to a piano. It produced more noise than Tim would have thought possible. While the racket continued, the Princess beckoned them to the balcony.

"Robert is alive?" she asked urgently.

"Yes. And he's here in the castle," replied Tim.

"As is your brother, Prince Briarre," added Sarre. "They are together. We have all come here to rescue you and the High King."

Princess Almea closed her eyes and for a moment

swayed as if she were about to fall. Then she opened her eyes and stood regally before them.

"You are sure my brother is alive?"

"Quite sure," answered Sarre. "He was imprisoned in the Duke's mines but he's free now."

"I hope you have come in time," said the Princess. "The Duke intends to execute us quite soon."

"Execute you!" cried both Tim and Sarre.

"And all those loyal to the High King," said Almea.

"But we were told the Duke can only become the rightful ruler of Tallis by marrying you, Ma'am," said Sarre.

Almea nodded. "That is so. But we also have spies. As yet, all they can tell us is that the Duke has found some way to become High King without marrying me. So, my father has been planning our escape."

Tim glanced at Sarre. "We understand the High King is unwell, Ma'am," he said.

The Princess smiled and shook her head. "He has pretended to be mad for a long time."

To Tim and Sarre's surprise, Erif suddenly appeared on the balcony and bowed to the Princess.

"We have almost completed the tunnel to the Warlock's chambers, Ma'am," he said. "We shall be able to enter it quite soon."

"We must all meet with Prince Briarre and Robert Quester," said Tim. "Is there anywhere safe in the castle?"

"What about the Killing Wind shelter?" suggested Erif.

"No one will have cause to go there now that the winds are safe."

"Where is it?" asked Sarre.

"Beneath the great hall," said Erif. "It was once a secret escape passage. They sealed it up years ago but opened it again to use as a shelter. The Duke doesn't bother to post guards, as it leads nowhere since it was blocked off."

"I will tell my father during dinner," said Almea.

"But how can you, if the Duke is there, Ma'am?" said Tim.

Almea smiled. "We have worked out a way of communicating by squeezing hands or tapping our fingers. My father and I can speak secretly at any time."

"Meanwhile, Ma'am, I will show our new friends the passageways," said the old Tregger.

Erif led them to a slightly darker part of the round wall in Almea's chamber and pressed a block of stone. A narrow crack opened, just wide enough for them to squeeze through. Sarre went first, then Tim, after pushing Josh through.

Inside, there was a narrow gap between the walls and even when the opening had closed behind Erif they could still see because the stones themselves glowed with a greenish white light.

"That must be phosphorus," said Tim, touching the glowing wall.

Erif hurried ahead, telling them as they went, "These ancient ways were made in all the castle buildings. The passages were created so Treggers could just appear whenever a noble rang a bell to call them. It meant we didn't have to walk through the usual corridors and get in the way. Gradually — some say it was because we used to play with them when they were children — the nobles came to like us more. As servants, that is."

When they came to a small recess that had shelves carved into the walls and a row of bells above them, Erif told Tim and Sarre, "This is where Treggers used to sleep in this part of the castle." Then, with a smile he said, "Are you fit? It's a long walk."

They both nodded, and Tim said, "Let's get going, then."

For nearly an hour, they trudged through the narrow, eerie corridors that branched off in all directions. Sometimes, snatches of conversation came through the walls. At one point, they could hear the clatter of a kitchen, then the sound of a soldier giving orders to other troops, and a few times, rushing water.

Finally, Erif held up a hand for them to stop, pointing ahead to where three Treggers were crouched over a Mossop Mole. The Mole was edging forward while one of the workers poured water over the cutting blades to dull the noise.

"Finished," said the one operating the machine. "Is the screen ready?"

"It's here," said another.

"We've tunneled into Stryker's workshop," whispered the Tregger operating the Mole. "And we've made a false-wall screen to hide the hole in the outer wall. While Stryker is dining with the Duke and the High King tonight, we'll break in and find out what secrets he's been working on."

"Can't we take a quick look now?" Tim asked.

"You could," replied the Tregger dubiously. "But be careful. Stryker could come in at any time."

"Can you keep Josh back here with you, please, Erif?" said Tim, before he and Sarre wriggled through the hole into the workshop.

The room was massive, at least a hundred paces square, and there were no windows. But it was brightly lit with gas mantles. Everything was extraordinarily neat. There were row upon row of workbenches, each one dedicated to a different activity.

One bench was entirely loaded with huge glass jars filled with various minerals; another was piled high with manuscripts. On some there were strange bottles in which wild creatures had been preserved in clear liquid. In one corner of the vast room there was something deeply disturbing: bodies of Treggers and normal-sized people were hanging from rows of hooks.

For a horrifying moment, Tim and Sarre thought they were real bodies, but on closer inspection they realized the lifelike figures were made of a waxlike substance that looked very much like flesh. Some had open compartments in their chests, revealing intricate clockwork mechanisms.

One figure of an archer had most of its outer body covering removed, which revealed its extraordinary inner workings.

"Automatons!" Tim murmured.

"What did you say?" whispered Sarre.

"*Automatons.* That's what clockwork figures are called."

Tim and Sarre were standing next to a large coffin-shaped box that stood upright and was made of rough branches of wood. In front of them, a large sheet of silk covered what was obviously two seated figures.

Just as they were about to lift the sheet, the door across the room opened, and they heard the sound of voices. Looking about desperately, Tim opened the rough-hewn coffin lid. It was just big enough for him and Sarre to squeeze into.

"I think you will be pleased, Your Grace," said a voice they both recognized.

Peering through gaps in the lid, Tim and Sarre watched breathlessly as the Duke came unerringly toward their hiding place. The Warlock Stryker tapped the figure of the archer, saying, "You may recall, I managed to bring this creation of Joseph Mossop's back from the Forest of the Southern Rim. It was just such automatons that made up the infamous ghost army of legend. I examined it in great detail and discovered the secret of how Mossop created those lifelike figures." Stryker sniggered. "Something of a paradox, since the figures were supposed to be *ghosts*."

"Get on with it," snapped the Duke.

Stryker turned to the shrouded figures and pulled away

the material to reveal astonishingly good replicas of the High King and the Lady of Tallis.

The Duke examined them intently, slowly nodding his head. Then he said, "They look like the real thing, Warlock — but will they work properly this time?"

"I am confident, Your Grace," said Stryker. "Not only have I worked out how to make these figures move like the people they represent, I have actually excelled Mossop in another way."

"What is that?"

"I can take the minds from living beings, control them, then put them into my mechanical figures."

"You're sure?" said the Duke, with rising excitement. "These dolls must obey my every order."

Stryker waved a hand toward his wax figures. "Command them, Your Grace. First, you must use the word *tarus* for the woman and *nagun* for the man. When you no longer require them, you say, *drogo*."

The Duke stood before the seated figure of the Lady of Tallis.

"Order her to kiss me," he said.

"She will obey *your* command, Your Grace," said Stryker. "Just use the word I told you; it will activate the mechanism."

"*Tarus*, I am your Lord and Master," said the Duke. "I order you to kiss me."

The waxen replica of the Lady of Tallis rose to its feet, arms outstretched.

"You are my Lord and Master," it said, and putting its arms firmly about the Duke's neck, it kissed him.

The Duke attempted to wriggle free but the figure held him in an unbreakable embrace. Finally, he managed to mutter, "Sit down! *Drogo!*"

The automaton released the Duke and he spun away, wiping his mouth.

"Agh! She tastes horrible," he complained. "And she's as strong as a Gurney's pig."

"I'm sorry, Your Grace. I didn't know you would want it to kiss you. The unpleasant taste is the special resin I used to cast the figures."

"Well, I shan't need it to do that again, so it doesn't matter."

"When will Your Grace execute the real Royal Family?" asked Stryker.

"I've given that some thought," said the Duke with sudden enthusiasm. "The business can only be observed by the most trusted of my men. Killing a king is a serious matter, you know. Even some of those who favor me would hesitate at such an act. At dawn tomorrow, I shall have ten of my best men stationed on the battlements to ward off unwanted witnesses. I shall personally execute the pair — you may watch, if you wish — then we shall spirit their bodies away in the punishment balloon tethered there.

"The men onboard the balloon will be trustworthy. They will bring it down in deserted countryside and dispose of the bodies. I shall then conduct a brief marriage ceremony using your mechanical figures. People will watch from a respectful distance, thinking they are seeing the real High King and Princess. Then there will be a tragic accident in which the High King and his daughter will perish, leaving *me* as the grieving husband and absolute ruler of Tallis."

"Brilliant, Your Grace. Simple and effective. Like all the best plans."

"Yes, I think so," said the Duke thoughtfully. "It would have given me great pleasure to torture them first but speed is of the essence in this plan. We know Prince Briarre and his companions have escaped and are bound to be on their way here. By the time they arrive, I intend to be installed as High King and ready to destroy them."

He slapped Stryker on the back. "Well, all this has given me an appetite for dinner. Just think of it," he sighed, "the last time I shall have to endure that idiotic old man's company and the arrogance of his detestable daughter."

As the workshop door slammed behind the Duke and his Warlock, Tim and Sarre leaped out of the coffin and hurried back to the hole behind the screen.

"Did you hear them?" Sarre asked the Treggers.

"Every word," Erif replied, and they raced back through the tunnels.

CHAPTER 32

The High King's Plan

Erif led Tim and Sarre through the Tregger passages that led to the minstrels' gallery above the dining hall. They could hear the High King and his guests talking loudly below them. It was easy for Tim and Sarre to edge up behind Hunter, Charto, and Prince Briarre and whisper to them as they continued to serenade the gathering of nobles.

Tim told them of the conversation they'd just overheard and of the Duke's intention to murder the High King and the Lady of Tallis at dawn. Then Tim and Sarre withdrew to hide elsewhere in the dark shadows of the minstrels' gallery to wait until the banquet ended.

It was clear from their behavior that the three other nobles accompanying the Duke and Stryker at the banquet below were not loyal to the High King. They leaned forward, listening to every word the Great Duke spoke, and laughed ingratiatingly at the barbed comments he made about the High King's childish antics. When they did speak, they left the High King and his daughter out of the conversation, acting as if they were already dead.

Finally, the Duke, barely bothering to nod to the High King and the Lady of Tallis, announced to his oafish companions that it was time to leave as the evening had grown tiresome.

When the unwelcome guest had departed, Sarre and Tim looked through the rails of the gallery and watched the High King. Earlier, he had been capering about the room with a candlestick balanced on his head, but now he slumped into his chair and rubbed his face with both hands. In doing so, it was as if he had erased the simple grinning mask, and a wiser, sadder face had taken its place. The Lady of Tallis was looking desperately about the great hall as the servants cleared the last of the tables.

"Are they all gone?" the High King called out softly when the last servant had departed.

"All clear, Your Majesty," answered a Tregger, and several of the little people emerged out of the shadows from where they were keeping watch on all the approaches to the hall.

"Robert! Robert!" the Lady of Tallis called as she rose to her feet, her voice breaking with emotion.

"Is it true?" said the High King, scarcely able to believe his ears. "Is my son really here with Robert Quester?"

Prince Briarre, Charto, and Hunter were already hurrying down the stairs from the gallery, carrying their Gurney instruments.

"It is true, Father," the Prince replied, running to embrace the High King, while Princess Almea ran across the wide banquet hall to fling herself into Hunter's arms.

"Isn't it wonderful?" Sarre murmured to Tim as they came down the stairs. "Have you ever seen anything so romantic?"

Tim shook his head. "She's probably never seen Hunter in one of his grumpy moods," he replied.

"Into the wind shelter, Your Majesties, I beg you," said Erif, lifting the trapdoor in the stone floor. Heeding the Tregger's plea, they all hurried down into the storm cellar. It was a dry musty place, the walls decorated with ancient weapons.

Josh was excited to see the High King, too. He kept jumping up to be patted and have his stomach tickled as Tim and Sarre told them what they had learned.

"Automatons that looked like me and Almea, you say?" said the King when they had finished.

"Exactly like you, Your Majesty," said Tim.

The King nodded. "You know, I would rather like to see them," he said, reaching out to take a double-headed battle-ax from the wall. "This belonged to my ancestor, Briarre the Bold," he said raising the ax. "I was taught how to use it in my youth."

"Your Majesty, we understand you had a plan of escape," said Hunter. "May we hear it?"

The High King shrugged. "I did have a plan, Robert, but recent events have made part of it redundant. My original intention was to wait until the next Killing Wind came and seize the balloon that hovers over the battlements of the main tower. We had masks strong enough to withstand the heaviest clouds of killing spores. But I'm told the Killing Winds have ceased. Besides which, we haven't yet solved the main problem."

"What is that, Father?" asked Prince Briarre.

The High King shrugged. "Pursuit, of course. The Duke has the best battle birds in the kingdom tethered next to his guardhouse. Even if we did escape, they could easily catch up with the balloon."

"Why not escape on battle birds then?" suggested Tim.

"Impossible," said Almea. "There are always soldiers stationed next to the battle bird cages. They are guarded constantly."

"But suppose the soldiers were called away," said Sarre.

"Only the Duke could do that," said the High King.

"And how would he do it?" asked Sarre.

"He would have them summoned with a special call from his battle trumpeter, of course."

"What makes the call special?" asked Tim.

"You couldn't imitate it, if that's what you're thinking," said the High King, shaking his head. "It takes years to train a battle trumpeter; the skills are passed from father to son. The point is, no one can copy the Duke's fanfare."

"What we need is a diversion that would cause the Duke himself to order the call to be sounded," said Hunter.

There was a silence, until Sarre said, "Tim has a brilliant idea."

"Do I?" said Tim, surprised. "How do you know?"

"Because I read your mind," she answered.

"I hope you don't do that all the time." Tim started to blush.

"Just tell them your idea, Tim," Sarre said.

"Well, it will need very fine timing," he began slowly as the idea continued to form in his mind. "We'll need the help of Treggers and, somehow, we must steal *all* of the battle birds; otherwise the Duke's men will be able to pursue us. And we'll need to overcome the guards on the battlements near the balloon. Could we do that?"

"Robert and I can overcome the soldiers guarding the balloon," said Prince Briarre.

"How will we steal *all* the battle birds?" asked Almea.

"Don't worry, I shall take care of the battle birds," said Charto.

"How?" asked Hunter.

"Never mind. Trust me, I am the greatest stealer of chickens in the Kingdom of Tallis," said Charto, grinning in anticipation.

* * *

Faint yellow streaks touched with pink were lightening the western sky as the Duke strode from his personal apartments and glanced briefly at his escort of carefully chosen men. As the company marched toward the High King's keep the Duke was so happy he was humming a tune.

"At last," he said to the Warlock Stryker, who strode beside him, "this is my day of destiny."

"I am honored to be with you on such an occasion, Your Grace," said the Warlock, glancing about warily. "There are fewer guards than usual," he noted.

"The fewer witnesses there are to these events the better," replied the Duke as they entered the High King's keep.

A captain of police flanked by six archers and the Duke's trumpeter leaped to attention.

"Rouse the High King and the Lady of Tallis and bring them to the roof of the tallest tower immediately," ordered the Duke.

The captain looked uncertain. "Your Grace," he said nervously, "the High King and the Princess are already up there."

"*What?*" snapped the Duke. "Follow me. On the double!" he commanded and began running up the stone steps several at a time, with Stryker and the guards close on his heels.

The Duke and his men emerged on the battlements of the tower to find the guards lying unconscious. There was evidence of a struggle. One of their charcoal braziers was overturned, its embers scattered about.

Immediately, the Duke looked up and saw the smiling

figures of the High King and the Lady of Tallis looking down on him from the basket slung beneath the balloon.

"Secure the balloon," shouted the Duke. "Trumpeter, summon the main guard."

But as the strange wailing trumpet call echoed from the tower, the High King raised his battle-ax and hacked through the cable with a single stroke. The gentle wind caught the balloon, and it drifted away toward the north with the royal couple waving a regal farewell.

A bitter bile of rage rose in the Duke's throat. "Bring the balloon down," he roared.

"How, Your Grace?" stuttered the captain of police.

"Use fire arrows, you imbecile," the Duke shouted.

The first arrows went wide of the mark.

Stryker flashed the Duke a warning look, and he quickly controlled his temper. His anger was now cold and determined.

"Steady yourselves!" he commanded. "Fire a spreading volley at my command. Are you ready?"

"Ready, Your Grace," snapped the archers.

"Fire!" shouted the Duke.

The volley of arrows rose into the sky, their flames brilliant against the remaining dark, and curved down onto the canopy of the balloon. For a moment, nothing happened. Then a great flame engulfed the balloon, releasing charred floating leaves to rise up into the air as the balloon plunged toward earth. The bodies of the High King and the Lady of Tallis tumbled down and smashed on the flag-stones of a garden pathway, just as the main guard arrived.

The Duke raced down the steps of the tower. "Recover the bodies and bring them to me in my private apartment," he said, stalking away.

"Yes, Your Grace," the police captain called after him.

"Your *Majesty*!" corrected the Duke coldly, glancing back at the distant crumpled forms.

Charto, Tim, and Sarre crept toward the lines where the nobles' battle birds were preening themselves in preparation for greeting the dawn. There were ten guards on duty.

But at the sound of the Duke's trumpet call the guard-house doors burst open. Soldiers streamed out, running toward the tower. The men guarding the battle birds joined them, leaving behind only the three grooms who were filling the feeding troughs.

"Quickly now!" said Charto. "The coast is clear."

Tim, Charto, and Sarre dashed toward the rows of cages.

The startled grooms fled when Charto shook his fist at them. As he hurried forward, Charto took a tiny dark green bottle out of his waistcoat pocket and uncorked it. Sarre and Tim could smell the heavy muskiness of the scent as he smeared it on his hands before entering the first cage of fighting cockerels.

Tim and Sarre watched nervously as Charto went to

work. The birds darted glances about, looking proud and dangerous in the early light. Their beaks and spurs could kill the Gurney with a single blow.

"Easy, my beauty," Charto crooned as he ran his hand over the first battle bird's back. Quickly, he did the same to each in turn.

"Start saddling them," he hissed to Tim and Sarre. "This is the one for me," he added. "What higher achievement than to steal the battle bird of the Great Duke?"

After throwing open the rows of cages, Charto, Tim, and Sarre mounted their chosen birds.

"The rest will follow me because of the scent," shouted Charto. "Head for the meeting place."

They soared into the air, Charto turning in a half-circle with all the freed battle birds following, their great wings beating the air.

Had the Duke arrived on the rooftop of the tower only a few seconds earlier, he would have seen Hunter and the Prince climbing over the battlements, after they had disposed of the guards. They'd slid together down a spider-yarn rope to the grassy moat below, then raced into the great courtyard where the real High King and the Lady of Tallis waited in hiding with Josh.

Minutes later, Charto, Tim, and Sarre landed their stolen battle birds, while the mighty flock of the Duke's liberated birds hovered overhead.

"Where's the Duke?" Charto asked, forgetting the usual formalities.

"In his apartment. We watched him storm off after they destroyed the balloon," said Almea.

Suddenly, the courtyard was filling with battle birds coming in to land.

"There are saddled mounts for us all," Charto shouted. "These other birds will follow us."

Within minutes the escape party soared into the air. Backs to the wind, they headed south for the castle of Lord Tredore with the rest of the flock trailing behind them.

Smiling with satisfaction, Bethen and Illya watched the flight of the High King and his rescuers from a window in Illya's tower.

"Hurry, now, Illya," said Bethen. "Have you got all your possessions?"

"Already loaded up," said Illya, but then she paused. "Oh, dear, I nearly forgot something precious." She opened a secret cupboard and took out a large roll of parchment. "We mustn't leave this behind."

Bethen sighed. "Hurry," she said.

In the Duke's private apartment, two of the archers had just laid the broken clockwork figures of the High King and Almea at the Great Duke's feet. He was at the window, watching in fury as the great flock of battle birds followed the escaping royal party.

"No more shall I hesitate," he hissed as he turned away and kicked the pathetic mechanical figures that the Treggers had stolen from Stryker's workshop well before dawn. "*No more!*" he roared. "Now it's war!"

He strode angrily away from the smashed automatons, shouting, "Captain, kill the old Chanters!"

"*Kill the Chanters*, Your Grace?" he gasped, appalled.

"Yes, *kill them*," insisted the Duke. "They can send thought messages to the outside. I want them silenced."

"As you wish, Your Grace."

"And call all my staff officers. There will be a council of war in my headquarters in half an hour." Then, to Stryker, he said, "Warlock, prepare your most dreadful weapons. The army moves at nightfall."

"Where to, My Lord?" asked the Captain.

"They have only one place of sanctuary from me," replied the Duke. "Tredore Castle."

"Give me your sword," Stryker ordered the police captain as they hurried away from the Duke's apartment. "I'll get rid of Bethen and Illya for you."

Relieved to have relinquished responsibility for killing two Chanters, the police captain followed the Warlock as he strode across the grass quadrangle toward Illya's tower.

But before they reached it, they heard a low buzzing noise, then the doors of an old stable block burst open. The High King's pigless carriage came hurtling out toward them, its gleaming, dark blue paint glittering in the sunlight.

Both Chanters wore goggles and long high-collared dust coats. Bethen was driving. Piled in the seat behind them were Illya's possessions: trunks, scrolls, and several large leather-bound books.

Stryker and the police guards scattered as the extraordinary machine swerved violently to sweep through their ranks, hooting loudly. As it did so, the roll of parchment Illya had nearly forgotten bounced out of the carriage and fell at Stryker's feet.

"After them!" he screamed.

"But all of the battle birds have escaped, Sir!" cried the Captain. "And no cavalry pig is fast enough to catch that machine."

Speechless with rage, Stryker stood shaking his fist at it. Fighting to control his temper, he picked up the scroll at his feet and opened it. His eyes widened in sudden comprehension, and a look of malevolent cunning spread across the Warlock's gaunt features. The escaping Chanters forgotten, he dismissed the guards with orders to prepare for the war council and hurried away to report to the Duke.

CHAPTER 33

The Siege of Tredore Castle

Months had passed since the High King's escape from the palace. Tim and Sarre, who were now serving in the High King's forces, crouched on firing steps on each side of a landing port within the great walls of Tredore Castle. Beneath them was a desolate scene.

The Great Duke's mighty army had besieged the castle and devastated the countryside around them. Acres of trees had been chopped down to build war engines, the moat drained away by the Duke's men and filled with rubble so they could wheel vast attack towers up against the walls.

The defenders had built tunnels from inside the castle

so they could undermine the Duke's huge catapults that hurled boulders against their defenses. The meadows had been churned to mud and the nearby rivers and streams fouled by thousands of attacking troops. The stench of decay was everywhere.

In the last weeks, Tim and Sarre's Tregger disguises had slowly worn off and they had returned to their usual shape and size. From their position on the firing steps, they were watching a desperate fight as Hunter and Prince Briarre, mounted on fighting cockerels, ran the Duke's blockade of fighting transporters that were circling the castle. Their birds twisted and turned to avoid the arrows of the Duke's pursuit troops, who were mounted on gigantic blackbirds. Hunter and the Prince dived toward the landing port, making their final approach.

"Ready," Tim shouted, and the company of archers he commanded drew their bows. Sarre was using her Chanter powers to detect any unforeseen dangers.

"Fire!" Tim shouted, as first the Prince, then Hunter, hurtled through the port and the blackbirds wheeled away. Four of the pursuing cavalry were wounded and three toppled to their deaths before they could fly out of range.

Hunter and the Prince dismounted next to the landing port and grooms mounted their battle birds to fly them down to ground level. Tim and Sarre hurried along the ramparts to go with Hunter and the Prince to the Royal Box, which was now serving as the High King's headquarters. Lord Tredore and the High King were standing with Princess Almea in front of a large map of Tallis. They looked relieved to see the two men as they entered.

Hunter and the Prince both shook their heads. They looked exhausted after their three-day scouting mission. Almea quickly hugged her husband, then reached for a pitcher and poured ale into two pewter mugs. The Prince and Hunter drank greedily.

"Is it true? Did you find out if the Duke has brought up a trained fighting hawk?" asked Tredore.

"It's true," said the Prince. "We only just managed to escape. We won't next time. It's much faster than our battle birds. Hawks are the future of warfare."

"What else did you learn?" asked the High King.

"Lord Renta's army is finished," said the Prince, with a nod of thanks to his sister as he put down the empty tankard.

"Is there nothing left of his forces?" asked Lord Tredore bleakly.

Hunter shook his head and took a deep draft of ale. He jabbed at the map. "The northern Lords loyal to the High King rallied at Renta's estate. They were going to march here in force, expecting to find the Duke laying siege. But the Duke, instead of attacking Tredore immediately, smashed them first in a surprise attack. He cut them to pieces."

"And what about Lord Nachua's force?" asked the High King, naming the other great army that had been expected to come and help defend Tredore Castle.

"He was coming by sea with his army," said the Prince.

"But a great storm scattered the fleet along the whole of the eastern coast. They'll be here eventually, but it's taken weeks for them to gather their forces together again."

As he spoke, Charto entered. "They're about to —" he began, but a great thudding crash suddenly shook the walls of the building.

"The siege machine?" asked Lord Tredore.

Charto nodded. "They've repaired it again. But they don't know it's sitting almost on top of one of our mines. As soon as the Mossop Mole is back I shall lead a raiding party. Will you give covering fire from the west wall?"

"I shall command the detachment personally, Charto," said Lord Tredore.

Charto saluted and was about to depart when the High King called his name.

"Majesty?" replied the Gurney.

The High King stood up and looked Charto in the eyes. "I have not had an opportunity to say this before, but I want to thank you for your bravery and loyalty throughout this siege."

"I am honored, Majesty," replied Charto, bowing his head.

"No, Charto," replied the High King. "It is *I* who am honored. Your people have not always enjoyed the respect you deserve in Tallis. It would be understandable if you had chosen not to take part in this war at all. Instead, you fight with gallantry for a people who have done little to deserve your loyalty. Your service will never be forgotten."

Tim felt as if half a lifetime had passed. In Tallis he'd found the meaning of true friendship, conquered his shyness, fought in a war, and met Sarre, who would never leave his heart.

Tim slipped into his grandparents' house and quietly climbed the stairs to his bedroom. He slowly took off the suit made for him by the tailor in Milchen and hid it, until he should need it again, at the bottom of his clothes chest. Then, with Josh at his feet, he sank gratefully into his bed and fell asleep wondering how he was going to convince the people of Enton that they could once more grow flowers.

Charto smiled at the compliment. "It is a pity the rest of my tribe cannot be here, Majesty. They hate the Duke more than anyone. With such friends we might drive this scum away."

"How many Gurney men are in the Forest of the Southern Rim?" asked Hunter.

Charto shrugged, "More than two thousand."

"We could never get word to them now that the Duke has brought a war hawk into the battle," said Lord Tredore.

Just then, an urgent drum roll and the shout, "Alarm! Alarm! Attack on the north wall," sent them running to the fighting balcony, the High King leading the way.

"They've taken advantage of a wind change," shouted a captain. "Look, they're sending more Killing Balloons against us."

The north wall was where the Duke's forces had made their most ferocious assaults and where he continued to batter them hardest with his siege engines.

"These must surely be the last of the balloons they have," shouted Hunter. "Masks on, lads, be prepared for boarders."

Although the wind from the north no longer killed, the Warlock Stryker had cultivated his own supply of the deadly spores and contained them in gigantic glass vessels. He'd also constructed vast, fireproof balloons. Their tactics were to fly the balloons at the castle, hurl the glass jars of killing spores onto the defenders, then launch an attack with assault troops from the boatlike containers dangling below the giant balloons.

The defenders were all brave men but they dreaded the killing jars. Strong leadership was needed to stop them from running in the face of such an attack.

"Masks on," shouted the Prince and Hunter.

"Fight hard, my boys," shouted the High King, before donning his own mask and clasping his ancestor's battle-ax with both hands.

Lord Tredore raised his arm. "Red company!" he shouted. "Give covering fire to Captain Charto's men below, they are about to attack the siege engine at the west wall. Gold company! Stand by to repel the balloons."

The fighting was long and hard before the balloons were finally driven off. Charto's troops had burst out through the Mossop Mole's tunnel and partially destroyed the siege machine. It was dark now, and they could hear the sound of Stryker's engineers at work repairing the huge weapon.

Sarre and Tim had joined the royal party for a meal in the war room. The food was no more than black bread, vegetable stew, and a few withered pieces of fruit.

After eating in silence, the High King pushed aside his plate and said, "It is time we planned a breakout."

"They would smash us to pieces, Your Majesty," said Lord Tredore.

"There is no alternative," said the High King briskly.

"Even if Lord Renta's men had arrived in time, our forces would still not have been enough to defeat the Duke. We have gambled and lost. I shall stay in the castle. But I order my son to fight his way out and take refuge in the Forest of the Southern Rim."

"I cannot go, Father," said Prince Briarre.

"You *must*," replied the High King angrily. "If you do not, our family line is finished. If you live, you will be a symbol for the people of Tallis to rally around."

Tim stood up. "May I speak, Your Majesty?"

The High King nodded.

"A *man* mounted on a battle bird couldn't outrun a fighting hawk, but Sarre and I might. We are much lighter. If we went on two birds, and without armor, we'd stand more chance, even if the Duke's men brought one of us down. We could each take a bird and slip out at night while you staged a diversion. When we find Charto's men in the Forest of the Southern Rim, we can join them up with Lord Nachua's army. We could beat the Duke yet."

Tredore shook his head sadly. "A brave thought, Tim, but it would take months to march an army from the Forest of the Southern Rim. By which time it will be all over here. The walls will have finally crumbled and we'll be finished. The only way is for the Prince to break out."

Tim persisted. "It would take more than a month if an army were marching. But Sarre and I have another idea."

Quickly, he outlined what they had planned.

The High King slowly nodded his head. "It might work.

It's highly original and simple, too. But how will you find Lord Nachua's army?"

"We already know where it is, Your Majesty," said Sarre. "Bethen and Illya are with them. They escaped from your castle and they are on the coast with the scattered fleet."

"Sometimes I forget you are a Chanter, child," said the High King with a weary smile.

"With your permission, we'll leave tonight," said Tim.

The High King stood up. "Lord Nachua is brave but he is also boneheaded. He would never accept the word of a boy, especially a commoner. Kneel down," he ordered Tim, and drawing his sword the High King tapped him once on each shoulder.

"Arise, Sir Timothy, Lord of Enton and Brother of the Dragon."

As Tim stood up, the High King took a ring from his own finger. "This was given to me by my father when I entered the Brotherhood of the Dragon," said the High King. "Wear it and even Lord Nachua will pay attention to you."

Tim and Sarre stood on the battlements looking over the massive lines of the Duke's army. A city of tents and camp-fires was spread out in all directions on the churned-up field below them. Well out of arrow range, men swarmed over the mighty siege engine, repairing it for the following day's attack. It was cold in the night air — autumn had long since given way to winter — and by morning a hard frost would have whitened the ground.

"Are you ready?" asked Charto, who had personally selected the battle birds they would ride. They had dispensed with all protection, even their saddle straps, to make themselves as light as possible.

"Yes," they answered.

"Sarre," Charto said, "be sure to watch your bird's beak, he doesn't like to be pulled to the right. Be firm."

"I shall be, Charto."

The Gurney leaned forward and kissed her forehead. "If I had a daughter I would want her to be just like you." Then he gripped Tim warmly by the shoulder and patted Josh whose head was poking out of Tim's surcoat.

In turn, Hunter, Princess Almea, and Prince Briarre embraced Sarre. When Hunter came to Tim, he shook his hand. "To think I didn't want to bring you," he said, trying to smile. Then he reached out and hugged him, saying, "Stay sharp, Tim. There's a long way to go."

From the battle positions on the far side of the castle, a cluster of fire arrows rained down on the nearest of the Duke's positions. A roar went up as a raiding party rushed from a gate, creating the diversion.

"Now!" said Charto, slapping each of the battle birds, and Tim and Sarre soared up into the dark night.

CHAPTER 34

Pursued by a Fighting Hawk

Their mounts heading into the wind, Tim and Sarre beat on through the night sky, heading south. Sarre was flying straight for the Forest of the Southern Rim to find the Gurneys, while Tim made for Lord Nachua's forces on the coast to negotiate a rendezvous of these two armies.

Tim began to think he'd succeeded in getting beyond the Duke's blockade, but as dawn came he saw one massive bird in pursuit — a fighting hawk! — far greater in size and strength than his own battle bird. Tim took a moment to steady his heartbeat. Then, looking back, he saw the hawk steadily climbing on a rising wind thermal to make its attack from a greater height.

It had no rider! The hawk would make its own decision when to begin its descent for the kill. Tim knew what to expect. When the hawk was ready to attack, it would snap its wings shut and hurtle down like an arrow, then suddenly spread its wings to brake the dive so it could snatch its prey in its talons.

Tim scanned the countryside ahead as light began to flood across the rolling plain. Far to the east he could see the faint blue line of the sea. Farther down the coast was the fishing village of Gulla, where Lord Nachua had set up his headquarters in order to rally his scattered forces.

The hawk was still climbing in anticipation of its attack, but the strong wind aided Tim. He'd thought of luring the hawk down to within range of Lord Nachua's archers or even into the sails of a windmill, but each scheme was impractical. Then another idea came to him.

His timing would have to be perfect, Tim thought, as he leaned forward to allow his battle bird to gradually lose height. They flew on across the countryside and Tim could soon see details of Lord Nachua's encampment.

A fleet of sailing boats under repair lay drawn up on the shelving shingle beach. From their battered condition and broken masts, Tim could see the severity of the storm they'd endured. But there was now a vast army camping beyond the dunes. The tallest tents told Tim where Lord Nachua's headquarters lay.

Swooping low over the camp, Tim saw everyone was looking up, some pointing to the hawk that was almost directly above Tim and obviously about to attack. Skimming the tents, Tim flew low over the village and along the beach. Then he rose in the stirrups to urge his bird on.

"Neck down, boy. Low as you can go."

The battle bird stretched out its lowered head and Tim steered it in to glide under the fishermen's spider-yarn nets that were raised up from the beach to dry. They formed a canopy above his head.

"Stop!" shouted Tim.

The cockerel spread its wings and came to a stock-still halt.

Overhead, the hawk had closed its wings and dived, but even its keen eyes hadn't detected the incredibly fine nets. Too late, the terrifying bird opened its wings to brake its dive, but within inches of Tim's head, its talons became hopelessly entangled in the nets.

Almost instantly, Tim and the hawk were surrounded by fishermen and soldiers, some with weapons raised.

"Stop! Don't kill the hawk!" Tim shouted. "We may be able to retrain it for ourselves."

Extracting himself, Tim asked a captain to care for his battle bird. "Feed and water him, please," he instructed. "I have to leave almost immediately. But first I must speak with your leader, Lord Nachua, I have a message from the High King."

Tim hurried along between two soldiers who were

escorting him to Lord Nachua's tent. A tall, red-faced man dressed in armor stood waiting as Tim approached. Unfortunately, he was not one of the Lords who had been rescued from the caves of Kanarki. Tim could see none of those Lords who would have recognized him.

Even before Tim could bow, Lord Nachua was shouting, "Who gave you permission to endanger my headquarters with that foolhardy trick, boy?"

Tim held out his hand, and the ring presented to him by the High King silenced the fuming Lord. "I am Lord Enton," he said. "I have orders from the High King."

"Orders? What orders?" snapped Lord Nachua. "Are they in writing? I must have written orders." He was unnerved by Tim's arrival and didn't want to make the wrong decision.

"You must march to Tredore Castle immediately," said Tim. "Once there, you will unite with an irregular Gurney force. Then, press home an attack to relieve the High King."

Lord Nachua looked around him and laughed nervously.

"Am I to take orders from a boy?" he asked no one in particular. "Suppose it's a trick."

To Tim's relief, Bethen and Illya emerged from a nearby tent. He was about to speak but Bethen held up a hand for him to be quiet.

"May I be of service, My Lord?" Bethen asked. "I could read the mind of this young man for you."

"Will you, Chanter?" Lord Nachua pleaded. "But be careful, he may be a spy."

Bethen winked reassuringly at Tim as she placed a hand

on his head. Then she looked up at Lord Nachua. "Your caution is most wise, My Lord," she said.

"It is?" said Nachua.

"Certainly. But this lad does have a message from the High King. If you bring quill and parchment I will be able to dictate it from his mind. It will be a direct written instruction from the High King."

"Written instructions. Excellent!" said Nachua gratefully. "Let it be done."

Tim snatched the pen, and Bethen whispered, "Slowly, slowly," then continued to murmur to him as Tim wrote down exactly what Nachua was to do.

"Here, My Lord," said Bethen, handing the parchment to Lord Nachua. "The High King has even drawn you a map. How clever you were to insist on this."

With written instructions clutched in his hand, Lord Nachua became the warlord. "The army marches within the hour," he commanded. "Carry light equipment only. The baggage train will follow. Each man to carry two days' rations and extra supplies of arrows. Captains, you have your orders, strike camp!"

A cheer went up all around the camp and Lord Nachua waved to his men as if the battle was already won.

"He's brave enough when he's fighting," said Bethen softly as they walked through the bustling camp. "Just timid when it comes to thinking."

"Not like me," said Tim. "People used to say I was timid about everything."

Bethen laughed. "Not anymore, Lord Enton," she said.

Tim realized she was right. It was sometime since he'd felt in awe of anyone.

"Hunter told me some things change as they come through a starway, Bethen," he replied. "Do you think it could it have made me braver?"

Bethen shook her head, "No, Tim. You were always brave; you just didn't know it. The hardest discoveries we make are always the ones about ourselves."

"How did you escape from the Duke?" Tim asked Bethen as they walked toward the groom who was holding his battle bird.

"In the High King's pigless carriage," she answered. "We reached Lord Nachua's army in it, but then I'm afraid we lost it in the storm when our ship went down. And poor Illya lost all her belongings, too."

"I wish I had time to hear that story, but I must go," said Tim as he mounted his battle bird.

"Sarre has found the Gurneys," said Bethen. "I received a message from her. You will see where they are when you reach the Forest of the Southern Rim."

The wind had changed by the time Tim set off, and he was able to travel faster as he headed south. On and on over rolling countryside he flew, the cockerel straining at its bit as they soared toward their destination. Tim recognized the ground they were passing over: to the west lay the smoking chimneys of Milchen, then there was the rich countryside that led to the Forest of the Southern Rim.

The forest soon spread out beneath him. As it was winter the mighty living trees were bare, but there was still a line of reddish gold across the horizon. The silvery reflection of the river came into view, then he saw a great star made of silk laid out on the treetops. Tim reined back the battle bird and they slowly descended into a huge Gurney encampment, but there were hardly any men left in it.

He found Sarre with two of the Gurney elders, fierce, heavily armed old men.

"I've seen Lord Nachua," Tim told Sarre after greeting the Gurneys. "His army is already on the march to Tredore Castle."

"The Treggers and the Gurney army have already gone to the petrified trees, as we planned," Sarre told him. "We hung on here to wait for you."

"What about the sails?" asked Tim.

Sarre nodded. "The Tregger river sailors are making them. They're going to act as crew and helmsmen."

Tim nodded and looked at the Gurney elders. "Those two can share our battle birds."

"I'm ready to go," answered Sarre.

Within minutes, they were above the forest with Tim and Sarre's birds each carrying an extra passenger. The fierce old warriors were shouting and pointing things out to each other, obviously relishing the breathtaking ride.

With the wind blowing to their advantage, and urging their birds on to their greatest speed, they flew, skimming the treetops, faster than ever before.

Soon, they saw the precipice on the horizon and instead of bare-branched trees in shades of gray and brown they began to pass over enormous red-and-gold–leafed trees.

Great silk arrows had been laid on the treetops pointing to where the Gurneys and Treggers were gathered.

"This way," shouted Sarre, altering the direction of her battle bird's flight.

Tim followed her down into the forest and, again, he was astonished by the sheer size of the trees. Finally, they saw a party of Treggers working to attach lines and an enormous sheet of silk to the outer branches of a specially selected tree. As they flew lower, they found the operation being repeated again and again the farther they traveled down the mighty trunk.

Tim judged they were no more than a third of the way down the full height of the tree, when they reached teams of Gurneys cutting through its trunk with diamond-edged saws.

They landed amid the branches and found Luxo supervising one of the teams of cutters. "Nearly through it," he said as Tim and Sarre dismounted and climbed along the great branch. Luxo picked up a fragment of the wood and said, "Incredible stuff, isn't it? So strong, but really quite light."

He held out the piece of petrified wood. "You see all

the tiny holes in it? Though it's no weight at all, no ordinary knife could cut through it."

"The last part of the trunk is almost cut through," called out the leader of one of the working teams.

"But there's still no wind to the north," said Sarre.

"It'll come," said Luxo confidently.

"What about the Gurney army?" asked Tim anxiously.

"They're already aboard," said Luxo, raising his eyes and pointing upward.

Sarre and Tim quickly ordered their birds to roost, then settled themselves on the huge branch, their arms wrapped securely around a smaller one.

"She's free!" came a sudden shout as the whole top third of the great petrified tree began to rise up through the forest.

Higher and higher it rose, buffeting against the other trees with an occasional crack of snapping branches, but all the time gaining speed.

"And here comes the wind!" a Gurney voice yelled as Tim and Sarre felt the first breezy gust.

Suddenly, the vast treetop freed itself from the surrounding forest and soared into the sky. A great roar of cheers and shouts of triumph went up from the Gurneys in the branches above Tim and Sarre. The wind filled the enormous silk sails that the Treggers had rigged to the tree's branches, causing it to topple forward and sail like a mighty ship over the great forest toward the north.

The wind blew harder and the extraordinary vessel ran

before it like a great clipper. The Gurneys were wild with the thrill of it and cheered boisterously as the Treggers trimmed the sails. Josh looked out of Tim's jerkin briefly but decided it was a mite too windy for him and nestled back down till it was all over.

It was an incredible sight — a vast tree sailing through the sky. It may only have been the top third of the mighty tree but even that was breathtakingly enormous.

An alarming thought suddenly occurred to Tim.

"How are we going to stop?" he shouted to Sarre above the rushing sound of the gale.

Making their way forward, they found the Tregger who was in charge of the sails. Tim remembered him from his first journey on the river.

"How are you going to stop, Captain?" Sarre yelled.

The Tregger was shouting orders to his yeoman, who was constantly ordering changes in the trim on the sails by means of flag signals. When he'd finished, he answered Sarre.

"Don't worry, we can lower her by trimming the sails. We'll come to a stop whenever I give the order."

They sailed on until, eventually, a lookout with a hailing horn shouted, "Milchen on the port bow!" They were low enough to see people in the streets staring up and pointing at the extraordinary sight.

They quickly left the town behind and hurtled on for some hours, changing course to head toward the coast.

When they passed over the river estuary, Tim and Sarre shouted, "Pass the word, we're close to Tredore Castle."

Just as the lookouts spotted Lord Nachua's army, the wind dropped and they slowed down considerably.

"Please don't let the wind turn and blow us back in the direction we've just come from," Tim murmured, but then he leaped up, saying to Sarre, "We'll be faster on the battle birds now. Quick, let's go."

Tim snatched up Josh and tucked him back inside his surcoat as they made their way to where their cockerels had roosted in the branches of the mighty craft, and remounted.

Urging their mounts on, Tim and Sarre soon reached the battleground. The transporters and fighting birds of the Duke's forces were no longer circling Tredore Castle but concentrating their fire on the breach in the north wall. Making a wide detour, Tim and Sarre saw that most of the high walls were finally near to crumbling away as a result of the relentless pounding from the Duke's siege machines. Lord Nachua's forces were close, but it was going to be a near-run thing. Across the battleground, the wailing notes of the Lord's battle trumpeters sounded.

"I hope we're in time," shouted Sarre as another great portion of the wall fell under the impact of a mighty rock. Siege towers were being trundled against the outer defenses in preparation for an all-out assault by the Duke's forces. The High King had committed all his battle birds to the fight; they swooped again and again onto the Duke's transporters.

The Duke had massed his forces for their final attack. Tim realized the defenders of the castle could all be dead before the Gurneys and Lord Nachua's troops even reached the castle.

"Back to the Gurneys!" he shouted to Sarre, and they wheeled their birds around to return to the sailing tree.

In danger of being becalmed, the tree was making only slow progress. Tim and Sarre landed on a lower branch and made their way to the Captain.

"Can you bring her down on top of the castle?" Tim called out.

"As you wish," replied the Tregger Captain.

Tim didn't want to take Josh into the battle, so he took the little dog out of his jerkin and said to the Tregger Captain, "Will you take care of Josh for me, please, and try to keep him out of the fighting?"

"He'll be safe with me," the Captain replied, and Tim handed Josh over, then ran off to borrow a loud hailer.

"Gurneys!" he shouted. "We are going straight into battle. Are you ready?"

An enthusiastic war cry roared up from the Gurneys who were crouching on the outer branches of the tree.

"I must go and tell Lord Nachua to attack immediately!" Tim shouted to Sarre.

"All right," she yelled back. "I'll go in with the Gurneys."

Tim remounted his battle bird and swooped down to

where Lord Nachua was forming his troops into fighting ranks. He needed no urging now. The enemy was before him and he knew what to do.

"Are you coming in with us, My Lord Enton?" he cried as Tim hovered beside him.

"No, My Lord," Tim replied, unslinging his Gurney bow. "I shall be more use attacking the Duke's transporters."

Lord Nachua reared back on his fighting boar and raised his sword. "Men of Nachua!" he bellowed. "For the High King and the honor of Tallis — follow me!"

His cavalry broke into a trot and the men at arms advanced on the double as the whole force thundered forward to attack the rear flank of the Duke's besieging army.

In all the confusion of the battle, Tim kept hoping to catch sight of Sarre, but he'd not yet caught even a glimpse of her. And now, with fire arrows raining about him, he swung his battle bird down beside the great tree that the Treggers had finally managed to tether at the top of the castle walls after the Gurneys had leaped from it right into the heat of the battle, already fighting as their feet touched the ramparts.

The High King's forces had been divided and were fighting off the besiegers from either side of a breach in the wall of the ramparts. On one side of the breach, Tim saw the High King and Lord Tredore fighting side by side as the enemy poured onto the castle ramparts from one of the Duke's assault towers.

On the other section of the breached wall, Hunter and

the Prince's troops were under pressure from two points of assault. Their men were gradually being beaten back. Tim could even see that the Lady of Tallis, dressed in a soldier's surcoat, had taken her place among a company of archers. It seemed as if they were about to be overwhelmed, but a young captain rallied a handful of men to make a desperate counterattack, and they were just able to hold off the Duke's men.

Then Tim saw Sarre. "She's all right!" he murmured with relief as he saw her swooping in and out of the melee on her battle bird. Too close to the Duke's best archers, Tim thought.

Again, the Duke's forces seemed to be about to overwhelm the High King's troops, but then the full force of the Gurney attack hit them and together with Lord Nachua's valiant assault from the rear they finally began to turn the tide of battle.

Suddenly, Gurneys were streaming about Hunter and the Prince's tiny force, shouting war cries and fighting like madmen as they forced the Duke's men to retreat from the castle walls, only to find Nachua's troops relentlessly crushing them as they fell back.

Tim wheeled away on his cockerel when he saw the Duke's personal transporter break away from the battle. With their troops almost certainly defeated, it seemed as if the Duke and Stryker, with their company of heavy archers, were about to flee. But instead they maneuvered below Sarre, who was hovering for a moment, dangerously close to the Duke's transporter. The Duke's archers sent a volley of arrows upward into her cockerel. The bird spun away, and Sarre, without her saddle straps to secure her, tumbled from its back to land among the Duke's archers in the transporter.

Tim was so close he even saw the look of pleasure that flashed across the Duke's face as his mighty carriage now turned and fled from the battle. Tim tried to follow but a screen of attacking transporters blocked his path. Instead, he landed on the battered castle wall and ran, dodging through the heaps of broken stone that littered the ramparts, searching for Hunter and the Prince.

He found them with a company of Gurneys who were already accepting the surrender of the attacking forces. Hunter and the Prince were crouching over the wounded figure of a Captain whose surcoat was soaked in blood. It was Urlica, the soldier who had saved the Prince and Hunter with his desperate counterattack on the Duke's forces.

Despite his wounds, the youth managed to smile at Tim, saying, "When you find Sarre, tell her I found my honor again."

CHAPTER 35

The Last Battle

The battle finally won, Tim had quickly retrieved Josh from the Tregger Captain and was now hurrying with Hunter and the Prince through the corridors in the ruined rampart walls, leaping over piles of rubble and skirting around groups who were tending to the wounded. The Prince had received a message that his father was badly hurt. As they approached through the smoke and dust, they could see that the High King's last position was still littered with the dead bodies of the Duke's men.

In their final assault, an arrow had struck the High King and penetrated the breastplate of his armor. He was dying, cradled in his daughter's arms, with Lord Tredore and Bethen crouched beside them. The Prince, Hunter, and Tim sank down by them, and Josh wriggled out from Tim's surcoat to lay a paw on the High King's grimy surcoat. He smiled fondly and ruffled Josh's head.

"I would have liked a dog like you," the High King said gently. Then he held out a hand to Lord Tredore whose grimy, unshaven face was streaked with tears.

"Good-bye, old friend," he said. "Remember the good times we had when we were boys."

"Always, Your Majesty," replied Tredore.

The High King reached out for his son.

"You were dead — but you returned to me. Tallis shall still have a High King. Do not grieve too long. I die happy."

He glanced around, unaware that it was his daughter who cradled him, "Almea. Almea," he called.

"I'm here, Father," she said.

He gripped her hand tightly, then beckoned to Tim and Hunter who had now been joined by Charto.

"You have been great and loyal friends to me. No man could ask for more." He smiled again weakly, and in a voice that was now no more than a whisper, said, "Remember me." Then he lowered his head for the last time.

Tim stood for a moment, his head bowed in sorrow, then tugged Hunter aside from the group.

"The Duke has captured Sarre," he said urgently, in a low voice.

Hunter looked down at the Duke's exhausted and defeated troops surrendering their weapons on the battle-ground below them, and murmured bleakly, "He'll kill her."

"I think not," said Bethen.

"What's to stop him?" said Hunter, replacing his helmet and tightening his body armor.

"He'll use her to bargain with," said Bethen. "Now he knows how valuable she is."

"As a Chanter?" said Hunter.

"More than that," replied Bethen. "Sarre has read the Duke's mind. He will keep her alive. What are you going to do?"

"What I set out to do from the first. Kill the Duke," said Hunter.

"I'm coming with you," said Tim, reaching for his Gurney bow.

Hunter hesitated, then seeing Tim's expression he gave a rueful smile. "Stay sharp, boy," he said. "There's a long way to go."

Mounted on battle birds, Tim and Hunter flew steadily toward the High King's palace. They knew more haste would be pointless. If the Duke was going to kill Sarre he would already have done so. If not, he would wish to bargain. But Tim could see that Hunter was in no bargaining mood.

Night had fallen by the time the Duke's transporter landed. Escorted by the company of archers, Sarre followed the Duke and Stryker without protest. She was completely calm as they entered the Duke's quarters and ascended a clockwork elevator to Stryker's workshop.

"Are you sure you can do this?" asked the Duke. "I thought she was a Chanter."

Stryker spoke proudly. "My powers grow with each mind I take, Your Grace. This child's mind will melt like snow. I have no doubt."

"Well, restrain her — just in case," insisted the Duke.

"As you command, Sir," replied Stryker petulantly, and with a rapid flick of his hand, he ordered the guards to "Strap her into the throne."

Sarre didn't struggle. She stepped forward to sit in the heavy, high-backed chair that had once been occupied by the clockwork figures of the High King and Princess Almea, and allowed the guards to chain her hands and feet.

Stryker stood cadaverously in front of Sarre, closed his eyes, took a deep breath . . . then slowly exhaled.

Sarre slumped forward.

"Is that all there is to it?" The Duke sounded dubious.

Stryker swayed for a moment, then recovered.

"She is mine!" he muttered triumphantly.

"Don't you mean *mine*?" the Duke reminded his Warlock sharply.

Stryker bowed slightly. "Of course, Your Grace."

The Duke nodded. "I'm going to wash away the stink of battle, then dine. I will see you in an hour." Then he turned to the Captain of his archers.

"I am expecting visitors. Warn me *immediately* of their arrival, then show them to my chamber."

Before leaving the workshop, the Duke seized hold

of Sarre's hair and lifted her head. She appeared to be lifeless.

"You haven't killed her, have you, Warlock?" he asked irritably. "We need her alive."

"Only her mind is dead, Your Grace," Stryker assured him.

Tim and Hunter saw the High King's palace at first light. As they approached, all looked serene and calm as the first rays of the sun set the dew sparkling on the lawns and gardens. Great dragonflies swooped over the clear blue waters of the mighty lake. All was silent but for the soft rustle of a gentle breeze through the trees.

They landed their battle birds in the courtyard before the Duke's keep and as soon as they'd dismounted, Tim released Josh from inside his surcoat.

The Captain of the archers saluted and said, "I have orders to escort you to the Duke's quarters, My Lord."

Hunter coolly handed the reins of his bird to a guard.

"There is a battalion of Gurney irregulars following aboard transporters," he said flatly. "If any treachery is attempted, you and all the Duke's men will wish you were already chained to a punishment balloon. Do you understand me?"

"Perfectly, My Lord," he said. "You must understand that many of the forces fighting for the Duke were just conscript soldiers following orders. We are regular troops, not the Duke's police."

Hunter nodded but didn't answer. He strode forward, Tim and Josh at his side, with the Captain hurrying to keep up.

When the doors of the reception chamber were thrown open, the Duke was standing at the window, hands clasped behind his back. He wore a black-and-white silk surcoat over silver court armor, a velvet cloak, a sword, and his great chain of office.

Still grimy from battle, the pair strode forward. Tim carried his Gurney bow with an arrow already notched and Hunter's hand rested on the hilt of his sword. Josh kept obediently to heel.

The Duke held up a hand, saying, "Warriors, restrain yourselves. At least until you hear what I have to say."

Hunter and Tim continued to stride forward, Hunter saying, "Release Sarre the Chanter to us now, or we will kill you where you stand."

"Please hear me out," said the Duke lightly. "Then, if you are of the same mind, I shall be happy to accommodate you. Although, I seem to remember the sword wasn't your best choice of weapon, Robert Quester."

The Duke crossed the chamber as he spoke, beckoning Tim and Hunter to follow. Guards threw open the doors as he approached and they entered a corridor that led to Stryker's workshop. They found the Warlock standing in the center of the vast room, wearing his snakeskin robes and carrying his staff.

As they approached the Warlock, Tim saw Sarre's

slumped figure chained to the wooden throne. He was about to run to her but Hunter put a restraining hand on his shoulder.

"Easy, Tim, easy," he murmured.

"Observe," said the Duke, seizing Sarre's hair again to lift her head. "Your little Chanter friend seems to have lost her mind. Now, you go to the High King and tell him I want an immediate pardon: none of my lands to be forfeited; and a standing army equal in size and equipment to his own forces."

"And why should he give you all that?" asked Tim.

"Tell the High King to consult with Chanter Bethen before he gives his answer." The Duke was looking smugly sure of himself.

"Why shouldn't we just take Sarre now?" said Tim.

The Duke shrugged. "If you wish. But she has no mind; you might just as well take one of those useless objects." He waved a dismissive hand at the automaton figures dangling behind the throne.

As they looked, one of them jerked an arm. Another twitched. The Duke suddenly looked less certain.

"Are you doing that, Stryker?" he asked uneasily.

"He's not doing it, Your Grace," came a high, disembodied voice, as a Tregger figure turned its head and gave the Duke a ghastly smile. Suddenly, all the figures appeared to come alive. They wriggled down from their hooks and began to advance.

Stryker stepped back, mortified, as two of the Tregger

machines scuttled forward to grasp the Duke. He twisted away in horror, throwing them off. Drawing his sword, he backed away and out of the room, screaming, "Stryker! Use your powers!"

The Warlock spun around to look at Sarre who was slowly raising her head. Her eyes were flashing with ever-changing colors. The chains at her wrists and feet broke off and whirled through the air.

Stryker raised his staff and pointed it at Sarre, screaming, "I have your mind, Chanter!"

Sarre now stood, speaking with infinite calm. "No, Warlock. You are mistaken. We Chanters have taken over *your* mind. You are finished."

"What will you do to me?" Stryker whispered.

Sarre shook her head. "I shall do nothing. You have already decided your own fate," said Sarre. "The punishment you had planned for me and my friends will now be yours. *Your* mind will see that it comes about."

A look of utter terror creased the face of the Warlock.

"No!" he screamed. "I beg you, be merciful."

"To save you from your own evil is beyond my power, Stryker," said Sarre.

The Warlock, raising his staff as if invisible foes had suddenly seized him, cringed away from her, beating at the air, struggling, flinching, screaming in vile torment.

"Whatever's happening?" asked Tim, looking relieved and puzzled at the same time.

"In his mind, Stryker is undergoing all the tortures he had devised for us. And to him, it is all too real."

The Warlock's screams were so terrible, even Hunter and Tim began to feel pity for the ghastly creature stumbling about the workshop.

"Can't we end it?" said Tim.

But the Warlock now fled from the room as though pursued by demons.

"Time to settle up with the Duke," said Hunter grimly and strode out of the Warlock's workshop.

Tim was about to follow but then thought to ask, "Are you coming with us, Sarre?"

She pointed toward the automatons. "Not yet. First, I must free all of the minds Stryker has trapped in these contraptions," she replied.

"There are *minds* in them?" asked Tim, incredulous.

Sarre nodded. "Stryker found a way to transfer the minds he controlled into these clockwork machines. He has the real people hidden somewhere in the castle. I shall need a little time to get them to their rightful owners. You go with Hunter."

"OK." And Tim ran from the room with Josh trotting at his side.

He hurried down the long corridor, looking for Hunter. He peered into room after room but there was no sign of him.

"Find him, Josh. Find Hunter," Tim urged the little dog.

Josh quickly picked up the scent and raced ahead, until finally he stopped and scratched at a section of the wall.

"Where, Josh, where?" said Tim.

The little dog leaped up and butted the stone carving of a flower. A section of wall swung smoothly open, revealing a pitch-black interior.

Warily, Tim and Josh stepped inside and the wall closed silently behind them. Despite the velvet darkness, Tim sensed he was in a vast chamber.

"Another intruder," hissed the Duke, his mocking voice echoing in the blackness.

Suddenly, bright lights flooded on, revealing an extraordinary sight. The walls, ceiling, and floor of the immense chamber were covered in mirrors that reflected an infinity of dazzling colors. It was like being trapped inside a thousand rainbows.

Then Tim realized that he, Josh, Hunter, and the Duke were standing in a chamber surrounded by a myriad of plinths, all bearing a Bloom of Kanarki. The reflections made it impossible to judge distance. The Duke could have been beside Tim or twenty paces away.

Both Hunter and the Duke had their swords drawn.

"Welcome to my private collection of Kanarki blooms, the finest in all of Tallis," the Duke boasted.

Hunter struck at the sound of his voice but his blade just hissed through empty space. Blinding light reflected from the thousands of glittering blooms.

Suddenly, the Duke casually flicked out his sword and stabbed Hunter in his arm. Hunter tried to return the blow, but once again his sword sliced through empty space.

"First," said the Duke lazily, "I will kill the boy's creature, then the boy, then you, Robert Quester."

The Duke stabbed again but Hunter managed to move away in time, with only a cut in his sleeve.

Tim had an idea. He put down his bow, reached for his slingshot, and fired a missile blindly. It struck home and with a splintering sound a great section of the mirrors shattered, leaving an area of velvet blackness.

"Hunter," Tim shouted. "Don't worry about us. Defend yourself; I'll destroy the mirrors."

He began to fire as fast as he could reload and more sections fell away, exploding in showers of glittering colored light. The Duke looked less certain now and began to move in a wary circle as the number of reflections were reduced with each of Tim's shots.

Now Hunter could establish the Duke's true position. His opponent moved catlike between the plinths of shimmering blooms but as Tim destroyed more and more of the mirrors, the Duke had no choice but to face Hunter.

Their blades clashed in a staccato rattle, flashing faster than Tim's eyes could follow. They battled backward and forward, darting between the plinths. It was clear they were well matched. But Hunter appeared to be gaining the advantage by the sheer ferocity of his attack.

Tim was sure he was winning, the Duke was completely

on the defense now and using all his skill just to hold off Hunter's remorseless advance. Then Hunter slipped on the shards of glass littering the floor, and the Duke thrust with his sword, piercing Hunter's side as he twisted away.

Hunter parried more blows from his kneeling position but as he strived to recover his footing, the Duke swiftly aimed a downward blow at his head. Hunter jerked aside and scrambled to his feet but a section of leather armor was sliced from his arm. With a malevolent chuckle of laughter, the Duke muttered, "Shoddy Gurney equipment, Robert!"

Slashing quickly, the Duke cut through another piece of the jewel-studded leather. This time from Hunter's shoulder.

"My armor is pure steel," boasted the Duke. "Quality always tells."

Hunter slipped to one knee again and the Duke raised his sword to make the killing stroke. For a fraction of a second the Duke's armored chest was exposed.

Hunter half rose and, using all his force, thrust his sword up to the hilt into the Duke's body. The blade pierced the steel armor as if it were cheap tin.

Hunter released his grip, and the Duke looked down in sudden disbelief at the hilt of the weapon protruding from his chest. His own sword fell clattering from his hand and for a moment he stood, swaying gently. Then, with a wailing cry, he reached out to grasp one of the sparkling Blooms of Kanarki, and crashed forward to lie still amid the glittering carpet of broken glass.

CHAPTER 36

Farewell to Tallis

Sarre and Hunter stood with Tim and Josh in the courtyard in front of the High King's keep, watching the descent of a vast State carriage, now drawn by black swans and bearing the body of the High King.

When it landed they walked toward the Lady of Tallis and High King Briarre, who had accompanied their father's body home. Bethen and Illya had also ridden in the funeral carriage.

"It's over, at last," Hunter said as he embraced Almea. "The Great Duke and his Warlock are finished."

Bethen and Illya nodded their satisfaction at the news, and Bethen suggested that they could all meet in the High King's private apartment.

Later, in the royal chambers, Tim, Sarre, and Josh

chose a corner in a window bay. Hunter and Almea sat with King Briarre on chairs placed in front of the fireplace. Charto leaned on the mantelpiece, while Illya and Bethen stood together in front of them all.

Hunter spoke first, addressing Bethen. "The Duke told us that you know something about Sarre. Something that would have made the High King give up half of his kingdom in return for her life."

Bethen nodded. "That is because he found a secret scroll called the *Chronicle of Tallis*. It must have fallen from the carriage when we escaped from the palace. We have recovered it now from the Duke's private chambers."

"What is the *Chronicle of Tallis*, Great Lady?" Charto asked.

"A genealogical plan showing all the High King's ancestors and descendants. It was kept by Illya," she replied. "From it, the Duke learned a great secret. Not even the High King or Princess Almea knew of it, because we Chanters always feared the consequences if Stryker ever learned to read their minds."

"What secret is this?" asked Almea.

Bethen now took her hand. "Do you remember when you lost Robert Quester?" she said gently.

The Lady of Tallis looked toward Hunter and shook her head. "Not very well, Bethen. I can recall very little of that time. It all seems cloudy, like trying to see through a mist."

Bethen smiled gently. "We know why that was, Almea. Because Illya and I took away your memory when we arranged your rescue from the Duke's guards. You, too, had been badly wounded in the fight on the boat and you thought your husband and your brother were both dead. Illya and I also believed Prince Briarre was dead. We searched for him with our minds but there was nothing. And we didn't suspect Stryker had taken away his mind. At the time we thought nothing else stood in the way of the Great Duke gaining the throne by marrying you. Knowing he would destroy anything that got in his way, Illya and I took certain steps."

"What kind of steps?" asked Princess Almea, puzzled.

Illya glanced at Bethen, who continued, "When we rescued you from the Duke, we discovered you were expecting a child."

Almea stood up. "A child?"

Bethen nodded. "You didn't know. You were terribly ill, wounded, and half out of your mind with grief for the loss of Robert Quester and your brother, Prince Briarre. Illya and I knew that if the Duke learned you were expecting a child he would attempt to kill it as soon as it was born. The child had to be kept secret — even from you. You gave birth during the time that Illya and I had clouded your mind. Afterward, we let you rest for more than a year."

"What about our child?" said Almea, clutching Hunter's hand.

"Can't you guess?" said Bethen. "I took her to the Forest of the Southern Rim for protection and discovered she was a Chanter — Sarre is your daughter."

Almea slowly turned to look at Sarre who had risen from her seat in the window. They hesitated for a moment, then rushed into each other's arms. Laughing and crying, overwhelmed with joy they held each other tight, until Sarre turned to Hunter. His brimming eyes shining with a chaos of feelings, her father lifted her off her feet and hugged her as if he would never let her go. And Josh raced about them all, barking happily.

The funeral of the High King took place, and under the new rule of High King Briarre of Tallis the kingdom was gradually being restored to its peaceful ways.

Tim knew it was time for him to go back to Enton. Hunter, now Robert Quester, would of course stay with his wife and daughter, the Princesses Almea and Sarre, to make his life in the kingdom.

Before Tim's departure, Princess Sarre made the necessary calculations on her Time Map, then they were to go to The Crack to fetch Tom Tagg. High King Briarre put the royal carriage at their disposal.

"A bit grander than a Gurney pack pig," said Tim as he bade farewell on the steps of the old palace. Bethen and Illya kissed him on the forehead, Princess Almea on both cheeks. Charto, who had been made a Lord of Tallis and the first Gurney member of the Royal Council, gave him a long hug. High King Briarre took his hand warmly and assured him there would always be a home for him in the kingdom.

Finally, Hunter shook his hand saying, "You have the letter to my lawyers. Everything I own on Earth is yours, Tim. I owe you more than I could ever begin to say."

Tim grinned as he said, "Stay sharp, Robert-Hunter. There's a long way to go."

Waving farewell, Sarre and Tim rose above the palace of the High King and set course for the Crack.

Tom Tagg, standing with the cave dwellers who'd been caring for him, gasped in wonder as they watched the magnificent royal carriage being gently brought in to land by the huge white swans. When he saw Tim and Sarre step from it the little boy ran forward, laughing excitedly. But when they told him Tim had come to take him home, to their horror he immediately turned away and ran off.

But a few minutes later he was back to present Sarre with a wonderful gift. A bunch of fresh wildflowers!

"Where did these come from?" she gasped.

"Just over there," said Tom with a sweep of his hand. "They're growing everywhere in The Crack. Don't you remember us planting them?"

"The packets of seeds!" said Sarre. "But it's incredible."

Tim laughed. "Surely, no more incredible than anything else about Tallis," he said.

When the royal carriage eventually landed on the Southern Rim, Tim remembered his apprehension when he'd first arrived in this unknown land. Now he was reluctant to leave. Suddenly, there seemed so much he wanted to say to Sarre. But he knew they were on dangerous ground. The swans were unhappy and kept flapping their great wings as if eager to depart. It was all the grooms could do to hold them in check.

Tim held Tom's hand as he looked for one last time at Sarre. She bent down to kiss the little boy, then looked at Tim and stroked Josh's head where it was sticking up out of Tim's jerkin.

"Will you be able to ask a girl to dance now, Tim?" she asked shyly.

"I think so," he answered, desperately wanting to say something more memorable. "I'll never forget you telling me the Chanter lesson of how not to be shy."

"When I told you to imagine that the girl you wanted to talk to was me?"

"That's right."

Sarre smiled. "I have a confession to make, Tim. That wasn't a Chanter lesson. I just made it up."

Tim shrugged. "Well, it worked — and you *are* a Chanter."

There was something else he wanted to do. Sarre decided for him. Leaning forward she kissed him quickly.

Suddenly, Tim didn't want to go at all.

"Remember me," she said.

"I'll be back," he replied. "I promise." Then, holding Tom's hand, Tim stepped into the pool of silvery colors — the starway was open.

They hurtled through the dark velvety tunnel, tumbling and turning against the soft walls until they were suddenly ejected.

Tim was lying on hard ground. Tom Tagg was beside him, and Josh was licking his chin. He looked up into a clear beam of moonlight that almost immediately faded. It was hot. All about him were piles of smoldering embers. It took him a moment to realize they were in the remains of the barn on Falling Star Hill. The wooden walls had partially burned away, but the tall stone pillars had kept the roof intact. Heaps of charred wood glowed everywhere but, the stone maze still stood, untouched.

Still holding Tom's hand and remembering Sarre's instructions, Tim walked back through the maze. The night sky was beginning to lighten in the east as they emerged onto the grassy slope in front of the house. Looking down the hill, Tim saw a solitary figure watching them. And so did Tom.

With a shout of joy, the little boy let go of Tim's hand and raced off down the hill, calling, "Mummy, mummy!"

Megan Tagg stood for a moment, motionless, then ran toward her son and lifted him into her arms.

Tim waited until Tom and his mother had left the hill before he and Josh resumed their walk down to his grandparents' house. Thinking about the letter from Hunter that he carried in his pocket, he murmured to himself, "Well, at least they won't have any more worries about making the plant nursery pay."

About the Author

MICHAEL MOLLOY was born in London in December 1940. In 1974, he was appointed editor of the *Daily Mirror*. In 1984, he became editor-in-chief of the Mirror Group Newspapers. In 1989, he left to become a full-time writer. He is the author of *The Witch Trade*, *The Time Witches*, and *Wild West Witches*. He lives in Ealing, London, with his wife, Sandy. They have three daughters, Jane, Kate, and Alexandra, and two dogs, Fred and Daisy.